# *What God Has Joined Together*

## *2nd Edition*

**OLIVIA SHAW-REEL**

*What God Has Joined Together, 2nd Edition*

© 2016-2021 by Olivia Shaw-Reel

Published by Olivia Shaw-Reel

**ISBN: 978-1-7360500-5-7**

# *Acknowledgments*

In 2016, *What God Has Joined Together* served as my very first #1 Amazon best-selling novel, and that was amazing, but let's remove the accolades. So many readers wrote to me expressing how my book helped their relationships and marriages. Seriously...*my* book? **WOW**! My prayer is that—much like *then*—it continues to bless and minister to those who read.

I am incredibly grateful to God for my gift, my family, my readers, my church family, and everyone connected to me. Your support truly keeps me going. Thank you. Thank you. Thank you!

*-OSR*

*"Therefore, what God has joined together, let no one separate."*

*- Mark 10:9*

# Prologue

"I want a divorce."

*Divorce…*

*Divorce…*

Divorce.

The four-word sentence echoed in her mind, specifically the dreaded *D-word* that no happily married woman wanted to hear. Happily married—at least that's what she felt. Obviously, by her husband's declaration, he didn't share in that same sentiment. Nylah was sure that she had heard her husband incorrectly as her head whipped around so that she could look him in the eye but his were already downcast, focused on his trembling hands.

"What—what did you say to me?" she questioned the man who had stolen her heart more than a decade ago.

This morning, as she washed their daughter's coarse hair, she had gotten a text to meet him at their favorite restaurant after work. He told her he would be sending a driver to pick her up and she was instructed to shower and get pretty. From there, they ate the most delicious seafood under low lights, sipped the finest red wine, and danced the night away under the moonlight barefoot at the lakefront. Currently, they sat hand-in-hand in the back of a limousine as the driver headed for their four-bedroom home. They planned to have a childfree evening of making love to celebrate their ten-year wedding anniversary. His out-of-the-blue confession posed a different plan.

She snapped her fingers, trying to get his attention but he didn't answer. "Bentley!"

*Goodness…*

He was handsome in his all-black attire, fresh haircut, and gold watch that gleamed in the darkening night. He looked far more mature than his 27 years and smelled of the new cologne she'd picked up for him. He was the definition of grown and sexy. And even with his revelation, he still made her heart beat rapidly in an unnatural cadence.

God, he was *everything* to her.

Nylah matched his fly. Her curvaceous body donned an off-the-shoulder cocktail dress. Mesh insets along her midriff gave her a classy but sensual look. On her feet were nude-colored heels with crisscrossed ankle straps. He had handpicked this outfit, down to the splash of perfume that she wore.

This evening was exactly what she hoped it would be; it was drama-free, relaxing and beautiful. Now, as he repeated himself, she could feel her world begin to turn upside down.

"I said, I want a divorce," he finally answered and lightly squeezed her hand, as if the caress would make things any better.

"Stop playin' like that," she laughed nervously. "Why—why would you say something like that, Bentley?"

She was unsure if he was joking or serious. His expression and the thickening tension pointed towards the latter as she fingered her curls. Her beautician had whipped up her unruly tresses two days ago and the curls were still full and voluminous. She stared at the man who she knew since they were snaggletooth and barely potty-trained—the man who had been her first date, first kiss, and who had become her first love.

Their worlds, since birth, were polar opposites. He was the eldest of five children and had two hardworking parents with little to nothing. Nylah was the only child to a mother who was a traveling nurse and a father who was an attorney. She was privileged, spoiled, and from the upper middle class, while he held the world on his young shoulders and was disadvantaged. He also suffered from lupus. Nylah had near-perfect health.

Bentley's father, a janitor at a local elementary school, had succumbed to heart disease in their adolescence and Nylah was there every step of the way. She and Bentley had fallen in love and gotten married, established lucrative careers, and had a beautiful baby girl. Things could not have been more picture-perfect.

Over the last few months, however, their marriage had been under attack and nothing that Nylah did seemed to help. She was cooking her best dishes, making love to her husband with all the special tricks she had learned over the years, and taking care of their daughter like any good mother should. Their communication was in shambles and his lupus was flaring up, all the while they studied to become elders in their evolving ministry.

Nylah stayed in prayer and was on her knees before God so much that her legs literally ached sometimes, and her throat would get sore from praying so intensely. The God-fearing couple was even taking marriage counseling at their church home. Nylah envisioned a lifetime with him, and thought that this night of laughter and love was a step in the right direction.

Oh, was she wrong.

Bentley removed his hand from hers gently and rubbed his face in uncertainty. "I'm…I'm not playing, baby. It's been on my mind *heavy* lately, and I just think it's what's best for us. We've grown apart…it happens to couples all the time."

"Yeah, but not to *US*. Wait a minute. Stop. Stop. Are you kiddin' me right now?" Nylah folded her arms and looked at him with an incredulous look. She could not believe he was carrying on this unfunny joke. Her lips, which were painted in a plum-colored lipstick, parted in shock. "Bentley, for real. This isn't funny, so stop it. You're ruining our night."

"Am I laughing?" he questioned coldly.

His calmness and straight face caused her to tear up. The corners of her almond-shaped eyes wrinkled, and she could feel herself grow warm with humiliation and anger. Her cheeks became flushed and soon, a streak of mascara made its way down her face with the tears accompanying it. Other than the blemish of running mascara, she resembled a doll the way she was made up with long, false eyelashes, blush, and flawless foundation.

"Why…why do you want a divorce? Where is this coming from?" Nylah croaked, her fists tightening on her lap. "You come at me with this on our anniversary, really? Are you seriously talking about a *divorce*?"

Her nightmare seemed to be coming true. There was something in his eyes all night and she assumed it was the stresses of his line of work. His smile had not quite reached his eyes, his kisses were cold and calculated, and his conversation had been strange. She now knew why—he had been planning to break her heart into a million different pieces all along. Like a slap to the face, she was stunned and felt numb. Her blood ran cold as she looked for the nearest bottle of wine to throw at him.

Bentley seemed to calculate her movements and grabbed her arm. "Hear me out. *Please* hear me out."

"Hear you out? What more is there to say? You just told me you wanted a divorce, Bentley! There is NOTHING you can say at this point! Get your hand off me!"

"Calm down," he hissed, but she raised her voice even more.

"I'm *NOT* calming down! I've been nothing but good to you for the last ten years," she openly cried and struggled to break free from his hold. "How could you do this to me—to *US*? Why did you buy me these things and take me out if you knew you were going to do this? How long have you been thinking about this and planning this?"

"Shhh. Shhh," his lips pressed together as he shushed her. "Nylah, you know you're my world. You know that. But things change. People change. Our marriage...*changed*."

*Thwack.*

Nylah cringed, as the sound echoed throughout the limo. Her hand throbbed instantly from connecting with his face. His head rocked to the side and a hand came up to press along his jaw, both in shock and in pain. His eyes locked with hers and grew darker with the realization that she had slapped him. She had actually inflicted pain on him. This was a first but judging by her growing animosity, it wouldn't be the last.

Nylah bit down on her lip and could not remember ever having so much restraint in her life. As much as she wanted to hit him again, she knew that violence was not the answer. Her mother had

12

always taught her never to put her hands on her spouse, or anyone else for that matter. If only her mother knew how heartbroken she was in this moment, she was certain that her antics would be excused.

Bentley stared back at her a moment more as he moved his jaw around and then licked his parched lips. Because of his fair skin, a bruise started to form on the left side of his face right away. Calmly and lowly, he began to speak, "I deserved that. I'll give you that much. Are you going to let me talk now?"

Nylah said nothing more.

"I wanted to celebrate with you tonight because I wanted to see if we could get that old thing back. I wanted to see you in your finest, while we dated like old times. I—I wanted to enjoy what was left of this marriage so that we can go our separate ways in peace."

"You *don't* mean that," she cried.

Bentley placed a hand on her knee cautiously. "I can't be the only one suffering in this, baby. I can't be the only one feeling like we've done all we can to salvage what we had. The excitement I once had for you and—for—for *us* is gone," he admitted, tears welling in his eyes. "As much as I hate to verbalize it,

I…I can't string you along like this anymore. It's hard to explain what I'm feeling, but please know that you didn't do anything wrong."

"Aaah." Nylah nodded, a bitter smile twisting her lips. "The 'it's not you, it's me' speech. *Wow*."

Bentley sighed. "Don't doubt my love for you. Please don't."

Nylah took in his sincere but harsh words and blinked back tears. Her eyes became glued to the scenic view outside of the limousine windows. She looked good but felt horrible inside. Plus, she was positive the food she'd eaten was starting to upset her stomach.

"Are you going to say anything, Love?" His nickname for her slipped from his mouth cautiously. "Please say something."

Even though she was inconsolable, she kept her head high as she said simply, "Say something? You want ME to say something? How about: 'go to hell, Bentley?' Does that work for you? 'Cause it works perfectly for me."

Nylah tapped against the partition and got the driver's attention. It rolled down slowly. "Hi, can you please take the quickest route back home? Mr. Rose and I would like to end our evening immediately."

"Yes, ma'am," the older gentleman responded politely with a Southern accent. His eyes met hers briefly in the rearview before the partition leisurely made its way back up.

Crossing her leg, and continuing to stare outside, Nylah kept silent the remainder of the drive to what was her dream home before the night began. It was once warm and full of love, but as she gazed upon its 2,200 square feet, she knew everything had changed forever. She could feel her husband's eyes ripping a hole in her side, but she refused to meet his gaze.

Finally, the limousine came to a stop in the familiar driveway decorated with neat rose bushes, marbleized boulders, and bustling accent trees and shrubs. He helped her out of the stretched vehicle, and then tucked her wrap around her shoulders. Nylah accepted the kiss he planted against her temple and closed her eyes. It was funny how quickly something so routine and sweet no longer meant anything to her.

"I'm going to go pick up Brooklyn from my mom's. I'll be back."

Nylah ignored Bentley's words and rushed inside of their home without another word or look back. The hardwood floors, stainless steel appliances, chandeliers, and multiple bathrooms and bedrooms no longer appealed to her. The paintings and their little handiwork that was placed around the house no longer seemed so special or sacred. For two years, Nylah had eyed this home. To her surprise, Bentley surprised her with it for her birthday last year. The joy from her fond memories subsided as she showered and settled in her walk-in closet turned prayer room.

Its walls were a solid mauve color, and a single painting was its only decoration. The artwork was filled with hues of red, grey, and black—it was something she had personally created back in college. The scripture scrawled across it, Nehemiah 8:10, was more fitting than ever as her eyes focused on the words.

Falling to her knees, Nylah recited the words over and over as she locked the door and crawled to a corner. "Do not grieve, for the joy of the Lord is your strength. Do not grieve, Nylah. The Lord is your strength."

After a moment, she did not pray as she intended. Instead, she looked to the dark ceiling and cried until her tear ducts could take no more. Perhaps tomorrow she would wake up and it would all be a dream…

When Nylah awakened the next morning, it was far from a dream. Her world was more like a nightmare as she realized her husband's words had actually happened the night before. She had actually gone through their divorce talk, and she had actually fallen asleep in her closet. With swollen eyelids and a tear-stained face, she finally emerged from her prayer room on all fours. Her stiff body had been in the fetal position all night. She needed to stretch; she needed a good cup of coffee, and to hear some good news from somebody…*anybody*.

Like an answered prayer, the pitter-patter of her daughter's footsteps greeted her as she settled on the porcelain toilet. Nylah closed her legs and chuckled because ever since she became a mother, she no longer had privacy even when she was half naked and harboring morning breath. This seemed to be no problem for four-year-old Brooklyn as she watched Nylah quietly handle her business and then wipe off.

Standing well under three feet with her head cocked to the side and her hands on her hips, Brooklyn looked at her in disbelief.

"Ummm, Mommy, where were you all night? I wet the bed and Daddy had to change my sheets."

Nylah put on her game face immediately and stared at her daughter through the mirror. As she saturated her palms with soap, she decided to push aside her heartache and gave her daughter the biggest smile she could muster up.

"Aw, baby. Mommy was talking with God and ended up fallin' asleep in the closet. I'm sorry I couldn't change your sheets." She finished washing her hands and smirked at Brooklyn's twisted pajama bottoms and disheveled hair. Her daughter was always a rough sleeper.

"S'okay," Brooklyn assured her, shrugging slightly. "Daddy gave me a bath, but he didn't use powder."

Like a gymnast, her daughter hoisted herself onto the counter so that she could look her mother in the eye. She reached out and patted Nylah's cheek. "Are you okay, Mommy? Your eyes are sad."

Nylah smiled at first her reflection, and then looked into her daughter's concerned eyes. She closed a hand over her daughter's much tinier one and gave it a comforting squeeze. Brooklyn was the perfect mixture of Nylah and Bentley, down to the thick hair, single dimple, cheeky smile, and beautiful toffee complexion. She had Bentley's smarts and freckles, while her outgoing personality, sass, and wittiness had Nylah written all over it.

"Mommy has you for a daughter, so that makes everything perfect. I'm fine, baby. Now, are you hungry? Because I'm starving." Nylah patted her stomach for effect. "You want to help me make banana nut muffins and eggs?"

Brooklyn did not need to be told twice. She all but somersaulted off the counter in her cartoon-themed pajamas and dove headfirst through the doorway.

"Hey, missy. Slow down," Nylah chuckled and followed behind leisurely, flicking the light off in the process.

She planned to figure things out with Bentley sooner than later. For now, she had to perform her favorite job and that was to be the best mother she could possibly be. Never mind how badly her heart ached and how crushed her feelings were.

Brooklyn Faith Rose was her number one priority.

# *Chapter One*

*Click, clack. Click, clack. Click.*

Nylah scraped the sole of her shoe against the concrete, feeling stickiness on the bottom. She turned her foot upward and wanted to cry at the sight of bright green gum nestled against the groove of her high heels. Her leopard-print shoes added a splash of color to her white blouse and distressed high waisted jeans. It was casual Friday at the office, and she chose a simple outfit, plus she had plans afterward much to her dismay.

The weeks that followed Bentley's declaration for divorce was intense to say the least. Instead of cooking four days out of the week, Nylah went down to just two days. Their pillow talk was rushed and uncompassionate and half the time they slept in separate rooms. Their usual morning kisses and sweet nothings were replaced with quick hugs when they parted ways. Things were instantly different, and Nylah could not help but to think that maybe another woman was involved. Bentley decided that they would attend one final marriage counseling session before they would agree or disagree on filing for divorce.

Their session would be starting shortly, and Nylah, still very much in love with this man, was at a loss for words. She knew that if he was happier without her, she would swallow her pride and give him what he wanted but she prayed the counseling would help them to make sense of everything.

*Ten years*, she thought, with a single tear making its way down her face.

As she drove from work to the family therapist's office, her mind went back to their sweet yesteryears. She thought about the day that she had fallen in love with him and knew he was the one. She thought about their beautiful wedding day, and the evening that she had wrapped up a pregnancy test for Christmas and revealed to him that after three miscarriages, God had given them a miracle baby.

Nylah's heart was filled with sorrow, and she still harbored her same feelings for him, but oh, how his heart had changed drastically. She vowed that she would not give up on him, and certainly would not give up on God.

Maybe, just *maybe*, things would turn around in her favor.

❖

"Good evening, Mrs. Rose! I'm glad you could make it."

Nylah had barely skimmed her knuckles over the door before it opened. A bubbly woman peeked around the door with a smile. It wasn't her normal therapist, but she looked friendly, nonetheless.

"How are you?"

"Doing okay, and yourself?" Nylah extended her hand and returned the warm smile. "Nylah Rose."

"Yes, I know exactly who you are, sweetheart. My name is Dr. Bloomberg, but please call me Carlotta. I'll be sitting in for your normal therapist this evening. I apologize for the inconvenience. She had an emergency. Are you still interested in speaking with me, or would you like to meet with Dr. Loren at a later time?" the woman spoke a mile a minute and was oddly chipper even though it was later in the evening.

Nylah perused the woman up and down with gentle yet judgmental eyes. The woman was motherly and had a pair of warm brown eyes. Her greying hair was slicked back into a lengthy ponytail that tickled

23

the back of her neck. When she smiled, her high cheekbones pushed against her glasses in an almost comical way.

"It's truly up to you, honey. I would be, in no way, offended if you wanted to wait," the therapist continued.

Nylah could feel the sincerity floating from the woman and lightly collapsed in the woman's arms, tears already forming. She decided that she felt safe with this woman and agreed to carry on their session.

"It's fine. We can meet. I—I just never thought I'd be meeting with someone to help save my marriage. This is all so new to me, and…confusing, and I'm just so tired of this," Nylah whispered, unable to stop from rambling, "I just want this phase to be over. I want to get back to how things were."

"Oh, shhh. I know, honey. Here…come on inside and have a seat. You are welcome to that tissue box on my desk. We can't mess up that beautiful makeup of yours."

As they waited for Bentley to arrive, Carlotta settled in a plush loveseat. Over small talk, they learned quickly that they had both attended the same college and were sisters in their esteemed sorority.

"I've got about 20 years on you, but I can certainly still step like nobody's business," Carlotta bragged, giving a smug smile. "Don't let the wide hips fool ya!"

Nylah giggled, slapping fives with the woman.

"Now, are you sure you don't want any refreshments?"

"Oh, no, thank you. I had something to eat awhile ago." Nylah crossed one leg over the other comfortably, playing with a piece of lint on the fabric of her shoes.

"No water? Anything?"

Nylah shrugged. "I'm fine, I promise. I'm just anxious to get going."

"Speaking of which. Tell me about yourself while we wait for your husband. I know you've gotten to know Dr. Loren pretty well, but I just want a brief overview of your interests and occupation," Carlotta explained and reached for a pen. "I have notes, of course, but I'd love to hear it from you directly. Oh, and I love that top, by the way."

Nylah eased off her heels, crossed her legs at the ankles again, and then unbuttoned the top of her blouse. She leaned back into the grey couch with a sigh. She intertwined her fingers and settled them on top of her stomach.

"Thank you. Who *am* I?" she asked aloud. "I am one of the sweetest people you'll ever meet. Hard-working. Accomplished, in my book. I have a passion for life, love, and laughter. Um, let's see…I am a senior copywriter for one of the biggest consulting companies in the region. I have a four-year-old who is my world, and I am madly in love with a man who no longer loves me."

Nylah ended her speech with a fake smile and then burst into tears for a second time. She heard the therapist maneuver around the room, and then soon felt the gentle tickle of tissue slipping through her fingers. Nylah dabbed at her face and hated that she looked so vulnerable.

Carlotta's eyes left the red scribbles of notes and met with Nylah's watery ones. "Why do you say that? Did he *tell* you he didn't love you?"

"No, but his actions show it. He asked for a divorce. He's distant and cold now. It's been this way for a few months now. I…I just don't know what to do."

The therapist nodded and was silent for a moment. She seemed to be gathering her qualms about the situation.

"I'll revisit what you just told me in a little bit. Can you tell me how you two met?"

"Sure." Nylah wiped her runny nose for a final time, and then sighed. "Our families have known each other since before we were born. Our mothers were college dormmates during their freshman year and remained close over the years. Naturally, he and I grew up together and became good friends as well. Our lives and families had complete opposite upbringings, but that didn't matter. We were all like one big happy family."

"Oh?" Carlotta lifted an eyebrow with interest.

Nylah picked at a stray thread on her blouse, continuing, "The earliest memory I have with Bentley is at three years old. We would take baths together, have play dates together, and just always be over each other's house. Well, he'd be over mine more because we had a bigger backyard." She giggled. "I am an only child, so his friendship has kept me sane for all of these years."

"That is beautiful," Carlotta spoke, as a gentle smile tugged at the corners of her lips. "So, you two remained close throughout your entire lives?"

"Yes. We were each other's shoulder to lean on when we got our hearts broken. We talked each other's ears off when things were going wrong with our families. We took each other to prom, we shared our first kiss, and we graduated with honors from every school we've ever attended," Nylah explained distractedly, shaking her head. "We've literally done it all together."

"That is such a rarity that it blows my mind…in a good way."

"Sometimes it blows my mind, too. People always say what we have is unusual, but it's just our history," Nylah said and wrapped her arms around herself. The cool breeze wafting through the open window was sending chill bumps up and down her arm. "It's all I know. *He's* all I know. I guess that's why it's so hard to think of divorcing and separating. I don't know any life outside of Bentley and don't want to experience it either."

"I see," the therapist spoke up and tapped her pen against her lips with each word. "When did things begin to change for you? When did you know the relationship wasn't just platonic, and that there may be feelings involved?"

Nylah did not need to think on it for long. She reminisced for a moment and then spoke from the heart. "For me, it was when we were in college. I began to notice how handsome and thoughtful he was. He was no longer just goofy and annoying, and brotherly. He became so much more. Bentley intrigued me and stimulated my mind unlike any of the other guys our age. For instance, I remember back in 2005 during majorette practice, he and the drummers from the marching band entered and…"

# Chapter Two

*September 2005*

*This was embarrassing. Correction: this was a HOT mess. Nylah shook her head in disbelief and looked at the group of exhausted women before her. They were panting with their hands on their hips.*

*"Ladies, y'all cannot be serious!" her usually mellow voice was decibels louder and met the ears of nine agitated majorettes. "Please start over. Five, six, seven, eight!" she counted off quickly and snapped her fingers with every word.*

*In her available hand, she pressed play on the stereo remote, and an R&B track blared through the speakers. Her petite body swirled around to face a large mirror, and on either sides of its reflection, were nine other bodies.*

*The room's occupants were all between 19 and 22 years old, all different shades of gorgeous melanin, and all different body shapes. Although tired, they were fine to say the least, in matching, nude-colored leotards and sleek ponytails. Nylah was the proud captain of the varsity majorette squad, and the only sophomore to have ever held such a position at Virginia College of the Arts.*

*"C'mon, ladies! Where is your energy? Start over!"*

*Groans and teeth sucking echoed off of the studio walls. The dancers looked distressed, while Nylah simply folded her arms underneath her C-cup breasts.*

*The music started up again, and just as quickly as they began to dance, she made them stop. "Seriously? That was worse than before. Majorettes pride themselves on sexy, precise movements. I'm willing to bet that nobody would come to see us, at this point, and I wouldn't blame them," Nylah teased.*

*A couple eye rolls and "no, she didn't" faces were caught in her peripheral vision. She made the dancers start over again and walked around the room. Her teammates continued throwing out previously rehearsed eight-counts. They looked worn, and although it was hot in the dance studio, they had another half-hour to go before anybody could pack up and leave.*

*Nylah stopped them again and sighed in frustration. She kicked off her ballet shoes that were tattered with close to 12 years of rehearsals and recitals. "Let's take a five."*

*Her roommate and close friend, Courtney, pulled the elastic holding her lengthy hair up and shook her head. Jet-black curls with aqua blue highlights flew everywhere before she bent over with her hands on her knees.*

*Courtney's chest heaved up and down as she spoke breathily, "What's the problem?"*

*"There's just no energy or umph to it," Nylah attempted to explain.*

"I thought it was perfect," one of the upperclassmen spoke up.

Her face was flushed and irritable. She was mad because someone younger and newer than her had become captain. Her dislike for Nylah was evident but Nylah could not care less. "Maybe YOU should show us how it's done…captain," she added dryly, mockingly.

"Get into first position." Out the corner of her eye, she saw a group of guys walk past, and then double back. They were definitely band members judging by their uniforms, sweaty foreheads, and the towels thrown around their necks. A few of them stood in the doorway, eyeing the women. "Can I help you all?"

"Don't mind us. Just seeing what songs you're rehearsing so we'll know what to play," the leader of the group said. Without permission, they began filing into the studio.

"Um, this is a closed rehearsal," Nylah said as politely as she could.

They continued gathering around and sitting down. Planting her hands on her hips, Nylah attempted to give a stern look. It obviously didn't work because all six of the guys found places on the floor and made themselves comfortable on the hardwood. It was then that she saw the drumsticks sticking out of some of the guys' bags and hands. They were a part of the *drumline. Her eyes zeroed in on one of the guys and her irritation soared.*

*"We'll be quiet," the leader of the group promised and winked.*

*He had gorgeous sandy hair that was braided neatly towards the back of his head. Dampened with sweat, his edges were smoothed against his caramel skin. No matter how handsome he was, he was interrupting them from being productive. Not to mention, he had been following her around campus for some time, trying to impress and get to know her.*

*No thanks.*

*"Whatever," she huffed and rolled her eyes.*

*She grew more and more annoyed by the second, but understood that studio time was a free for all. Nylah ignored the guys' smug grins, and gathered her girls' attention, with a clap. Some were already giggling and blushing over these cornballs. She just wanted to look good for next week's performance.*

*Nylah slid the remote towards the group and announced, "We're going to take it from the top. Since y'all are sitting in, can you play the music for me at least?"*

*"I got you. Just tell me when to start."*

*She twirled around on the heels of her ballet shoes, dug the clingy material of the leotard out of her butt, and then raised her arms into first position. She started her countdown off, nodded to the drummer, and then began dancing.*

*The R&B crooner's voice brought out her alter ego and it was like a chain reaction. Nylah swung her hips fiercely and threw her neck and arms with attitude. She snapped her back extra hard, dropped her body low, and then brought it up slow. Her audience of drummers and surrounding dancers stepped back for a second. They were clearly speechless and in awe.*

*Nylah did not dare look in the mirror at anybody's face, but she had to admit, she was feeling herself. The others in the room seemed to agree as some stood, a few of the girls covered their mouths with their hands, and one of the drummer's mouth hung open. Whispers could be heard faintly, and Courtney walked towards her quickly.*

*"Nylah, hold up…"*

*The routine was far from complete, so Courtney's words were ignored as Nylah continued to dance. Her ankle stiffened and her toes pointed beautifully before she moved into her final stance. It was time for the signature cartwheel into a split. Spinning quickly, and then shooting her arms up towards the ceiling, Nylah bent at the waist. She cartwheeled twice, and then landed with her legs stretched out until they could go no further. She pointed her toes for added elegance. As cocky as she wanted to be, Nylah knew her performance was perfect.*

No one clapped, no one moved, and no one said anything. Her flowing ponytail had worked its way down, sweat now coated her hairline, and she felt her patience growing thin.

"Any questions? Are we understanding the umph I was talking about?"

Courtney, still standing just a few feet away, motioned Nylah to follow her. She was widening her eyes like a crazy woman.

"One sec," Nylah said, looking back towards the other dancers. They were whispering and laughing now. "What are we cacklin' about? Speak up. What? I got y'all speechless?"

"All for the wrong reasons." Asia, the upperclassman with a bad attitude and bad overbite, chuckled and began gathering her belongings. She looked at the clock. "It's four thirty. Time to go."

Nylah was confused. The room seemed to erupt in laughter now except for one of the drummers, and Courtney simply shook her head. As everyone filed out, she stood up, and walked towards her friend. "What was that about?"

"I tried to get your attention, but you kept waving me off."

"Because I don't like being distracted while I'm dancing," Nylah snapped at her. "What was so important that you needed to interrupt me anyway?"

Courtney threw her hands up and backed away from Nylah. "Look, you've been snapping all day, and that's not cool. Before I say something I regret, I'm gone. Check yourself...literally."

Nylah watched her friend walk out and then screamed in frustration. "Why does everybody have an attitude TODAY?" As she gathered her things, she continued to mumble to herself.

"Too much estrogen," another voice entered the room, and it was a member of the drumline who had busted in before. He was no stranger to Nylah. In fact, he was her best friend.

Standing at an awkward six feet and three inches was Bentley Rose. He had been quiet earlier and looked shy but pleasant. Braces covered his teeth, and he had a forehead full of acne. His boyish face held a look of understanding, as he held out a sweatshirt. "You might need this."

"I'm mad at you! You knew I had the studio, and you let your boys take over like that."

"Chill out," he demanded with amusement on his face. "It's not that serious."

"It IS! I'm already irritated, and that rehearsal went nothing like how I wanted it to go."

"So, it IS true? Interesting," Bentley raised his eyebrows, and offered his sweatshirt to her again.

"What's true?"

"Girls are always irritated when they're on."

"On what?"

"Their period. I never understood what my mom and sister meant by that."

"What are you talking about?" Nylah gathered her things and wanted to give her cornball of a best friend a piece of her mind. She decided to bite her tongue. As a child of God, she was working on her mean remarks towards people. Her face, however, still needed deliverance. "Boy, bye. Please keep it moving. You were foul for that."

He was silent, so she glanced back, and he was biting back laughter. Nylah was unsure about what he found so funny. "Why do you act so stuck up when we're in public? But in private, you're all goofy and huggin' up on me. You're the foul one!"

"Why won't you shut up?" Nylah growled and rolled her eyes.

"You SURE you don't want this?"

"Why would I want your dingy sweatshirt, Bentley?" she screamed. "I would advise you to leave me ALONE."

"Alright." He gave up and followed behind her as they left the studio.

They headed in the same direction and Nylah forced herself to cool down. She was unfairly taking her frustrations out on the same person that she rode the bus with every morning

37

*since kindergarten. This was the same young man who she once took baths with, and shared playpens with. Her attitude needed checking and Bentley was just the person to do it.*

*"But since we're giving advice, I would advise YOU to put this sweatshirt around your waist. You...uh, had an accident."*

*Nylah gave him a crazy look, before she understood what he was implying. Her face grew red in embarrassment, and her mouth became dry. It all made sense now; she recalled the drummers and dancers laughing, Courtney attempting to get her attention, the sweatshirt offers from Bentley, and even her moody attitude.*

*She dusted her backside off and felt moisture. It only absorbed further into the material of the leotard. Nylah's fingertips were completely red when she brought them back into view, and then it occurred to her. After 19 years, she was finally starting her period at the WORST possible time.*

*Bentley—whom she knew like the back of her hand after all these years—had a knowing smile on his face now.*

*"I'm so sorry," she whispered and tucked her arms behind her back. She attempted to cover the red stain that she knew was making its presence known below the curve of her butt.*

*He tossed Nylah his sweatshirt and said nothing more. She quickly tied it around her waist to cover up, and they waited for the bus in silence. When it pulled up, she saw that there were very few seats available and cringed. They would have to sit by each other in the only two spots nearest to the driver.*

*"Ladies first," he spoke, extending his arm out.*

*She sat down, still embarrassed, and kept her legs closed tightly. Mom had warned her about a woman's time of the month, but she assumed that her athleticism had given her a pass. Most girls started their cycles in middle school. Not Nylah. She was always the exception to this stuff.*

*Nylah was probably the ONLY college girl wondering how to insert a tampon properly. Just like she was the only college girl on the bus looking at the guy sitting beside her. An entire football team was scattered behind them, but she was intrigued by what she saw.*

*Bentley's head had dipped low to read a book. He was dressed in off-brand clothes and a pair of Air Force Ones. Nylah looked at his build. He was a little on the thin side yet had the broadest shoulders and towered over most people. Since they were little, he had always been different. He was sort of weird and sort of fascinating. He also had a pair of the warmest brown eyes that she had ever seen, and his eyebrows were better shaped than hers. Nylah knew that if he developed a better skincare routine, he would look handsome.*

*"You forgive me?" The bus hit a pothole and their shoulders collided. "I'm...sorry."*

*"You're good," he looked over, clearing his throat. "Of course, I forgive you."*

*"You're my best friend, and I love you," she mused. "I hate when we fight."*

*"That was a fight?" he chuckled.*

*She playfully hit him. "You know what I mean. You've always been the same though. I appreciate guys like you."*

*"Guys like me?"*

*Nylah nodded. "Genuine…original…thoughtful. You came back to give me your sweatshirt while everybody else joked about it. That was so sweet of you."*

*"Hey, I grew up around all women, so I've seen some things in my life, plus, you're like my little sister," Bentley shrugged his shoulders. "It was nothing."*

*"Well, it was something to me. Thank you again," she emphasized and rubbed her hand over his. Eventually, he turned his hand under hers, fully enveloping it.*

*The two rode in silence for the remainder of the way, holding hands and trying not to blush whenever their eyes shyly met. Her stop arrived shortly after, so she stood to scoot around his legs.*

*"Have a good evening, Bentley."*

*"You too, Nylah."*

*She waited on the corner for the bus to continue its route, and when it finally passed, she caught Bentley's eyes again. He waved a final goodbye, and then Nylah started on her way home.*

*All smiles.*

*"I think I'm in love with my best friend," she gushed to no one.*

# *Chapter Three*

"Well, it was a pleasure getting to know you two, your history, and your marriage better. I just want to thank you for entrusting me for your final counseling session," Carlotta declared and looked from Bentley to Nylah and then back again.

Nylah had done most of the crying and talking, while Bentley, who arrived more than a half-hour late, offered few words.

"Did this clear up some things for you two? Are you interested in returning to delve deeper?"

"Yes."

"No."

The two answered at the same time, and then looked at each other. Bentley repeated himself, "*No.*"

The therapist peered over her wire-rimmed glasses. "Any particular reason? You seem like a match made in Heaven and have just as many similarities as differences. You're even able to finish each other's thoughts, whereas most couples talk over one another. There has been no infidelity or lies. Plus, Bentley, you mentioned how she takes great care of you when you're sick. Surely, that's something to hang onto and work on, right?"

"It's the same thing I've said before, Doc. I plan to take care of her and be in our daughter's life as if we never separated, but I don't think we were meant to be anything more than friends," Bentley confessed. "Once we put a title on what we had, things began to change for me, and I don't want to ruin our friendship or the history we've built. I love her too much for that."

Nylah squinted in confusion. "If you loved me so much you wouldn't hurt me like this. Just say it. Did you meet someone? Are you seeing someone and you're just afraid to tell me?"

Bentley huffed and ran a hand over his face in frustration. "No, of course not. I'm man enough to tell you the truth if there was ever anyone involved. I just...I just can't explain myself in a way that you would understand or support me."

"See, that's the thing," Nylah said and felt another round of tears escaping her eyes. "I love and support you in EVERYTHING you do, sometimes more than I support and love my own endeavors. You don't see or appreciate that. You *never* did."

"Please don't cry. You know I hate it when you cry," he pleaded and reached for her hand.

"Then stop giving me a reason to!" she screamed so loudly, it felt like the walls of the office shook. She ignored his puppy dog eyes and yanked her hand from his. Her bottom lip quivered so much that she was sure that she favored their daughter whenever she didn't get her way. "I'm sorry, Carlotta. We're done here. Thank you for trying to help."

Bentley spoke through clenched teeth, "Love…"

"*Don't* call me that and don't touch me. Go ahead and do what you want to do. I've given it my all and obviously that wasn't enough. I'm not about to sit here and beg for marriage!"

"Mrs. Rose, wait," Carlotta called and stood to her feet. "Bentley, do you mind if I speak with her privately? Please?"

Reluctantly, he excused himself and closed the door gently, putting the women in complete silence. When the focus was solely on Nylah again, Carlotta ordered her to sit down again. She fiddled with something on her desk and came away with a Bible. It was one of Nylah's favorite pieces of literature and she was so familiar with its contents, but she was confused about why it was being paged through.

"Now, I know you two grew up in the church and are still heavily involved, so I just want to offer you a reminder and this is totally off the clock," Carlotta explained just above a whisper.

With the tip of her bubblegum-colored tongue, she moistened her index finger and thumb, and then turned to a page. Her fingernail skimmed over the black words and cream pages until she found what she was searching for.

"Are you listening?"

"I'm listening," Nylah responded lowly.

Her voice was hoarse from raising it, and a headache was gradually forming from all her crying.

Carlotta began to read with authority and assurance, "'From the beginning of creation, God made them male and female. For this reason, a man will leave his father and mother and be united to his wife, and the two will become one flesh. So, they are no longer two, but one flesh. Therefore, what God has joined together, let man not separate.'"

As she completed the scripture, Nylah nodded and stared back in silence. She continued to wipe absently at her face and was sure that every drop of makeup was long gone. A calm took over her as she continued to listen to the therapist.

"I'm no pastor nor do I have any degrees in theology, but I *am* deeply rooted in the infallible Word of God. What I can say about this situation is everything under the Heavens has a season. While God may have confirmed that this marriage was orchestrated *by* Him, it may not necessarily be the season for it," she explained and took Nylah's hand. "Knowing that scripture and what God says about your relationship, wipe away your tears and give it to God. If it's meant to be, it *will* be."

"But it hurts so badly," Nylah cried.

"Oh, honey, I know it does. I've been exactly where you are, and it didn't break me. I stood on faith, just as you should. I have divorced and remarried the same knuckleheaded man twice," she joked. "But in all seriousness. Trust me, your story is much like mine. I had to learn how to trust God though it all, and the moment I let Him take over is when things began to fall into place. Just promise me one thing."

"Yes, ma'am?"

"Promise me that you'll call me when you two figure it out. Visit me sometime. I know it had to be

God that placed us together, because you remind me so much of myself when I was your age. Don't allow life's circumstances to steal your joy, and always, always, always keep the faith. I know it's easier said than done, but if I did it, I know you can because I wasn't a Christian like you. I was in the world and hopeless, but I still knew the power of God. You hear me?"

With a lengthy, parting hug, Nylah nodded against the therapist's shoulder. "I hear you. Thank you so much for everything, Carlotta."

"It was my pleasure, baby," she bade a final goodbye and then closed the door behind Nylah.

Bentley, who had been dropped off by a coworker, sat in the waiting area with his head in his hands. He seemed to be frustrated while Nylah now felt renewed. Because of his illness and past seizures, he did not like driving around on his own, so Nylah knew that she would have to take him back home.

They rode with just the sounds of smooth jazz as their background noise and the occasional sniffle. Nylah gripped the steering wheel and focused on the dark night ahead of her. Her stomach growled and she remembered that she had not eaten a decent meal all day.

"I see somebody's hungry," Bentley teased, his voice breaking the silence.

Nylah suppressed her smile.

"You want to stop and pick up something?" he asked and looked over. "My treat?"

"*Your* treat? Oh, that's all I need to hear," she joked and the two shared a laugh.

"There's that beautiful smile," Bentley mused while he drummed his fingertips along his thigh. "I was beginning to think that I had taken it away."

"No, you didn't. It's been a long few weeks, but I'm actually okay," Nylah declared, as she slowed down at a stoplight.

Bentley sat up and cleared his throat. "Listen, you deserve a man that has it all figured out."

"I do, but it doesn't change the fact that I *wanted* you. I *needed* you." She looked over, her eyes not quite meeting his eyes. "It doesn't change the fact that I loved and *still* love you. It doesn't change that this divorce caught me off guard and was never an option in our eyes, well, at least mine. It just…doesn't make sense to me anymore and I'm done wondering what went wrong."

Finally, she took a deep breath and finished her thought. Her voice broke slightly, "I've said all that to say…tonight was all the confirmation I needed to move forward."

She kept her eyes forward until she felt Bentley's cautious hand pull her face around. His hand was warm around her delicate chin, and his attractiveness and unmoving gaze made her blush as if they were dating for the first time. Her cheeks became flushed and then she sighed into the atmosphere knowing that his heart no longer matched hers.

Bentley leaned forward and their lips collided passionately. The world seemed to vanish around them as they kissed like it would be their last time. Nylah's heart broke further as she concluded that it was indeed a farewell kiss. While beautiful and sense heightening, it was short-lived, when a horn blew behind the vehicle.

Nylah broke away and wiped her lips. Bentley sucked on his bottom lip and looked quietly out of the window. Things were quiet for a moment except other passing cars, the faint hum of the engine, and the ticking of the turn signal every so often.

"Baby," he finally spoke as she proceeded down the road. "No matter what happens, and no matter where life takes us, you will *always* be my first love. You will always have my heart and be the number one lady in my life. No one can replace you or what we built. You hear me?"

"I do," she whispered.

"I love you for all eternity, just as I vowed on our wedding day, and Brooklyn will *always* be well taken care of. Please don't ever forget that, for as long as I'm living, what's mine is yours," he added with sincerity.

Nylah believed every word that he said, but she still could not believe that they even had to have such a conversation.

"You promise nothing will change between us?"

"I promise."

That night, for the final time, they made love, cried, prayed, and planned for what the future would look like under two roofs.

# *Chapter Four*

*A year and a half later…*

"Girl, what are you smiling about?"

Nylah glanced over to her girlfriends who were fingering their wine glasses and giving her side eyes. This was supposed to be a night of laughter, forgetting life's problems, and enjoying all the foods that they had given up for their diets. Instead, Nylah had been quiet, thoughtful, and distant much of the night. While watching a chick flick, her mind had wandered back to Bentley. No matter what she did, he always consumed her thoughts, it seemed.

Their untimely divorce was the shock of the decade to the family and friends who believed longevity was theirs. To this day, it was one of the most embarrassing and hurtful experiences of Nylah's life. But their friendship remained solid as they created a healthy living environment for their daughter. As more and more time passed, she was able to heal and move forward with her life...*almost*.

It didn't help that Bentley was now engaged to a gorgeous, aspiring swimsuit model, and Nylah had a new man for the last few months. Everything she had ever mapped out for her life seemed to be shredded before her eyes. Although the divorce eventually became a mutual decision, and they had been separated for nearly a year, it just felt weird.

"Nylah? You alright?"

Her thoughts were jumbled but she focused on the crazed looks that she was receiving, nodding, "Just was thinking about the last time Bentley and I…"

"Uh uh. Less thinking and more drinking," Yara encouraged, refilling her glass with the ice-cold champagne. "Why are you even thinking about him? We said no talk of the opposite sex tonight."

Nylah wasn't a big fan of wine, however, since meeting up regularly with the girls, she had probably drunk it more in the last few months than she ever had in her life. It was nasty and made her lose her mind half the time, and did she mention how nasty it was? Still, she accepted the glass and sipped away.

"This man was my life. It just still feels surreal. I never imagined that my marriage wouldn't last."

"But just think," Kandice spoke up, always the rational one. She leaned to turn down the old school R&B that they were listening to. "You two ended on good terms, and you're still the best of friends. He's happy…you're happy. You've both moved on. What's the problem?"

"You have to let it go sooner than later," Liliana added, shrugging, and causing half of her champagne to spill.

"I know, I know," Nylah sighed, and nibbled on a chocolate-covered strawberry. "I just need to focus on the bigger picture. Taking care of our baby."

"That's right. As long as YOU feel good about it, that's all that matters. You *do* feel like you've made the right decision, don't you?" Ivy paused from slow dancing in the middle of the floor and looked over with raised eyebrows.

Without hesitation, Nylah nodded and answered, "I really do. I'm just trippin'."

"Girl, you're always trippin' and messing up somebody's vibe," Yara said, giggling uncontrollably. She was hosting this week's ladies' night at her house and had cooked meatballs and a kale salad. It was a good thing she was already home because she clearly could not handle her liquor.

"Shut up," Nylah extended her foot, playfully kicking her friend. The girls all erupted into laughter then, and just like that, the memories and mention of Bentley were long gone.

More than an hour later, Nylah was pulling up in her driveway and stumbling slightly in her unstrapped high heels. She had only downed two glasses of white zinfandel but could tell that her head was already throbbing because of it. This was her first time drinking so much in a long while, and she was glad that she could get away from the norm for just one night. It was the weekend, and her daughter had been with her father the last three days, so she had the house to herself.

Or not.

The silhouette of her boyfriend grabbed her attention as she fumbled with the keys. He was blocking the light from the patio and looked to be holding his own bottle of liquor in one hand. "So, we're just not answering phone calls now? Is that what we're doing?"

It was too late for this.

"What?" Nylah brushed past him into the house and dropped everything on the couch, her body included.

"I called you three times tonight. What are you doing out this late?"

"I'm sorry, Malik. Is it that serious?" She kicked off her shoes and sighed. The strands of hair that had fallen into her face blew upward, and then settled back in their original spot. "I was at Yara's. There was music playing, and we were laughing. I probably had my phone on vibrate and couldn't hear you. Calm down, baby."

He didn't look too impressed as he took another swig from the long-necked brown bottle. But he calmed down, placing his bottle on the table, and joining Nylah on the couch. His head lolled to the side, settling on her shoulder. "You gotta start telling me these things. I was worried."

Her heart melted at his sweet words as he kissed along her collarbone. "I promise not to scare you ever again. C'mere."

The two kissed.

"Can I run your bath water? Rub you down?" He looked at her with glazed, bloodshot eyes. She grinned and shook her head.

"You can do both of those things, and then leave," she teased, and then put her finger over his lips. "I'm still standing on my promise. No sex, and I mean that."

He looked disappointed and shook his head. "It's been THREE months. How much longer? You can't be making these demands when you come in here looking like *this*."

Clearly, Nylah's little black dress, fishnet stockings, and exposed cleavage were too much for him. She grabbed his hand and led him to the master bedroom. "When you put a ring on it, you can sample all the milk you want. Until then, continue to court me and respect my wishes. You got that, big boy?"

Nylah could feel his eyes on her backside, but then she stopped in her tracks to get his attention again.

Finally, he answered, while biting his lip. "Yeah, yeah. I got it."

As promised, Malik ran her bath water and popped in a CBD-infused bath bomb. He also massaged her feet and back, and then left. With no Malik around to scold her, with no friends to take away her erratic thoughts, and with no daughter to ask her what was bothering her, Nylah cried herself to sleep as she had done every night since signing the divorce papers.

# Chapter Five

"*Mommmmmyyyy*! I'm hoooome!"

The weekend flew by and the little person who had stolen Nylah's heart from day one, burst into the master bedroom. Brooklyn Faith wore two long ponytails, a tutu, and big sunglasses that nearly covered her entire face. Nylah could not help but to chuckle in amusement. "Hey, diva! I mean, baby. I missed you."

"I missed you too. Look what Daddy got me," she said and wiggled her shoulder. Nylah noticed the new fancy, purple purse that sat there.

"Oh, that is too cute." She bent to hug her daughter and kissed her forehead. "Is Daddy outside or did he drop you off?"

"Daddy's right here," another voice entered their conversation.

Nylah tore her eyes away from Brooklyn's excited face to slowly look up at the doorway. She was greeted by a half-grin and a bouquet of flowers. Her ex-husband leaned coolly against the doorframe rocking a pair of dark jeans, tennis shoes, and a hooded dashiki. He looked like he had stepped out of the pages of a men's fashion magazine.

This man had completely reinvented himself from the day that Nylah fell in love with him until now. His closet now consisted of the finest suits, shoes, and designer garments. No longer awkward and shy, he now exuded sexiness and self-assurance, and she always admired how far he had come along. Not to mention, he had made hundreds of thousands of dollars from his landscaping business, rental properties, and his fast-food restaurant ownership. Nylah was proud of the man he had become. If there were ever a definition of 'rags to riches,' it would be Bentley.

"These are for me?" She motioned towards the fragranced bouquet, knowing good and well they were. He always bought her flowers and had not stopped even after their split.

"These are for you," he repeated, walking forward. He pulled Nylah into his arms for a hug, and then kissed the side of her face. His cologne entered her nostrils deliciously. "I know I'm a few days early, but Happy Birthday, Love."

"Aw, you didn't have to do this," she murmured and then buried her nose in the carnations.

They were her favorite. "Thank you. These are lovely."

Bentley was always doing something sweet and thoughtful. To this day, most people didn't understand their friendship and love for one another. They had literally been in each other's lives since childhood, and they vowed to grow old together, just not as a married couple. Nylah was still getting over the shock of their divorce, but moments like this made her more comfortable.

It was time to take Brooklyn to her dance academy just a few blocks up from Nylah's home. They would normally walk down, but it was scorching out, and she didn't want her daughter's eczema to flare up. No parents were allowed to sit in on the rehearsals, so after dropping Brooklyn off, the two decided to eat breakfast at a nearby café.

"So, how've you been? How's your mom doing?"

"She's been okay," Bentley exhaled heavily and shrugged a shoulder. "I've got her all moved in at her new assisted living complex, and she seems to like it so far."

"That's good to hear. I haven't seen her in forever. How's the wedding planning going?" she asked nonchalantly, peeking over the menu. Nylah could not care less about his response, but she was just making conversation.

He sipped on his glass of water, and it seemed to go down the wrong way. He choked for a second while Nylah looked on with raised eyebrows. "Aw, man. Excuse me."

"That bad, huh?" she joked.

"No wedding talk, please," Bentley said and wiped his mouth with a napkin. "Jazlyn is workin' my LAST nerve with her extravagant spending and all these grand ideas. She wants to fly out to Jamaica for the ceremony, and then go to Hawaii for the honeymoon."

"Does she have Jamaica and Hawaii money?" Nylah rolled her eyes, sitting up a little straighter. "Better yet, does she have a job yet?"

"Not exactly. She's just doing her little modeling gigs here and there, but that's about it. I'm paying for all of it," Bentley said, rubbing his forehead in frustration. "It's stressful."

She shook her head and reached out to touch his hand. "It's written all over your face. We can change the subject."

"How about you and…uh…?"

"Malik," Nylah completed his sentence. She placed her menu at the corner of the table and folded her hands in front of her. "We're doing well. Everything's still fresh, and we're taking things slow."

She studied him for a moment, sensing his next question. "To answer your question. *No*, he still hasn't met Brooklyn, and I'm trying to keep it that way for as long as possible."

"Good choice." Bentley winked, as their waitress walked up at the same time. The young woman openly gawked at him and fumbled with her pen and pad. Nylah could not blame her.

Since their younger days, Bentley had transformed into something special. Confidence now oozed from his pores, his skin had cleared up, and he had a sex appeal that could not be ignored. Even now, dressed casually, he had turned heads from the moment the two stepped into the restaurant.

"We'll both have a veggie omelet, American fries, and orange juice with ice, please," he spoke and waved his hands in front of the girl's face. She giggled nervously, scribbled on her notepad, and then turned around. Nylah watched as the poor girl miscalculated her steps, ran smack into another waiter holding a tray of drinks, and everybody went down with a loud crash.

Bentley held back his laughter, and Nylah was reminded of the days that they would go out on dates, late at night. It used to be him and her against the world. Those were the good old days.

*Wait.* There she was daydreaming and reminiscing again.

"I'm sorry. What did you say?" She snapped out of her thoughts and read his full lips as he repeated himself.

"You okay?"

"I'm fine. What were you saying?"

"I was saying we have a housewarming this Friday. I know it's last minute, but it's something Jaz came up with. You and…uh…"

"*Malik.*"

"…yeah, him. You guys should stop through."

"I guess I could and *should* meet the woman who's going to be in my daughter's life," Nylah said, slicing into the warm loaf of complimentary wheat bread with a butter knife. "How does she feel about me coming?"

Bentley cocked his head to the side. "It doesn't matter. I invited you, and I want you there. I'm the king of *my* castle." He balled his fist and beat on his chest in a manly way.

"Well, the king has spoken," she teased. "Just text me the details. We'll be there."

"It'll be fun. Good food, games, drinks, and I can finally meet…" He pretended to forget her boyfriend's name again, snapping his fingers.

Nylah threw a piece of bread his way, laughing, "His name is Malik! I'm going to need you to remember it!"

After breakfast, when the check came, Nylah reached for her purse, and he slapped her hand away. "Girl, what are you doing? I've got this."

"No, let me pay for my own portion. You've done enough."

"I could never do enough for the mother of my child. Stop acting like you don't know how I operate, woman," he fussed and then winked at her. He tucked his credit card in the leather booklet and then flagged the waitress down.

A few minutes went by before she returned with a frown on her face. "Mr. Rose, I'm afraid your card has been declined. Do you have another form of payment?"

"*Declined?*" Bentley asked in shock. He looked confused, staring at his card, and then back up at the waitress. "I have over twelve grand on that card."

She seemed to be unmoved by his explanation, tucked her hands in her apron, and then waited for one of them to give her another form of payment. Frustrated, Bentley reached into his back pocket, pulled out a hundred-dollar bill, and then eased it into her hand.

"Keep the change. Thanks for your hospitality," he offered her a final smile and wave, and then looked at Nylah. "It must be Jaz. She's been doing so much shopping for the house; it's not even funny. She must've maxed the card out."

Nylah shook her head and then rolled her eyes. "Twelve grand, though? That's pretty ridiculous. Why do you allow her so much access? At least wait until you two get married." She watched him grab his phone and send a text message. "I also hope you have a prenup in place."

Bentley didn't agree or disagree, or even acknowledge her statement. Instead, he clapped his hands together once and then motioned for her to get up. "You ready to pick up the youngin' in charge?"

The two swung back by the studio to pick Brooklyn up, and then parted ways. While Nylah straightened the house, Brooklyn went on and on about how much fun she had in her class. She had learned a few new techniques and received a lot of compliments on her purse.

"You want to show me what you learned?" Nylah asked, as she hovered over the stovetop to make Brooklyn lunch.

"It's a surprise. No peeks allowed!" the child spoke sassily, one hand on her hip. "I hope you and Daddy can come to my recycle."

"You mean your *recital?*" Nylah corrected her, "And of course we'll be there, baby. We always come out to support our little superstar."

Brooklyn looked up from her drawing and held out her pinky as she talked, "You promise?"

Nylah walked over, locked pinkies with her, and then gave her word. "I promise."

"Aye, baby! You in here? Jaz!"

Bentley strolled through his home, looking in every direction and shouting in each room he passed. The handsome, 28-year-old tossed his keys on the marbled kitchen countertop, and then called out to his fiancée again. His agitated voice echoed throughout the house and received no response, so he figured that she was in somebody's salon, getting her weekly manicure and pedicure.

Boxes were still neatly stacked along the walls and the aroma of fresh paint was intense. Bentley could not wait for maintenance to fully complete their new home, and he was ready for the housewarming to be over and done with. There was no telling what his woman was up to. She had been borrowing the card all week and judging by the embarrassing restaurant encounter a half-hour before, she had borrowed his card one time too many.

"JAZ!" Bentley called out a final time, and then heard the faint sounds of female laughter and chatter. It sounded like she was chilling out back, poolside, with a few of her equally high maintenance friends.

*Ugh, here we go,* he thought.

Ducking his head out of the door, he spotted her and two other women splashing around in the pool. It had been a gift from his employees and was put to use every weekend. Jazlyn was a party girl in every sense of the word; she hated to cook or clean and did not watch anything other than *Love & Hip Hop* and *America's Next Top Model* reruns. Although they were opposites, their attraction for one another was high.

As much as he hated to fornicate and sin, her love was addicting. She made him feel 18 all over again.

"Can I speak to you for a second, Jaz?" he asked and then waved to her friends. "Hello, ladies."

"Hi," the women cooed, eyeing him head to toe appreciatively.

"What's up, baby?"

Jazlyn never budged from her poolside perch. Her toenails glittered with fresh polish and her dark hair was now highlighted with color—completely different than when he'd seen her this morning.

She held a glass of champagne in one hand and an assorted box of chocolates in the other. He looked from her, back to her nosey friends, and then rolled his eyes. One was blatantly staring at his groin

67

while the other was looking back and forth between he and Jaz in amusement.

"Can I speak to YOU for a second?" Bentley repeated. "*Now?*"

"What's the rush?"

"Because I said so, Jazlyn. In the house...NOW!"

Deepening the tone of his voice, Bentley watched as his fiancée looked at her friends in humiliation, pulled her legs from the cool water, and then sauntered over. She kept her eyes on him as she angrily snatched her robe closed and then followed him into the house.

"You want to tell me what you're so upset and pissed about?" she questioned, slamming the side door shut. "How dare you talk to me like that."

"I can ask you the same thing. You want to tell me what's up with my credit card? I tried to use it this morning at breakfast, and it was declined. What's especially hilarious is that I specifically gave you a budget and you went over it. Why is my card maxed out? Do you know anything about *that?*"

Jazlyn looked down at her short and squared fingernails. "Breakfast? Who did you go to breakfast with?"

"Of ALL the things I just said, that's what you choose to focus on?" He shook his head incredulously. "If you must know what I do with MY own money and MY time—during Brooklyn's dance class, me and Nylah grabbed something to eat. It's no big deal. We go out often. Answer my questions!"

"It's a VERY big deal, Bentley," Jazlyn forced through gritted teeth. "Do you see me going out with exes and having lunch with people I used to sleep with?"

Bentley rubbed the back of his tense neck and could feel himself grow more and more agitated. They were having yet another disagreement about her spending habits and she wanted to turn the blame on him. It was a typical Jazlyn move and one that he was beginning to catch onto.

"Where did you spend my money, Jazlyn? I'm not waiting for the month to be over to get a statement. What did you buy? More shoes? More clothes? What?"

Nervously, she twisted her fingers like a reprimanded child and then looked him in the eye. "I booked a three-night stay in Cabo with a friend. I didn't want to tell you until the week of the trip because I knew you would be mad."

"*Mad* is not even the word." It was his turn to speak through gritted teeth. Bentley's patience had officially grown thin. "You're just being reckless…with MY money. We discussed getting furniture for the house and things for the wedding; I said nothing about booking lavish trips with friends. Of course, I'm not happy with you."

"Don't be upset with me," Jazlyn pouted and wrapped her arms around his neck. Her lipstick-covered mouth kissed along his face, and then she snaked her tongue out to run along the curve of his earlobe. He shuttered instantaneously, which caused a thin smile to creep along her face. "Please don't be upset."

"Jaz, stop. It's—it's not going to work."

"I know I've been bad, but I promise I'll make it up to you," she all but purred.

"Oh yeah? How?" he asked, giving into her seductive tone. He couldn't help but to toss his frustrations aside for the moment as she slid her tight little body against his. She was magnetic and he could not stay angry with her for long.

Jazlyn told her friends to see their way out, returned to him, and then dropped her robe. The swimsuit that barely covered her womanly parts was moist against her skin and water still dripped from her lower half onto the floor.

All was forgiven. All was forgotten.

## Chapter Six

The workweek flew by, Friday rolled around, and before Nylah knew it, Bentley's housewarming was beginning in another hour. Malik was in her bedroom, watching a basketball game on the edge of the bed, while she stood in the bathroom trying to tame her hair with the flat iron. "Baby, come zip me up," she called out.

He never came.

Nylah rolled her eyes and bounced around barefoot in the skintight, ruby-colored dress. It was backless and hung to skim the tops of her thighs.

"Babe?" she called out to Malik again, and then gave up the battle when she heard the faint sounds of the sports commentator. Malik had more than likely fallen asleep while waiting for her.

She scurried out to the room and was surprised to see him standing by the nightstand. He was reading the small, white card that had come with her flowers from Bentley. Leisurely, he held the card up and then looked over at her. "He's still giving you gifts?"

"Please don't start."

"Nah, I'm going to start because every time I turn around, he's sending you flowers, taking you out to eat, or you're going to the movies with him. Is there something you want to tell me?" Malik asked and grabbed the flowers.

"We have a daughter. What do you expect? We're always going to be in each other's lives. It's not like we're sleeping around. What are you doing, Malik?" Nylah watched in disbelief as he threw her carnations away.

"That's the last gift you'll ever receive from him. Believe that." Malik settled on the edge of the bed and continued his basketball game.

"Are you serious right now? It was just a nice birthday gesture, especially since I don't recall my man buying me anything," she pointed out and slid her earrings in one by one. She twirled around and stomped back into the bathroom, and then zipped her dress up angrily. The zipper broke in the process, and Nylah screamed out in frustration.

"It wasn't meant for you to wear that anyway," he commented. "*Way* too short and *way* too tight. I don't need any other reasons for Bentley to be after my woman."

"You're beginning to piss me off!"

73

Malik rushed into the bathroom, and she could hear his teeth grinding together. It was so intense that she cringed as if she was doing the grinding. "What did you say to me?"

"I said, you're beginning to piss me off. That's my child's father. You knew exactly what you signed up for when we met. Stop all of that," she challenged him and shimmed out of the dress. She would have to find another outfit because this one obviously was not going to work.

Nylah ducked around him to head back out into the room, but he grabbed her arm. She was glad that Brooklyn wasn't in the house to witness their altercation. His grip tightened with each word. "Stop acting out and get ready. I already don't want to go."

She yanked her wrist from his death grip, and then rubbed at the bruising area. "Then don't go. But don't you ever…EVER put your hands on me again. You hear me?"

"Yeah. Whateva."

Nylah watched Malik storm out and then looked in the mirror. She was not sure why he was so insecure and overprotective, but he had truly lost his mind grabbing her like she was just some dude off the street. She glanced down at her throbbing flesh and shook her head.

Nylah changed into a gold bodysuit and added a few accessories before deciding things were as good as they were going to get. Malik was sitting on the couch when she made her way down the staircase.

"What did you decide to do?"

"Look, baby, that won't happen again. I'm so sorry," Malik apologized while his eyes watered. He reached for her, and without a fight, she gave into his charm. Malik was not one to show emotions, so Nylah knew that he had made an honest mistake by grabbing her.

"Please forgive me. I'm so in love with you, and I don't want you to ever doubt that. It's just that money is tight right now, and that frustrates me. It's killin' me that I was unable to buy you anything for your birthday, and he did."

"I know, baby. I'm sorry if I was out of line. I love you too." She kissed his lips slowly and sweetly. "Now, let's go before we miss this gathering."

He licked his lips and grabbed her butt. "Maybe that's not such a bad thing. You're lookin' good."

Nylah propped her hands on her knees, bent over, and danced for him playfully. The excitement in his eyes made her laugh as she dodged his hands. "Ah-ah, no touching. Let's go."

The couple made it to the Rose household in record time, thanks to Nylah's lead foot. There were about 75 attendees, most of them dressed to the nines, snotty and privileged, and far different from Bentley's usual circle. She admired the ambiance and décor in mild interest. Everything from the rugs to the lamps, and even to the door handles was brimming with gold. It was no wonder Bentley's card had been maxed out.

Nylah shook her head, already dreading coming but knowing her ex-husband needed her support more than he let on. Her eyes searched out the woman in question—the woman who had somehow stolen his heart and the woman who she didn't want in her daughter's life though she had no choice.

*Bingo.* Nylah's heart tightened as she zeroed in on the Afro-Latina. Jazlyn was as uppity as she imagined her to be—beautiful but not Bentley's type. She walked around the house in a faux fur with only a swimsuit underneath. The house was incredible, but the way she pranced around like she was paying a single bill was beyond Nylah. She just knew that she was on some hidden camera show.

"Who is she? Like a model or something?" Malik asked, looking Jazlyn up and down. Like Nylah, he was trying to hold back his laughter.

"*Aspiring* swimsuit model," she corrected and shook her head.

"Why is she *literally* in a swimsuit though? Who does that?"

"She's tacky. That's why."

At that moment, Jazlyn turned and looked at them.

"Hello, I'm Jazlyn. Welcome to my home." She hugged them both dramatically, and then eased her long fingers down the faux fur. "I'm sorry, I'm not good with names or faces. Who invited you?"

*No, she didn't.*

"Hi." Nylah extended her hand and watched Jazlyn reluctantly take it. "I'm sure you've heard my name come out of your fiancé's mouth before. Nylah Christiansen."

"Nylah…? Oh, I haven't heard of you, sorry."

Jazlyn's sarcastic words were ignored. She was attempting to push Nylah's buttons. Obviously, she was aware of who she was. "This is Malik, my boyfriend, and that pretty girl sitting poolside with the other kids? That's my daughter."

"Oh, well, nice to meet you. Enjoy a few drinks, refreshments, and stick around. We'll have a raffle in a few minutes," she said and smiled pleasantly.

Nylah rolled her eyes and waved Bentley over. With a smirk, he embraced her for a long while. "Hey, Love. Glad you could make it. *Malik.*"

"*Bentley.*"

Nylah watched as her past and present partners stared one another down for a second. Only when Jazlyn cleared her throat did they glance away from one another, and she breathed a sigh of relief. They each had big egos, and Nylah wanted to be sure that tension never arose between them. If they were all going to be in each other's lives, they had to all act like mature adults.

Jazlyn made her way to the center of the room again and got everyone's attention. Then she pulled on Bentley's arm, dragging him from Nylah.

"Baby, would you like to do the honors?"

Bentley's face was hilarious. He looked exhausted, perplexed, and ready to strangle Jazlyn. "Do the honors of *what?*"

"Our raffle, duh. We have a best-dressed prize, worst-dressed prize, and first to arrive prize."

Bentley shook his head, placing his wineglass on the table. "Since when did we agree on this?"

"Bentley, really? Remember you said…"

Nylah watched in amusement as they talked through their teeth in frustration. Her ex-husband raised his hands in defeat and was clearly not in the mood for an argument. "Okay, okay. You can go ahead and give the prizes out. Wrap it up though. I have to work in the morning."

Jazlyn blew hot air from her mouth, but then composed herself, and tapped her fork to the glass. "Can I have everyone's attention, pleeease?" When the chatter died down, she deposited her wineglass on an end table. She clapped her hands together and turned to address everyone with a cheesy smile.

"I am so appreciative of all the gifts and love you've given us tonight. Thank you so much for coming out. As my thank you to our guests, I do have prizes for a few people tonight. Starting with *you.*"

Nylah watched in utter disbelief as Jazlyn singled her out.

Jazlyn dramatically bent down to grab a gift bag and then handed it to her. Still speaking to the crowd, she continued, "*This* woman gets the worst-dressed prize for her underwhelming taste in this gold jumpsuit from a couple seasons ago."

Nylah's jaw nearly hit the floor.

Jazlyn continued, "Inside the bag is a $50 gift card to one of my favorite boutiques downtown. Enjoy."

"This woman? Worst-dressed?" Nylah repeated.

Some people, including Malik, found her antics amusing. Bentley looked infuriated. Then there was Jazlyn. She had a grin on her face, and it took everything in Nylah not to wipe it off.

"*Excuse you?*"

"What? You don't shop there?"

"No, heffa, I'll show you where I shop. Malik, hold my clutch." Before Nylah could *really* react, Bentley took the gift bag from her hands, shoved it in Jazlyn's unexpected hands, and then apologized.

"Look, I'll call you tomorrow. I don't know what's wrong with her. Y'all get home safely," Bentley said and hugged her a final time. His eyes were on his fiancée's in shock and fury.

"Get your girl, B. Get your girl," were Nylah's last words, as she broke free from his arms.

Nylah's irritation stayed with her for the next couple of days, and she just had to vent to someone.

"She did *WHAT*?"

"Girl, yes," she said into the phone.

Nylah told Yara word for word what had gone down at the housewarming with Jazlyn. Her blood was boiling still, and it was a blessing that it was Sunday, so that she could get some praise and worship in. "Malik and a few other guests laughed. That upset me even more."

"That wench better HOPE I never run into her. Well, did Bentley at least put her in check?"

Nylah maneuvered around the spacious condo, while she pinned her hair up, shimmed into a pair of nude-colored stockings, and then smoothed on some powder foundation.

"Yes. That, at least, made me feel a little better. I don't know why she doesn't respect our relationship. She has to accept the fact that I had him first, and that I'll *always* come before anybody in his eyes," Nylah mimicked his voice as she talked. "At least until the wedding, anyway."

Brooklyn was tugging on her stockings in the bedroom over and making all sorts of sounds. Nylah peeked in at her, as she still balanced the cell phone between her shoulder and face. "You need help or you got it?"

Her face was reddened with frustration. "I can't get it, Momma."

Nylah wrapped up her conversation with her friend and then helped her daughter with the stockings. They would be late to church if they didn't put more pep in their step. "C'mon, baby."

She placed her hand on Brooklyn's head, done up in Shirley Temple curls, and led her out to the attached garage.

It had been a while since she walked into the doors of her longtime worship center, but she was looking forward to renewing her membership and commitment. Nylah could remember it was Bentley that had first gotten her into the routine of giving God just two hours of her week. For the longest time, she would keep up with the days and never miss a service. Nowadays, Nylah was looking at BET broadcasts of televangelists and counting that as her church time.

Prayer was also out of the door much of the time since the divorce. She no longer felt like God could hear her. Lord knows, she had been drinking lately, growing angrier quicker, feeling unhappy more, and was finding it harder and harder to flee temptation with her thoughts.

Although she had not slept with Malik yet, there were many instances where Nylah wanted him to take her to new heights sexually and cure her loneliness. There was only so much that her vibrator and a porno could do.

She had to get it together. If not for her own salvation, Nylah needed to show Brooklyn the *right* way.

# Chapter Seven

*Bentley*

His head was killing him.

*Pounding.*

Aching.

Without pain medication handy, Bentley briefly wished something, *anything,* would take him out of his misery. The throb in his head was so piercing that his eyelids were lowered in agony, and not even painkillers could ease the pain. Bentley knew why he was suffering, just as he was aware that he had to continue with his day. Only one person in the world understood his discomfort, and she was so far away from him at this moment.

For several agonizing moments, his body was immobile as he leaned against the shower wall. His waist was still wrapped in the towel that he had placed there a half-hour before. His fingers massaged his temples deeply a few times, and then he exhaled as if it would make the twinge go away.

The room spun around him then, and dizziness brought Bentley to his knees. It was a good thing Jazlyn was asleep in the bedroom, because as the towel unfastened and fell from his body, the remnants of last night's Buffalo wings and steak fries made their quick escape upward and out of his mouth. He cringed as the bathroom became filled with the pungency of vomit.

"Have mercy, God."

It did not mean it was the end of the world for him; it just meant that he had to take it easy for the next week or two.

Bentley was accustomed to his imperfect health, as it was the late-night restlessness, early morning vomiting, excruciating migraines, and faking normality that made up much of his young life. With no one to take care of him or even fully understand his body's functionality, Bentley mustered up the courage to crawl around the bathroom, clean up the mess, and go on with his morning routine.

It was a Sunday—one that Bentley had never seen before, but one that he was grateful for, and one that he planned to praise God for. Since he was a child, he had been raised in the church and was taught how to live and breathe by the Bible. For the most part, his life had been a proper reflection of the Word of God. Other than tattoos and a few curse words when he was *really* upset, he had waited until his wedding day to have sex. He and Nylah had also conceived Brooklyn long after their wedding vows were exchanged, and he had been a faithful husband while their marriage lasted.

Only lately did Bentley begin to backslide and find himself sleeping in on days that were once reserved for God. Jazlyn had never been a churchgoer and was no help. Oftentimes, she would throw a leg over his waist and coax him into staying in to eat breakfast in bed with her. She would demand that he make love to her during their steamy showers and any willpower was out of the door. Even his tithing was slacking, and his money was staying in his wallets now instead of filling the collection plates. It was not intentional, but it was slowly becoming his reality. Bentley's father was probably turning over in his grave at his actions and God certainly was not pleased.

Bentley had to get himself together and be a better example for Brooklyn.

Eventually, he found enough strength to rewash and move from the bathroom to the bedroom. Jazlyn's soft snores could be heard as he tugged on clothing, sprayed cologne here and there, and then brushed his hair. Bentley wedged a granola bar between the thick, sculpted lips staring back at him. He chewed lazily, in vain. Hunger was not there but the medication that he had taken would need some food to accompany it.

Two weeks prior, Bentley had shopped online, bought this outfit with the coordinating dress shoes and bowtie, and was ready for the world. But something was missing as he peered into the mirror. There was something not nearly as fulfilling in his life, and it had felt that way for a while now. Usually dropping a couple hundred dollars on new clothes and sneakers gave him a particular satisfaction, and yet all it amounted to now was hundreds of dollars foolishly wasted.

"Looking good but feeling bad," Bentley spoke aloud.

"Hmm?" Jazlyn rolled over and mumbled, "What did you say?"

He ignored her sleepy inquiry, still disappointed in her actions. She had blatantly disrespected and embarrassed his child's mother, and he was not okay with that. The two had a long, heated discussion once everyone cleared their home that night. He recalled their yelling matching with a cringe.

*"All right, have a good night. Thank you."*

Bentley closed the door behind their last guest and whipped around to glare at his fiancée. His smile disappeared and a scowl took over his striking features.

"Are you crazy?"

Jazlyn was standing in front of their bar with her faux fur thrown over the back of the couch. She shimmied out of her swimsuit in the middle of the room. He was unsure why she had worn the ridiculous outfit in the first place. She was idolizing Beyoncé way too much in his opinion.

"Crazy? No. Fabulous? Of course," she said playfully and tossed her swimsuit to the floor.

Bentley ignored her naked body and could not remember a time where he was ever so angry with her. From the credit card incident to now, he was not sure what had gotten into her, but he hated the woman she was becoming. Jealousy looked good on no one.

He spoke firmly, "You're joking and I'm being serious."

"I was being serious too. Your baby's mother needs help in the wardrobe department. I was just being helpful." She shrugged innocently. "Didn't you say that we should all be one big, happy family and love on one another? That gift card was more than generous."

Bentley moved swiftly to the master bedroom, and she tiptoed after. His voice had raised decibels as he tried to prove

88

*his point, but he did not want his daughter to hear them arguing. He had tucked her in a little while ago in her bedroom.*

*"You know that wasn't your intention, so stop lying. You were purposely trying to embarrass her, and I'll never be okay with that."*

*"You act like I called her out of her name."*

*"Jazlyn, I'm going to say this once, and I'm not going to repeat myself. For as long as I have breath in my body, you will never disrespect me, my child, or my child's mother like that again. You hear me?"*

*"Whatever."*

*"Do you HEAR me?" he repeated and cuffed her forearm in his grasp.*

*She looked down at where his hand was, raised a perfectly arched eyebrow, and then spoke up when he removed his hold on her.*

*"I hear you," she said and settled on her side of the bed, "and if I didn't know any better, I would say you were defending her because you still have feelings for her."*

*"Yeah, well..." Bentley shrugged out of his clothing and then joined her in the gigantic bed. Roughly, he yanked the blanket up to his ear. "We all know you don't know any better."*

*Jazlyn stared at the side of his face in disbelief for the remainder of the night.*

Bentley broke free from his thoughts and stepped leisurely through a sunny paradise of full-bloomed flowers and well-trimmed bushes that the landscaper had done. His eyes lifted as he took in the gorgeous outside world.

A sprinkler was going off not far from where he walked. One droplet settled atop his nose, and it seemed to warm immediately against his flesh. Bentley smirked at the innocence of God's surrounding creations, not even bothering to wipe where the tiny puddle had formed as he settled in the *Cayenne S Hybrid Porsche*. Truly a blessing from above, the earnings from his businesses had made this dream truck possible.

KB, one of his favorite Christian rappers, met his ears as he pulled from the three-car garage. Church was calling and nothing or no one would stop him from getting there.

A short drive over led him to the parking lot of Abundant Faith Christian Worship Center.

"It's a full house today," Bentley said thoughtfully, searching for a parking space.

The first image that met his eyes, as he pulled further in, was a breathtaking one. It was one that made him smile, and was one that always drew him in. The image of his ex-wife and daughter threatened to make him jam on brakes, but it would prove dangerous and reason for a collision as other churchgoers drove in behind him.

Nylah Estelle Christiansen—even her name was sexy and captivating.

Bentley had not seen her in over 36 hours, but his heart tripled in beat as he took all of her in. As he parked, he remembered the first time that he brought her here. Because she was new to the whole church thing, she had been timid, unsure, and awkward. Bentley could remember her grooving to the praise team before an usher came over and told her that her skirt was too short, and her dance moves were inappropriate. From then, she had done her best to dress conservatively and act decently.

Bentley loved her for trying so hard. He fell deeper in love when she gave her life to God with him by her side and had joined the church all in the same day. He also recalled how comfortable she grew in the house of the Lord, joining the young adults' choir and praise dance ministry, and from then on, everyone loved her. Bentley was happy to see her here.

"Good mornin', Daddy!"

His thoughts were interrupted as he looked down at his little nugget running up. Nylah and Brooklyn were matching from head to toe in the same-colored clothes, accessories, and shoes. Their hair was similar as well; there were curls for days.

"Morning, Princess. You look beautiful," he glanced up and added, "Both of you."

Bentley was convinced that his ex-wife was still one of the most gorgeous women to have ever graced the earth. She was stunning in all white. It was the rightful color to mirror her angelic personality. Her long, thick hair was loosely curled and gathered over a shoulder, and a wide smile touched her crimson-tinted lips. His daughter tugged at the headband on her head and asked if he liked her new dress.

"I love it. Who picked it out?"

"You, silly!"

She giggled and jumped around for a bit. Nylah looked like something was on her mind as she skimmed through her tiny handbag for whatever piece of cosmetic. Truthfully, Bentley thought she looked perfect already. Her 5'3" height was extended by inches, and the high heels explained that difference. He always loved her in heels, and not that she lacked any, but they gave her an undeniable sexiness and even more confidence. This was especially true the way the straps wrapped along her calves and allowed her pretty toes to peek out just slightly.

"Are you okay?"

"Yeah, why do you ask?" Bentley looked to where Nylah was frowning and examining his face. She pressed the back of her hand to his forehead and then the underside of his neck.

"Boy, you are burning up! Do you have another infection?"

Bentley could not help smirking. It was just like Nylah to pinpoint exactly what was wrong with him. Jazlyn had not even noticed that he was not feeling well lately, and yet the woman he did not live with, was diagnosing him and taking notice of his fatigue and discomfort. Nylah knew him almost as much as she knew herself. To this day, it was still impressive how in tune she was with him.

"I'm fine, I promise," he chuckled, "I haven't been taking my antibiotics like I should but it's cool."

"It's *not* cool. You haven't had a kidney infection in over three years. You *have* to take better care of yourself," she commanded and gave him another stern look. "For real."

"I hear you. I hear you."

Worship would be starting shortly, so Bentley decided to take action. There was no sense in standing around, looking silly. "Are we sitting together? Or you want to sit by Momma?" he asked their daughter.

Brooklyn grabbed his hand and then looked back and forth between them. Her face scrunched up. "Can I sit in between you until it's time to go to children's church?"

Nylah shrugged and he agreed. "Let's go. Ladies first."

Brooklyn took off running, spotting her friend near the back row. "So much for that seating arrangement," Bentley joked. "By the way, welcome back."

"I know, right? Same to you. It feels good to be back." Nylah turned then, heading for the building but not making it very far before a crack in the cement tripped up her step.

"Careful."

Bentley offered his arm to her. Reluctantly, she took it, and softly thanked him. He continued holding onto her arm, as he walked with her, "I didn't know you two were coming today."

"Well," Nylah smiled widely this time and nodded. Her teeth and smile were even prettier than when they were younger, and they seemed to glisten in the morning light. "Friday was just the push I needed to realize I need God again."

"I can't apologize enough about that. I don't know why Jazlyn acts that way."

They settled in the second to last row, and his arm naturally came around to sit around her shoulders. Nylah jokingly frowned at him, and then settled further in her seat. The usher who had seated them, leaned in, and whispered, "I'm so happy you two are back together!"

Before Bentley could protest, the middle-aged woman was tending to another couple coming in, and all he could do was laugh. "As I was saying, Jazlyn is usually so mellow. I don't know what it is, but you get under her skin."

"It's not rocket science, B. I had you first, and if I wanted, I could have you again. That thought probably kills her each time she sees me."

Her words flowed so easily and confidently that it caused him to whip around and look at her. She kept her eyes on the praise and worship team setting up near the pulpit. The more Bentley stared, the more uncomfortable she seemed to get.

"Had me and could have me again if you wanted?" he repeated.

"Shhh. Church is starting," Nylah said simply, leaving him hanging. She stood to her feet, a tambourine in her hand, and beat it against her palm to the music. She smelled amazing as she moved around.

Finally, still watching her, their eyes locked for a moment's time, as she placed her tambourine on his lap. The corners of her mouth lifted just briefly, and she shook her head in amusement, "This coffee ran right through me."

All at once, her smile left and so did she. The switch of her hips and head full of curls was the last thing he saw as she headed for the restrooms and never returned.

# Chapter Eight

"Why did you leave earlier? You okay?"

Bentley knew he was not tripping. Nylah did not pee at church. She had found their daughter in children's church and left. After service, he stopped by to make sure everything was okay.

Brooklyn was asleep on the couch with a coloring book on her lap and crayons in her hand. She was a picky eater and had begged for a grilled cheese sandwich and homemade fries. Remnants of it sat on the plate just a few inches away from her. Nylah prepared regular dinner at the stove with her back to Bentley. She had changed from her dressy attire to lounge shorts and an oversized shirt that stayed closed with only one button. He recognized it as one of his old work shirts.

"I was tired," she said simply, and stirred her pot of jambalaya.

In the oven were buttery dinner rolls. The aromas were doing something to his stomach. Jazlyn had not cooked today. Correction: Jazlyn *never* cooked. It was just something that she had not taken the time out to learn, and instead, had become an expert in making reservations and placing fast-food orders. This was something that he missed from he and Nylah's marriage. A brotha could appreciate a home-cooked meal every once in awhile.

"I hear you," Bentley said and drummed his fingers along the countertop. He watched her move around the kitchen fluidly. The way she sprinkled seasoning here and there, tasted her creation, and then plated the food was all so mesmerizing. "Can I stay for dinner or is your man coming through?"

"You can stay for dinner. Malik is out of town on business."

"Where to?"

"I'm not sure. He didn't say, and I didn't ask."

"Oh." Bentley raised an eyebrow and nodded deliberately. "Okay."

"What?"

"I didn't say anything." He grabbed a ceramic plate and placed two scoops of jambalaya at the center of it. He was starving and planned to eat every piece of rice, Andouille sausage, green pepper, and onion.

Before sitting down with Nylah to eat, he moved Brooklyn to her bedroom and tucked her in.

Then he returned to the living room, led prayer, and then dived in.

"Church was good. Pastor preached his behind off."

"What was the topic?"

"How to live a purpose-driven life. He's doing a part two message next week."

Nylah looked distracted. Even as Bentley talked and she responded, he noticed how her eyes did not quite meet his, and how she looked away shyly. Something was definitely off with her.

"What's wrong, Love?" He put his fork down and eyed her. "Did I do something?"

"No, not at all." She dabbed her mouth with a napkin. "I told you, I'm just tired."

"You must think I'm Malik. I know everything about you, just like I know how you look when you're tired. You rub your eyes and laugh a lot whenever you're sleepy. When you're angry, your eyes well up and your cheeks become flushed. When you're deep in thought or concentrating, you bite your bottom lip. When something's REALLY bothering you, you don't talk as much and look away from me just like you're doing now. I know you, girl," Bentley ranted with sincerity.

Shocked at his accurate assessment, Nylah smoothed hair out of her face and then bit her lip. She seemed to catch his knowing look, and then placed her chin in the palm of her hand and leaned forward. "I just don't get it."

"Get what?"

"I don't understand why you're with her. Jazlyn is *nothing* like me."

The conversation was not what Bentley was expecting and he was sure that his expression reflected his surprise. He chose his words carefully, "No, she's not. You and I both know that."

"So, why did you start dating her? Why did you propose to her?"

"The same reason you got with Malik. You and I didn't work out, so we chose other people who completed us. Am I right?"

"Wrong. Malik doesn't complete me. I've been with him for three months. I'm still learning his ways. But that's neither here nor there. Can you honestly say you're ready to marry that girl?" Nylah asked and stood up.

She moved to throw away her napkin and soda can, but Bentley took it from her. "Sit down. We can clean up later."

Doing as told, she settled across from him again and then looked at a placemat. "Love, look at me."

"Please stop calling me that," she commanded softly.

"I've called you that for years."

"Exactly." Nylah looked up, and he noticed the tears welling up in her eyes. "You called me that when we were married and in love. We're no longer in that same space, so don't call me that. It's disrespectful to your future wife."

"Okay, whatever you say." He shrugged and placed his hand over hers. "Where is all this coming from? What brought on this conversation? I thought things were okay between us."

"I don't know." Nylah looked away, and the first tear made its way down her cheek. "I guess I just saw the way you two interacted. She had on a swimsuit and fur for goodness's sake, Bentley. That's so childish and unlike you to choose someone like…like *that*. I just don't get what you see in her, or why we divorced in the first place. To this day, we've never gotten the closure we needed. It…it just hurts, you know?"

"It hurts you to see me with her?"

Nylah was quiet for some time and then nodded. Her admittance was almost incomprehensible as she stood again. "Please leave."

"Whoa, wait. Why do I have to leave?"

"I'm done discussing this and should have never brought it up. Forgive me. Kiss Brooklyn goodbye and leave."

"See, I hate when you do this." Bentley followed behind her into the bathroom where she pulled a fresh hand towel from the cabinet and wiped her tear-ridden face. "This is one of the reasons we grew apart. Why do you walk away when we're talking? Why do you shut down like that?"

"So that's really one of the reasons? Oh, please."

"One of the reasons, yes, and you know that. You grew up spoiled and always getting things your way so it's no surprise that you feel entitled all the time. I grew to accept that about you, but I never loved it."

Her face began to change as he continued.

"We also divorced because things became a routine. We would eat dinner the same way, make love the same way, go to work and come home the same way. You were and will always be my best friend, but it just didn't work out. *That's* why we broke up."

For the longest time, Nylah stared at him. Her eyes never left his, and he watched as tear after tear fell down her beautifully sculpted cheekbones. Finally, her mouth opened and out came the statement that broke his heart in a million different pieces. In fact, his soul downright shattered.

"So, I bored you, is what you're saying? That's something NO wife ever wants to hear her husband say."

"I didn't say that. I said our routine became…"

"Boring!" she finished his thought. "In so many words, that's exactly what you're saying. So, that's really how you feel? Wow. Nice. And here I thought I was putting down some of my best stuff inside and outside of the bedroom."

"Love…I mean, *Nylah*, don't do that. You know that's not what I'm saying."

Quickly, she pulled away from him and moved from the bathroom to the kitchen. He was close on her heels, regretting the way he was hurting her feelings, but wanting to make things better.

Nothing he ever said seemed to come out the right way.

She swept forcefully, wiped down the table angrily, and then threw dishes into the sink one by one. As she threw the items, she mumbled to herself. Bentley watched as one of the plates broke in half and shards of glass flew out of the sink.

Unaware, Nylah continued to rant, cry, and throw the last of the silverware in the soapy warm water she had run minutes before. She spun around on her bare feet and stepped right into the mess she had made, including one of the sharp pieces from the plate. A pained look took over her pretty features and she fell a few feet away, catching herself awkwardly on her palms. Her foot bled immediately and with a curse, Bentley ran to her aid.

"I got you. Shhh. I got you."

"Do you think it'll need stitches?" she shrieked and tried to keep her composure. The more she bled, the more she panicked, so he hoisted her in his arms. Bentley wrapped a towel around the area to apply pressure, and Nylah nearly passed out from the pain.

"I don't know, but we're going to get you to a hospital, okay? It looks bad and I don't want you to…Nylah? Keep your eyes open for me. Nylah!"

"Mmhmm?" she whispered, just seconds before her eyes closed involuntarily and she passed out from the agony. Even though she was a mother and had seen some crazy injuries on Brooklyn, blood was always something she could not tolerate.

Bentley grabbed her keys and headed for the attached garage, all while struggling to keep her upright. In the process, he forgot the most important thing in the house…

Their peacefully sleeping Brooklyn.

# Chapter Nine

*Nylah*

"All right, Ms. Christiansen, we are all done here. I'm going to set you up with a three-week appointment to get those stitches removed. Please keep your foot elevated at all times," the Asian doctor instructed, as she swiveled around in her chair and grabbed a clipboard. "Is there anything else I can do for you while the meds wear off a bit?"

Sluggishly, Nylah gave the doctor a thumbs up signal and then shook her head. She was in and out, sleepily, and was grateful that she did not feel any pain. A large piece of glass had been removed from her foot and six stitches were now keeping her from using her right foot. It would be a long journey ahead of her while she learned to maneuver on crutches, but she was glad to still have a fully functioning limb.

Nylah could not believe she had snapped like that during their talk to the point that she had put them both in danger. His words had cut deep though, deeper than any cut. Bentley seemed unaffected by her blowup and was only concerned with her well-being. He had gone into Hulk-mode as he hoisted her in the air, and then carried her to the car. She appreciated him being there, although this had been her entire fault.

"Can I go home tonight?"

"Absolutely. Do you have someone living with you that can assist you, should you need anything?" the doctor stood and asked. "We want to keep you off of your foot as much as we can."

One by one, she eased her fingers out of the blue latex gloves, and then tossed them into the trashcan. She turned to Bentley. "Are you able to tend to her if necessary?"

"No, he doesn't live with me. It's just me and our dau…" Nylah's words broke off and her heart skipped a beat. She looked around, searched for Brooklyn, but saw nothing but the empty hospital room. She looked over to Bentley, who was yawning and growing even sleepier. He stood above the wheelchair that she would be taking down and leaned into it lazily. "Where is Brooklyn? Did you grab her?"

Her ex-husband's eyes became as wide as saucers. He looked around the room for added confirmation, and then covered his face with his hands. "No, I was carrying you, remember? Oh, my

God. We have to go right away. Are we done here?"
Bentley asked the woman and stood to his full height.

They rushed from the hospital to the gated
community where she lived and were relieved that
there was no house on fire or anything suspicious
looking. "I can't believe this," Bentley mumbled,
waiting on the security gates to open. "How could I
be so irresponsible?"

His eyes were glazed with unshed tears.

"We've always been responsible parents. This
was literally an honest mistake. Don't beat yourself up
over it. God was covering her," Nylah said and placed
her hand over his briefly.

She noticed that there were two cars out in
front of the house, and they blocked the garage doors.
One of those cars was Malik's. The other was
unfamiliar.

As the two entered the house with Bentley
holding her in his arms, they noticed the remnants of
broken ceramic still on the floor. There was a tiny
puddle of blood and then splatters of it leading to the
doorway. Malik sat in the corner of the living room,
holding Brooklyn in his arms, and wore an angered
expression on his face as he saw the pair enter
together.

"Nice of you to come back home and retrieve your daughter," he said simply, watching Bentley leave out again. "How can you leave a five-year old sleeping by herself? What kind of parents are you?"

"Malik, it was a mistake. I got hurt and was bleeding, and it distracted us from grabbing her. You see that she's okay. You know I don't usually do things like that, and we haven't even been gone that long."

"It was long enough," he reasoned coldly. "And what if she *wasn't* okay? What if an outlet started burning, or the neighbors' house went up in flames and no one knew she was inside?"

"I understand that, and it's eating me up inside, but don't do that. Stop playing the blame game. It's been a long day." She eased into the wheelchair that Bentley had brought inside.

He chuckled and shook his head in disgust. "It would've been an even longer night if you had returned home and she was dead."

"Stop talkin' like that!" Nylah screamed. For the first time since all of this had happened, tears ran down her face in guilt and shame. Had it not been for her blowup, she and Bentley would still have been at home with Brooklyn, and she would have not been put in harm's way. Malik's words crushed her spirit more. As harsh as he was, he was absolutely right.

"And stop rubbing my daughter's back like. Her *parents* are home now. Why are you even here? I thought you were out of town on business." Bentley scowled. "You gave him a key, Nylah?"

"Yes, but…" She rolled forward in the wheelchair and extended her arms. Her words faded as she examined Brooklyn's face and body. "Baby, wake up, Mommy and Daddy are so sorry we left you. Are you okay?"

She rubbed her eyes with her balled fists, and then all at once, fell forward against Nylah's chest. She was out like a light once more and seemed oblivious to everything going on around her. "See, she looks and is acting fine."

"You might want to tell that to the social worker who's here, searching the premises," Malik said simply and stood to his feet.

"Social worker? MALIK! What is a social worker doing at my house?" Nylah raised her voice, looking from him to Bentley, and then back again in panic. "Why didn't you just call me? Why would you report ME?"

"What kind of game are you playing, man?" Bentley asked him.

Malik shrugged. "I didn't have to call or report you at all. Your neighbor, *the social worker*, who's nosey, might I add, stopped over, and realized you weren't home. As I was pulling up, she was coming down the stairs. I told her I could leave a message, but she wanted to drop off some kind of pie that she made everyone on the block. We both walked in the house and that's when we saw Brooklyn on the couch, crying, and asking where you were," he explained. "You dug your own grave with that one."

Bentley stepped around Nylah, exhaling loudly. He began rolling up the sleeves of his dress shirt. "Aye, man, it's time for you to go. Get out of the house." Bentley pointed with his thumb, motioning to the door.

Malik was sarcastic as he spoke, "That's a strange way to say *thank you*, but I'll accept it."

"I'm thanking you by not bashing your head in for entering the house while nobody was here, and for letting some woman in the house!"

"She's the neighbor!"

"She's still a stranger, bro!"

"Nylah can speak for herself."

"I'm speaking on her behalf!" Bentley shouted. "Nobody was here—so, how much sense did that make to let someone in? *You* shouldn't even be here when she's gone!"

"Oh, but someone *was* here, Bentley Boy." Malik leaned forward, grinning smugly. "Your daughter, remember? The one you left."

"Don't call me that. Get…out…of…my…house," Bentley challenged him and stepped closer, while he spoke through gritted teeth. Their chests pressed together.

Malik waved his hand in dismissal, almost catching the edge of Bentley's chin on the way down. "This is not your house. This is my woman's place."

Bentley chuckled with controlled anger. "Exactly, and I'm paying the mortgage and utilities on your woman's place, so it's mine too. Now, what? You're heading in the wrong direction. The door is behind you."

Malik continued to walk towards the living room, ignoring Bentley's request to leave, until Bentley's patience wore dangerously thin. Nylah could literally see his restraint snap and knew all hell was about to break loose. He grabbed Malik by the shoulder, roughly throwing him around to face him.

Already anticipating a fight, Malik turned in defense and reached out to throw a punch, but Bentley was much quicker and faster. He ducked and then grabbed Malik around the legs and slammed him down onto the floor. The sounds of bodies slamming together was rough and intense. The men began to tussle while Nylah sat in disbelief.

"Stop it, guys! Bentley, that's enough! Malik, stop, please! GUYS!"

She could not stand up like she wanted to and break up the fight. Brooklyn stirred awake to see her father fighting and being aggressive and cried out. Nylah attempted to shield her daughter's eyes and turned their bodies in the opposite direction. Her screams to stop went unheeded as they punched and roughed up one another. Their bodies rolled around, fists slammed into walls, and items from the countertops fell over and crashed to the floor.

This was not how she expected things would go down.

A woman jogged up from the basement after hearing the commotion and looked horrified. It appeared to be the social worker and neighbor that Malik had mentioned. Sure enough, it *was* Jessika, from down the street, and she did, in fact, work for Child Protective Services.

Nylah grew warm all over, hating the fact that Malik had let her in. Her eyes were wide with shock as she surveyed the scene. This probably did not help their case at all. Nylah squeezed Brooklyn tighter and waited for the madness to end.

"Hey! Hey! STOP IT! Who is the biological father here? What is going on here?" the woman yelled, "Stop it! NOW!"

The men broke free from one another reluctantly. Nylah watched as Malik dabbed his bloody nose with the bottom of his shirt. Bentley's face looked untouched except for a scratch above his eyebrow. His knuckles appeared bloody and raw, and his clothes were ripped.

"Answer me! Who is the biological father?" the woman repeated.

Nylah tore her eyes away from the heavily breathing men and looked at her neighbor.

"Jessika, I know we don't know each other very well, but you know me enough to know that this," Nylah made a circle of motions with her hands, "isn't something I ever engage in. I have never had problems on this block, and I've never left Brooklyn home by herself before."

"I understand that, but I'm a mandated reporter. I'm sorry. I have to say something if I see something, and this, as you put it," Jessika made a circle of motions with her hands like Nylah had just done, "is alarming. This isn't a good environment for the child, no matter what."

Jessika fished around in her purse for a badge, flashing it at Nylah and then Bentley. Then, she walked over towards Malik leisurely. "Sir, this is a private matter. Can you please leave the room as I speak with the parents?"

"He can leave the house. I'll escort him out," Bentley volunteered, but Malik shrugged him off.

"Do I have to call the police?" the woman questioned.

"No, absolutely not," Nylah pleaded. She felt like the world was spinning and caving in on her. "This was just a big misunderstanding. We're okay. She's okay. See? No injuries or distress, Jessika. I don't understand what you're trying to do."

"I have two eyes and can very well see that," the woman disputed, and seemed to grow agitated. "But there's a bigger picture here that you aren't understanding. A child was left unattended for over an hour, I'd assume, and she was placed in danger just now. Do you understand what could have happened had she awakened and turned on the stove, or lit a candle? Do you understand what could have happened had she fallen and seriously injured herself, with no one home to help her?"

"We do, trust me, we definitely understand," Bentley spoke up this time. The desperation in his voice was high. "But we've taught our baby what to do and what not to do. She knows how to call 911, and she's familiar with the next-door neighbors if she needed anything. She would have never done any of those things you mentioned."

Jessika held her hand up. "Never say never. I have literally seen it all. Ma'am, sir, I'm sorry but for the time being, I'm afraid I have to take your daughter with me and have her placed in another home for the next few nights, or at least until a family member steps up. If you know of a trusted individual, I'd be more than happy to make the connections and we can get her settled in this evening."

"No, no, no. Wait…wait. There will be NO rehoming my child. I understand and appreciate your concern, but lady, you brought over a PIE! Had you not done that, you wouldn't have known our daughter was even here!" Bentley yelled.

"And if I hadn't brought the PIE, who knows what could have happened while you were away?" Jessika challenged, her cheeks reddening and her voice cracking. Her hands shook as she gripped a cell phone in one hand and her purse strap in the other.

Nylah butted in, trying not to lose control of her emotions, "Jessika, please, you KNOW us. You're a mother, too. You KNOW how much this little girl means to me. This…this was a mistake—an emergency. You see my foot. You see the glass on the floor and the blood. We rushed out of the house, and she was so quiet in the room…and…and…"

Bentley dropped his head in frustration.

"Please don't take her from me," Nylah wailed, holding onto Brooklyn tighter. "We've always been good parents. This was an honest mistake, and…and…we would never hurt her or intentionally put her in harm's way. I know it looks bad, but please don't do this."

Jessika sighed, looking around the room and blinking back tears of her own. After a moment, she apologized under her breath and then reached for

Brooklyn, but Nylah yanked the child away again. Jessika offered a lopsided, sympathetic smile.

"I don't doubt that it was a mistake, but it could have been costly. Now, you two have a beautiful, overall SAFE home other than the fighting back there. There are three working smoke detectors, outlets that are higher up and away from her reach, and no visible weapons or items that could seriously hurt your daughter. There would be no reason that you two could not get her back over the next few weeks, or so."

"Next few weeks, or so? Are you kidding me? What all do we have to do?" Nylah panicked. "No, I'm not accepting this. I have to spend WEEKS away from my child? No!"

Bentley placed his hand on her shoulder and attempted to comfort her. No matter what pleas she threw out, the woman was adamant. As skinny as she was, she was also extremely strong. Nylah could hear the arrival of police officers outside, probably to assist Jessika. She grabbed for Brooklyn again and gave one final pull. Brooklyn broke away from her arms and continued to scream at the top of her lungs, even as the woman read them their options and then told them that she understood that mistakes happen.

"If you really understood, then you wouldn't take my child from me for seven whole days or longer! You have children too, and yet you're putting another mother through this. Go to hell, Jessika! You and your bland pies!" Nylah screamed through the tears.

"I'm going to leave you with my business card. Give me a call when you're ready to give me some names of relatives or responsible caretakers for Brooklyn. As per state law, you cannot see or be in contact with the child until CPS has completed its investigation."

There was no longer any remorse or empathy in the woman's voice. She had a job to do, and unfortunately, that meant breaking Bentley, Brooklyn and Nylah's hearts in the process. She was no longer the neighbor and "semi friend" down the block—she had betrayed them in unimaginable ways, and the worst part of it all, they could not do anything about it.

Brooklyn cried harder as the evening air surrounded her outside, and she looked back at her mother. Nylah's heart broke even more when Brooklyn called out for them. Nylah eventually turned her back on the hysterical child, unable to handle her being whisked away.

"I can't believe he did this," she cried, referring to Malik. "Why…why would he do this to us? He knows I've never neglected her a day in my life."

Bentley slammed the door behind the officers and Jessika, and then watched the police car pull away with their daughter inside of it. With his palm pressed to the window, he eyed the taillights until they disappeared into the night. He screamed at the top of his lungs, until he literally ran out of breath.

"I'm going to fix this! She'll be back tomorrow. Mark my words, Nylah. I'm going to make it all better. Brooklyn, baby, I'm going to make it all right," he vowed into the atmosphere, finally succumbing to the emotions that tugged at his heartstrings.

Eventually, he helped Nylah up into the bed hours later, and they cried themselves to sleep. Just like that, in the blink of an eye, *everything* had changed for them.

# *Chapter Ten*

The days that followed Brooklyn's departure proved tumultuous. Thankfully, Bentley's sister had come forward and taken Brooklyn in, so they knew she was in good hands. It still didn't take away the embarrassment, shame, emptiness, and guilt they felt. Plus, sister or not, they could not speak to Brooklyn and that was torture.

While trying to heal, Nylah also had to force herself to eat and do normal activities. Bentley was helpful and would spend most of his time at her house, much to Jazlyn's dismay. Every day, the two worked with representatives from the Child Protective Services offices. They were even instructed to take a few online courses on safe and efficient parenting. The icing on life's pitiful cake was that they both had to go to court in order to get Brooklyn back. The hearing was scheduled three weeks out, and while it was a humiliating process, Bentley and Nylah were determined to prove themselves as fit.

Nylah understood that every case was unique, and not every child had it as good as Brooklyn. She understood that the system was being "safe than sorry," and pulling Brooklyn out of a potentially dangerous situation, no matter how skewed the facts were. She understood that in a case where a child really was being abused and neglected, that this was merely procedure, and the system ultimately put the child's needs first. She understood it all.

However, Nylah still could not believe how their character and integrity was being questioned. They were the best mother and father that they could possibly be, and no one gave them grace even though it was the first and only costly mistake that the two had made as parents.

Nylah had officially cut Malik off and reluctantly forgave him in her heart, but she knew that she could *never* forget what he did to their family. Instead of calling to notify her of what had taken place, Malik had taken matters into his own hands. His actions had separated and broken up her family, and that was unacceptable. He had caused so much damage, and Nylah would not allow him to enter her home or heart ever again.

Brooklyn would be returning home hopefully sooner than later, so Nylah planned to let her eat up all the cake and ice cream that she desired. She was also planning a pizza and tea party, something that

Bentley was looking forward to. He had even agreed to put one of her princess crowns on and talk to her stuffed animals as she always asked of him.

"How're you holding up today?" This was Bentley now, talking to her while he sat in his office, many miles away. His voice sounded tired, and he was more than likely going to pull an all-nighter at work. "Did you get any sleep last night? Have you been eating?"

Over the long week, their exchange of words had literally become a routine. He would always ask the same question and she would always give the same answer. This time was no exception as Nylah felt a lone tear escape her eye. "I'll be better when she's back in my arms."

"I hear you, Love. But please don't make yourself sick over this. I need you."

Nylah did not even bother to correct Bentley's words, and pulled her legs up against her chest. She put the phone on speaker, laid it on the kitchen table, and then rested her head sideways against her knees.

"Be careful out there."

"I will," he whispered. "Hey, you remember that song you sang when we were in junior high?"

"I sang so many," she chuckled.

"You know, the one during our 7th grade talent show? Sing it for me."

Nylah's mind raced back to sweeter yesteryears when there was no obligation to be an adult, pay bills, or have responsibilities. She could barely remember what the song was, so to think that he remembered was mind-blowing. Finally, with a minuscule grin, it came back to her remembrance.

"Oh. 'The Storm is Over Now,' I think. You remember me singing that?"

"Yes, like it was yesterday," in his voice, she also heard a smile, along with overwhelming emotion, "Sing for me, Love."

"I'm honestly not in the…" she began to protest but he cut her off.

"Sing it. Minister to yourself. Encourage yourself with the words," he said simply. "And in doing that, it'll help me right now. *Please*."

As she swallowed the lump in her throat, Nylah thought back to the powerful lyrics. Kirk Franklin had always been one of her favorite gospel artists, and his song certainly spoke to her spirit and their situation. Right now, she was literally in her darkest hour, and perhaps Bentley was onto something. Nylah did as told and decided to encourage herself through worship.

She closed her eyes, continued to relax her face against her folded legs, and then sang every line, every word, and every note that fell from her parched lips.

Although there was no background music, no instrumental, and no audience besides Bentley, Nylah careened her neck to sing more loudly. The more she sang, the more her spirit was revived. The sadness she felt was leaving little by little; in its place was joy, peace, and overwhelming hope.

Bentley sniffled through the phone, and he seemed to be crying tears of joy too, as they sang the encouraging words together.

A heart-wrenching cry flowed from her diaphragm as she thought of Brooklyn. Only God knew how the little girl was feeling each day, not being able to see either of her parents. Nylah prayed that her daughter was eating and sleeping at least, and that she did not feel abandoned by them. She could not wait to hug Brooklyn's tiny body against hers.

"You okay?" she asked after a few moments. Bentley had grown so quiet. When she stopped singing, she realized she no longer heard the tapping from his fingers, against his keyboard in the background. Nylah no longer heard the sounds of copy machines spitting out paper, fax machines whirring with new messages, or any of the traditional office noises. She just heard silence. She didn't even hear his breathing.

*"Bentley?"*

He never answered. Nylah stayed on the line another few minutes, hung up, and then tried to call him again, but did not hear another word from her ex-husband. She sent him a text, bade him a goodnight, and then buried herself in the warm covers.

Her pillows, like every night, became her tissues. They caught every tear that fell from her eyes. Nylah continued to weep for another hour, and only stopped when she received the shock of her life as the front door opened.

Reluctantly, she heard approaching footsteps and expected Malik to be begging as normal or vying for another chance at love. After all, he had never given her back the key to her place. She even thought it was one of her parents dropping by to comfort her. But it was none of those individuals. It was the one person that she needed most, besides her daughter.

It was Bentley.

Bentley had sped all the way over, in the middle of the night, and now stood before her. He had come through for her, as she needed him to, yet had been too afraid to ask. Though he looked rougher than she had ever seen him look in his life, he was also beautiful and a sight for sore eyes.

"Did I wake you?" he croaked.

"No, no. Sit down," Nylah ordered.

She scooted further up in the queen-sized bed and felt the blanket puddle at her waist. She wore a gold, satin nightgown, and her hair was wrapped in a silk scarf. Her face was painted in warm, salty tears, and the mascara from this morning had given her eyes a raccoon look. Nylah was a mess, but he did not seem to mind.

Bentley dropped his workbag and yanked off his tie. Nylah threw the covers away from her body and tossed her legs onto the side of the bed. All at once, they ran towards one another and embraced tightly. It did not matter that her foot was swollen and sore and she had to limp to him. It didn't matter that he smelled like a hard day's work. None of that mattered.

He picked her up and twirled her around as he buried his face in her ample bosom. Nylah cradled his head with her arms and kissed the top of his head. It was like a movie scene, but their emotions were the real deal. The two were hurting and there was no place that Nylah would have rather been than with Bentley.

# Chapter Eleven

*Bentley*

*Bzzzz. Bzzzz. Bzzzz.*

"You've got to be kidding me," Bentley mumbled.

Nah. He wasn't going to believe that his sweet and surprisingly deep sleep had been interrupted by a caller, followed by a series of text messages. If Bentley hadn't been so tired the night before, he would have put his phone on silent.

Reluctantly, he left his dream and then opened his eyes with a few blinks and back of the hand rubs. Moisture from the night had dried against his eyelids, so he blinked to rid his vision of it. Just as soon as he got his eyes opened, the bright sunlight peeking through the blinds caused him to snap his eyes shut again. The continuous vibrations coming from the phone irritated him, but when they stopped, Bentley found a comfortable spot again and fell asleep.

*Bzzzz. Bzzzz. Bzzzz.*

The caller would not let him sleep in as another round of calls and text messages came through. This was just disrespectful. Bentley removed his hand from the warmth of the covers, and then blindly felt for the phone against the top of the nightstand. He turned off the mobile device entirely, not even bothering to check the missed notifications. Whoever it was could leave a message. There were no real emergencies, since he was here with Nylah, and Brooklyn was with his sister.

"Who is that?"

He scooted closer to Nylah, wrapped his arm around her hip, and then mumbled, "Nobody."

"You sure you don't want to check? It could be Jaz, or a work associate, or someone calling about Brooklyn."

Bentley shrugged and sleepily looked at the back of her head. The scarf from last night had worked its way down and her hair was all over the place. He chuckled to himself, and the sound made her glance over her petite shoulder.

"What's so funny?"

"Your hair looks a mess," he pointed out.

Nylah's hand came up and she felt her head. Her fuchsia fingertips ran through her hair, as she attempted to give the tresses a presentable look.

Eventually, she joined him with a hearty laugh. "Whatever."

"You were always a rough sleeper."

Nylah's mouth hung open. "I am not! You're the one who was snoring last night."

"Snoring and sleeping all over the place is two different things," Bentley mentioned with a playful look on his face. She was smiling and it was exactly what he wanted to see after the week that they had endured. "Look at us now. You have ALL the covers, and I'm sleeping on less than half of the bed."

Nylah, still amused, looked down at how they were laying. Sure enough, Bentley was on his side and was barely covered with the blankets. She, on the other hand, was fully covered and had both legs stretched out. Nylah erupted into a fit of giggles and apologized.

"No need to be sorry." He admired her bright smile and combed through her hair with his fingers. "I was teasin' anyway. I love your hair like this."

"Thanks." She blushed.

He leaned forward and placed a feathery light kiss on her forehead. "How did you sleep?"

"Honestly? Probably the best I've slept in a really long time."

Bentley's heart skipped a beat, and he bit his tongue from asking why she was feeling so refreshed and well-rested. "That's good, Love."

"What did I tell you about calling me that?"

"I can't help it." He shrugged boyishly, grinning. "You were my first. That was my special name for you."

Nylah rolled her eyes, and then looked over at him. "It doesn't matter. Like I said before, that's disrespectful to your future wife."

Bentley chuckled and turned onto his back to stare up at the ceiling. "And her cheating on me isn't disrespectful? Trust me, a little nickname won't hurt anybody."

The words slipped out so easily and harshly, that he had to blink to realize what had happened. He had already said too much, and he knew she was going to say something. It was just a matter of time. Things grew quiet.

"Bentley," she said.

"Hm?"

"Are you joking or are you just being goofy still?"

He kept quiet for a little while longer, instead, playing with his thumbs. Then, with a heavy exhale, he finally answered her with a quick nod. It was not his intention to stir up such a conversation so early in the morning, but he had already run his mouth.

"I'm serious. She stepped out on me."

"What's going on?" Nylah turned completely towards him, propping her chin in her hand. "How do you know she's cheating? Did you catch her in the act?"

Bentley smirked a little, and then closed his eyes. "Bank statements. All that spending she did on my card went towards him. I guess I should've figured it out sooner. Who goes out of town on business but never returns with receipts or pictures from the trip?"

Nylah shook her head in disbelief and watched him closely.

"I've given that woman the best of me, *no*, all of me. I gave her *everything*," he hissed.

As much as he hated to grow angry, his emotions got the best of him as he poured his frustrations out. He appreciated how Nylah listened intently beside him, and how she placed her hand on his chest. It provided all the comfort he never knew he needed.

"I've dealt with her high standards and uppity personality; I've looked past her spending habits and tried to make this work. I could deal with all of that, but another man? That's what I have a problem with."

"Of course. You don't deserve that, and you shouldn't have to put up with that," Nylah added, and the hand that was on his chest began to rub up and down.

"He's obviously a clown, too, because there's no way he thinks she's paid for all of that stuff without a real job."

Nylah nodded. "True. But she had to have lied to him like she's lied to everyone else. Like, girl, come on. I've never known a supermodel to have a resume as short as hers."

Bentley chuckled. He realized she was trying to make him laugh.

"I mean, no offense," Nylah added.

He felt her hand skim lower and lower until her arm was thrown over his waist. She rested her head in the crook of his neck and blew out hot air. Clearly, she had brushed her teeth before he awakened because there was no tartness to her breath.

Bentley only smelled remnants of minty toothpaste and mouthwash.

Quietly, she continued to speak against his chest. "So where does that leave you two? You know, with the wedding and all?"

"I don't know. I honestly don't know." Bentley rubbed his hand over his hair, smoothing it down, in frustration.

Nylah nodded and brushed her lips against his cheek. "Don't let it stress you out. Whatever you do, don't let it get the best of you. I feel like this is something that needed to come out *before* the wedding to help you avoid some mistakes and heartache down the line. Even though it hurts now, it was for the best, Bentley."

"Yeah, you're right."

"I am, huh?"

"That's no surprise. You always know what to say, huh?" Bentley looked down and questioned.

She made circles against his lower stomach with her fingertips and smirked. "Sometimes. Other times I don't really mean half of what comes out of my mouth. I just like to hear myself talk."

"So, what does that mean?" Bentley added to the joke and pulled her body on top of his. She straddled his waist and situated each of her thighs on either side of his hips. The two stared at each other playfully. "So, were you lying all of those times we made love? Were you just making sounds because you like to hear yourself?"

Nylah's eyes widened in surprise. Still, she kept her game face on and played along. "Oh, no, no. *Never.* When it's good, it's good, and baby, I never had to fake that."

Bentley bit his bottom lip and chuckled, happy to hear her say that. As a man, no matter what your age or marital status was, hearing a woman you've been with say you were good in bed was *always* music to the ears.

"Okay, so it wasn't then? Well, let me think…" he pretended to think.

Nylah sat up straighter, playing with the sprinkle of fine hair across his chest. She remembered a time where he didn't have any.

"You're thinking awfully hard," she teased.

"Oh, I got one." Bentley knew they were just playing around, but he couldn't help his next words. He had been meaning to address this with her before and hoped she didn't shy away. "Did you really mean it when you said you could still have me if you wanted to?"

Nylah snorted as she laughed. "I had a feeling you would ask that. Bentley, honestly, that's something *you* have to think about. I feel like I could still have you if I wanted, but it's obviously up to you. Are you tempted by me? Could you fall for me again?" She wiggled against him and giggled again.

He swallowed hard, not really sharing in her same playfulness. He was serious as he spoke his next words, "Many times I've thought about it. *Having you.* Winning you back. Loving you all over again."

Nylah's teeth gradually disappeared behind her full lips, as her smile faded.

Bentley ignored the direction the mood had shifted. The door to being vulnerable was opened and he had to take it.

"Answer me this: all those times that you said you loved me—were you just talking to hear yourself?"

He could literally hear the thumps that her heart made, beating purposely with nervousness, anticipation and want.

"Oh, I loved you," she finally answered in a whisper, "and I still do. That was never fake, and you know that."

Bentley moved his head up and down on the pillow, studying her with adoration. "My love for you was never fake either. I feel like after all these years, you thought that. You probably blamed yourself for the way our marriage crumbled. You probably thought of yourself as not good enough, but that was never the case. *You* were the prize all along. *I* was the fool, Nylah. It was all me, baby."

Although their eyes were locked, Bentley noticed from his peripherals as the strap of her gown fell from her shoulder. She rushed to ease it back up, but he stopped her hand. She was not wearing a bra underneath the light garment, and even though he wore boxer-briefs, he could tell that she was panty-less as well.

This was not good. This was not good at all.

But no matter how hard he tried to push her off his waist, they only drew closer. The harder he tried to think of something else, the more excited he grew at the thought of Nylah being on top of him. It had been forever since they made love or intimately touched, and it had been painful the last time they did it. It did not hurt in the traditional sense, but emotionally.

Bentley knew her body, just like he knew her thoughts, and right now, her body was speaking an entirely different language. She was longing for him, and he desired her in unimaginable ways. Although they were divorced and had moved on, Bentley could not lie. Their history seemed to flood his thoughts day in and day out. Just last week, he had a dream about her and with Jazlyn looking on, he had apparently moaned Nylah's name in his sleep.

This was all so confusing, but they never moved from their position. They never talked about the temptation they felt, nor did they decide to flee from it. Bentley did not stop Nylah, and Nylah certainly did not stop Bentley.

Instead, with passion as high as the sky, and with all the pent-up frustrations and emotions from their trying week, Bentley eased the gown down the front of her body and allowed it to puddle at her waist. Nylah began to drop her head with shyness; it was something she always did when he stared at her naked body, but he caught her chin on the way down.

"Look at me. You are beautiful."

As he basked in her brown skinned beauty, his eyes filled with hunger, appreciation, and an unexplained protectiveness to shield her from the world. As selfish as it sounded, he prayed that he would be the *only* man to enter such a precious territory. Other men didn't deserve her. Heck, Bentley didn't even deserve her.

He gently touched every curve, crevice, and inch of her. He made love to his ex-wife, as if they had just consummated their vows. He explored her body like they were newlyweds all over again. He painted her skin with his tongue and tugged at her hair with his fingers.

Bentley forgot about all his problems, as he drowned himself in her love. He forgot about the pain of his daughter's absence, as she pleased him how he liked. He even seemed to forget that he still had a fiancée, as he ordered Nylah to switch positions for a fourth time.

In that moment, he did not care about anything other than pleasing her and making her forget that a Malik ever existed. He was once the king of her castle, and her protector. He was once the only one handling her body and stimulating her mind.

After all, the two had lost their virginities to one another, and had never looked back.

More than an hour later, Nylah's head collapsed onto his shoulder, and she fought to get her breathing under control. Bentley, who was gasping for air, and still holding her backside in his palms, could not remember their lovemaking ever being so erotic and sexy. In the time that they had been separated, something incredible had happened and as bad as it sounded, he wanted to experience her body and love again and again.

So, after a quick nap, they made love a second time.

"What...what was *that?*" Nylah questioned breathily. Her hair was drenched in sweat and her body was sticky with moisture. She looked like she had gone for a dip in the pool.

"We needed that," Bentley admitted shamelessly. "As wrong as it was, I needed that. I missed you."

"I missed you too," she confessed and held the covers up to her bare chest.

"You were so good," he whispered.

Nylah smiled shyly, bit on her bottom lip, and then leaned in to kiss him one final time.

As good as this felt, the slipup was not supposed to happen. But to make matters worse, they had not used protection. This was crazy. Bentley kept his eyes closed and focused on breathing. He and God had to have a long talk. He had some explaining and apologizing to do for his actions.

"Where do we go from here?" Nylah asked. "That wasn't supposed to happen, no matter how we look at it, but...where do we stand now?"

It was Bentley's turn to shake his head in disbelief, and he could not believe that he was saying his next words.

"I won't lie. That was amazing, Love, but...like you said, that wasn't supposed to happen."

Nylah's eyes narrowed, dreading his next words. "And what about Jaz?"

Bentley scratched his chest. "I'm still going to try to make things work with Jaz. I'm going to take her to couple's counseling or something. We still have some layers to peel before we get married, but I'm willing to put in the work if she is."

"But she cheated," Nylah reasoned.

"Yeah. But she told me she wouldn't do it again...and I trust her. I really do."

For the longest time, Nylah stared at him. She did not blink, did not speak, and did not move. Bentley kept his eyes on the ceiling fan above them as it spun at a gradual speed. Then, with effortless grace and poise, she tossed the covers from over her legs and stood up.

"Get out."

"What?" he asked.

Nylah's face took on a different look, and she seemed agitated. Naked, with just tears and sweat running from her pores, she pointed towards the door. "Get out," she repeated. "*Please* leave."

"Nylah, talk to me. Why the sudden change? I know we had sex, but why are you acting like this? Did you think I was going to propose all over again and we were going to get back together? It's not that simple. I'm just trying to make sense of everything."

Before he could move, the back of her hand smacked the side of his face. He moved his jaw around in disbelief and shook his head. She was never the violent type, but lately, she had gotten more and more physical with him.

"Nylah, I'm not going to leave with you mad at me like this. What's wrong?"

When she spoke again, it was controlled and barely audible. It pained Bentley to see the tears running from her face, and the look of humiliation on her beautiful features, especially after the incredible night and morning they had shared.

"Bentley, if I have to ask you again, it won't be nice. Put your stuff on and leave."

Quickly, he did as told.

# Chapter Twelve

*Nylah*

"I slept with him."

There was silence on the end of the phone and then a piercing scream. Nylah pulled the phone away from her ear, already anticipating the shrill of disapproval. "You WHAT?"

"Momma, I slept with him," Nylah repeated and cringed at the words that echoed throughout the bathroom.

She was still in shock too. Since Bentley's departure, she had pretty much been idle. She only moved to cook breakfast, watch a half-hour rerun of *Criminal Minds*, and now, she soaked in the bathtub. Nylah had lit a few candles, turned off all the lights, and was watching the flames dance from across the room. Her mother went into panic mode, quoted the Bible a few times, and then started to explain how to be a lady.

"*Moooom*," she whined, already regretting revealing her secret. "I know how to be a lady; I know all about those scriptures you just gave me, and I know it was wrong. I wasn't telling you to be lectured or scolded like a child. I was just telling you what happened in MY moments of weakness. Why must you *always* go to the extreme with things?"

"Obviously, you don't know how to be! Sleeping with him only complicated things, and more than that, God is not pleased with you. He's engaged, Nylah! He's not *your* husband anymore, and you had NO right to invite him into your room and..."

Nylah cut her off, "I didn't invite him over for sex. It just sort of happened. With everything going on, we just needed comfort. We were talking and encouraging each other, and one thing led to another. It was never my intention to sleep with him."

Her mother sighed and called out to her father in the background. "I just can't believe what you're telling me. I never thought you would be so irresponsible with your child and your body, Nylah. I didn't raise you to be a homewrecker, and God certainly didn't give you the spirit of confusion. You've caused all this discord and for what—one night of pleasure? I hope it was worth it."

Nylah took the phone from her ear, stared at it, shook her head, and then continued talking to the woman that had birthed her. "You just said something very true."

"What's that?"

"You didn't raise me to be a homewrecker. As I recall, Momma, you didn't raise me at all. It was the nannies that took care of me while you were away. Just like now, you and Daddy are off on some vacation and haven't checked in on me not once since Brooklyn was taken! The only reason we're talking is because I CALLED YOU!" she screamed and for the second time today, felt the warm tears welling up in her eyes.

Nylah stood up in the bathtub and stepped out one foot at a time, carefully and painfully. She reached for her towel and crutch, all while balancing the phone between her shoulder and ear.

Her mother began to speak, but she cut her off again. "Listen to me! Do you know how it feels for your daughter to be taken from you because of an *honest*, genuine mistake? Do you know how painful it is to watch a neighbor—*no, no*, a SOCIAL WORKER—remove your daughter from your home because you appear to be UNFIT? Do you know how it feels to have your character and intentions questioned?"

"Nylah—"

"No, you don't know. You didn't bother to create a relationship with me, but you're so quick to speak on what's right and wrong in the Bible. You're so quick to point fingers and judge, aren't you? Well, what does the Bible say about child abandonment every month, or whenever you and Daddy decided to get away? *Huh*?"

Her mother was silent on the other end.

"You're missing one key Bible verse. 'Judge not, and ye shall not be judged.' So, for you to sit here and talk to me like I'm some side chick, who slept around, is enough. I've had enough of your judging! When's the last time you visited your *only* grandchild, Ma? I'm grown now! This foolishness has got to stop. If we're going to peel back the layers and JUDGE ME, let's peel back your layers too, because I learned discord from YOU!"

There was a long silence in Nylah's ear—no breathing, no rebuttal, and not even the sounds of the background TV. Then, as expected, there was a *click*. Clearly, a reality check was too much for her mother as she disconnected their call without a single word. That was just like her mother to talk Nylah's ear off about her shortcomings and then want to run off when she gave her a dose of her own medicine. Nylah knew that she should not have gone off like that, but she could no longer contain her emotions. Her mother's infamous blame-game had not helped at all.

Nylah only wanted her mother's compassion and wisdom in this moment, and for her to tell her that things would be okay. She was not looking for validation or blame and had not asked to be judged for her emotional decision-making this morning. Much like when Nylah was little, her mother was still unsure how to be understanding, empathetic, and nurturing. All Nylah could do was pray that someday she would have the mother-daughter relationship that she desired.

As she dried her body off and then rubbed Cocoa Butter over her damp skin, the doorbell rang. Nylah was sure that it was Bentley returning. He had probably run into problems again with Jaz and needed to vent. She would politely send him back home. Nylah could not face him after this morning. It would be like reopening a wound.

She rounded the kitchen counter, unsteadily, and attempted to look through the tightly closed blinds. She could not make out the silhouette at the door, or the car in the driveway. It was much too dark outside.

"Who is it?" Nylah called out.

"Bentley," she heard faintly. "Open up. I just want to talk."

*Of course, it's you,* she thought.

Nylah could not help but to roll her eyes, because she knew her ex-husband like the back of her hand. Either he had developed a cold since this morning, or he had something in his mouth. Whichever the case, he was muffled and hard to understand. He probably wanted to apologize and sleep over again, but Nylah planned to shut all of that down. She tightened the towel around her body, unlocked the door, and then hobbled away.

"So, what brings you over? You found out more information on Jaz?" Nylah kept her back to him and limped over to the stove. She prepared a cup of tea, and then sipped at it deliberately. "Let me just be clear about something. What happened this morning cannot, and will not, happen again. You hear me?"

Bentley stepped in the door and then closed it gently. The lock was latched. One by one, he removed his shoes, and then walked over to her. She heard his movements and did not turn. She wasn't sure she had the courage to even turn around. But he decided to make a move first. Soon, she felt his arms come around her waist.

"I hear you," he answered.

All she smelled was liquor. Bentley was never one to just get sloppy drunk, so it took her by surprise as she began to choke at how terrible he reeked. There was not only alcohol in his system, but something illegal too. He had been smoking tonight.

Nylah pried his arms away from her body and then looked over her shoulder. To her surprise, Bentley was much shorter and darker. He was Malik. "What are you doing here?" she yelled.

"You let me in," he said.

That could not have been truer. Instead of Nylah checking to see who it was, she had believed him when he said that he was Bentley. Now, here they stood, face to face. Her heart thumped nervously.

"Get out," she ordered. "You did that on purpose!"

"I knew you weren't going to let me in, so I lied," he admitted, and looked down at her bare shoulders and legs.

Her skin was still glistening with moisture from the bath. All the relaxing and stress relieving that had taken place in her bathroom had all disappeared with her mother's phone call and Malik's current antics. To add to what had taken place between she and Bentley, the day could not have gotten any worse.

She swallowed hard and prayed that he would not give her trouble.

Stumbling over nothing, Malik followed behind her as she led him to the door. "After what you pulled, I told you I didn't want you over here. That hasn't changed. My feelings are still the same."

"What happened to forgiving and forgetting?" Malik slurred and reached for her. She yanked her arm away from his clammy hands and he lost his balance. Nylah watched as he fell to his knees before her. "I NEED you, Nylah!"

"Please, stop. Don't make things worse. Plus, you're drunk. Go home, and we'll talk about this another day, but tonight is not the right time," she pleaded.

Her ex-boyfriend stared at her with his low, bloodshot eyes and open mouth. He was a mess. He was so drunk that he could not focus on her eyes, nor could he stand to his full height. It was then that Nylah noticed the pocket-sized, dark brown bottle sticking out from the back of his jeans. Malik tugged at it, twisted the top off, and then took a long swig.

"I'm not leaving," he said simply and burped.

"Malik, do I need to call the police? Stop acting like this and leave before I *really* get angry."

Standing on his feet again shakily, he cornered her against the door with his arms. His chin sat on top of her head, and he began to cry.

"Shouldn't I be the angry one? How do you expect me to live without you? You were the best thing that ever happened to me. You completed me. I loved you. I still do," Malik, again, confessed.

If there was one thing about liquor, it was the truth that came out of consuming it. Even still, she knew he was inebriated and did not fully realize how tightly he was holding her against the door, or how heavy his chin was baring down on the top of her head.

"Malik, I broke up with you because your actions caused my daughter to be taken away! You didn't even try to fight for us or prove to Jessika that I was a good mother. You were so caught up in seeing me and Bentley that you just ran your mouth and let your emotions take over. Brooklyn hasn't been home since."

"I'm sorry, okay? Dang, woman! Why won't you let it goooo?"

Nylah attempted to twist out of his grasp. "You're hurting me. Get up!"

In her struggle to push him away, the towel that was tied around her body came loose. He took notice in her bare body instantly and leaned back to admire everything that she had withheld from him. Naked before his eyes for the first time, Nylah tried to cower away, but his strength outnumbered hers. Malik held both of her hands in one of his, and then relaxed into her again. His body weighed her down and she became immobilized.

"Why did you make me wait? I was faithful to you. I did everything you asked of me, but still, you couldn't see past your baby's father. It was always Bentley this, and Bentley that. Blah, blah, blah. I could never compete with him," Malik incoherently spoke again and then hiccupped.

Nylah struggled to breathe and cover herself, but because of the way that they were positioned, she could do nothing. The man she once trusted and loved tugged on her roughly. She watched as his eyes took on a darker look. He was officially crazy, and it was not just the liquor talking. Like a ragdoll, he grabbed Nylah by the neck, and threw her into the wall. She landed face down and became dizzy immediately.

"I gave you flowers, but you were never happy with them. *He* gave you flowers, and you would put them in a vase and keep them for months, even after they shriveled up and died," Malik said. "I tried to take you out, but you always said you were too busy. *Bentley* got to take you out just about every morning. I was NEVER good enough for you! You didn't even let me make love to you to SHOW you how much I cared!"

Out of his mouth came curse word after word. Nylah was called every name in the book. He threw paintings at her from the wall; he slammed coasters from the dinner table down onto the glass, and he threw sculptures to the floor. Her well-kept house was turned into a war zone in a matter of seconds, and he continued to trash it, even as she screamed for him to stop.

Nylah could not reach for her phone and making a run for the door was out of the question on her injured foot. There was no way that she could escape his rants and wrath. Nylah only prayed that he would not go a step further to prove his point.

As he took a breath in between ransacking her home, he took another swig from the bottle in his back pocket. Malik did not need any more alcohol in his system. It was making him crazier and crazier. He pulled her hair in his hands, forced her neck to stretch backward, and then poured remnants of the liquor down her throat. Nylah choked in disgust as she tried to clear her airways, and some of the liquid burned her nostrils as it ran backward.

When the bottle was fully empty, he threw it to the wall, and glass shattered everywhere. Then, zooming in on her exposed lady parts, his eyes seemed to widen with excitement.

Nylah watched in fear as he tugged at the belt looped in his jeans, and then unzipped his pants. "You...should...have...given it to me! Now I have to take it! Come here, Nylah!"

"No, Malik. NO! Please don't do this!"

# Chapter Thirteen

*Bentley*

Bentley still could not believe what had gone down between he and Nylah. Whiffs of her perfume and natural scent lingered on his body, and all he could think of was the way she had looked at him when she kicked him out. In all the years that Bentley had known her, Nylah had never looked so confused, hurt, or angry. To think that he was the cause of her sadness and frustration bothered him. The guilt stayed with him the entire day. He knew he had to make things right.

But first, Bentley needed to confront Jazlyn and confess some secrets of his own to her. It would be like an eye for eye; Bentley telling her that he found out that she was cheating, but then Bentley confessing to her that he had slept with Nylah. This could be dangerous, and he searched the vicinity for any weapons, before calling her to the kitchen.

Jazlyn came in somber and with her eyes low. "Where were you last night? I called your office *three* times and they said you left early, so I called and text your phone, but you never picked up. What's going on, Bentley?"

He sat down with a sigh. "I could ask that same thing, Jaz."

"What are you talking about?" she frowned and asked.

"Who is Ryan?" The moment Bentley asked her, Jazlyn's face fell, and suddenly she focused on her fingernails. "My eyes are up here. Who is RYAN? His name was in our bank statement memos. Who is he?"

She was quiet. She swallowed hard and it echoed throughout the kitchen. "Ryan is a friend."

"What *kind* of friend?"

"Just...a friend." She shrugged, still avoiding his eyes. "He's someone I met at the mall last year. He has a small photography business, and I told him I wanted to be a model, so I could help him launch his portfolio. We exchanged numbers and have been cool since. He's literally just a friend, baby."

Bentley's eyes narrowed. "Did you sleep with him?"

"Of course not, Bentley! I would never do that to you."

"Then what *did* you do? Don't sit there acting like the victim! What did you do, Jazlyn?" he yelled.

His voice had become decibels louder, and she could feel the heat coming from his pores as he grew angrier and more exasperated.

"He just…he buys me nice things and I send him…um…" she trailed off.

"Send him *what?*" He looked her up and down, not sure he wanted to hear what was next.

"I send him naked photos of me in exchange for things. That's *all,*" Jazlyn pleaded and reached for his hand. Her voice was shaky and remorseful as she added, "I promise I've never slept with him! I swear to God I would never do that to you!"

"What were the trips and big purchases for?"

"We all took a vacation—me and the girls, Ryan, some of his friends."

"On *my* dime?"

Jazlyn nodded. "On your dime, but I swear to you, we didn't sleep together. I'll pay you back…every penny. Just…please, don't leave me."

Bentley shook his head and looked down at her petite fingers that were intertwined with his. As disappointed as he was in Jazlyn, he was even more upset with himself and the news that he was about to give her.

"I forgive you." And he really did.

"You do?"

"I do. Because nobody is perfect, and who am I to judge or condemn you for making a *mistake*? I forgive you, Jazlyn, and I would hope that you would do the same for me."

"What are you talking about?" she asked with confusion etched on her face. "Bentley, what did you do?"

"Baby, I…" he cleared his throat. "Last night, I…well, this morning…"

She pulled her hands from his roughly, "You slept with her, didn't you?"

Emotionless, he nodded and looked her directly in the eye. "This morning. It was not my intention to cheat on you, or to sleep with her, or to hurt you like this. But I did it, I regret it, and I'm sorry."

Before Bentley could say anything else, the underside of Jazlyn's hand slammed into his cheek. The slap produced a sound that was so loud and high-pitched that he knew it would qualify for the Guinness Book of World Records. Jazlyn had hit him with a force so hard that he was sure that the neighbor's dog could feel the tremor too. Bentley gritted down on his teeth and then felt his face.

"I deserved that," he whispered.

Another slap followed. Then another. And then, she began to beat on his chest with her balled fists until she broke down crying. Only when she semi-calmed down and her hits lessened, did he embrace her and rock her back and forth in his arms.

"Shhh, I know. I'm so sorry that I hurt you," Bentley spoke against her hair. "You didn't deserve any of this."

"How could you do this to me? We were supposed to get married! You lied to me! You did the ONE thing I said not to! I knew I shouldn't have trusted you being friends with her. How stupid was I?" Jazlyn cried.

Bentley normally had an answer for everything, and yet nothing that he said to her would soothe the hurt she felt. No words of remorse or professions of love would ease her resentment and sorrow. He had broken her heart, and although she had done her dirt too, he had committed the ultimate betrayal.

Bentley only had himself to blame.

"You should be tryin' to get your daughter back, and yet you're over there fooling around with her? What kind of parenting is that? I see you're not as worried as you said you were!"

*That was a low blow,* he thought and turned his back to her. She was erratic and screaming as loudly as her lungs would allow. Bentley was never good with confrontation and figured he would walk away.

Jazlyn kicked him out of his own place, and he knew he would give her space for just the night. As easily as he could have gone to a hotel, or made arrangements at one of his rental properties, Bentley wanted to check in on Nylah again. He was unhappy with how things had ended earlier between them, and he needed her to know exactly what he was thinking and feeling.

The second Bentley pulled in the driveway to Nylah's house, he slammed on brakes as he saw moving shadows behind the blinds. The neighborhood was normally quiet, but alarming sounds permeated the cozy home that their daughter would have been in. Shouts and loud noises came from the home that his ex-wife rested her head in. A few concerned neighbors were peeking out of their windows, but no one looked to be heroes. No one seemed to want to get involved. Then there was the unknown car parked out front and center.

Nylah wasn't one to just invite people over, and especially not at a time like this. For the most part, he knew her circle of friends and the cars they drove, and this random car wasn't ringing a bell.

It had to be Malik.

His teeth clenched as he put two and two together, and quickly exited the still running car. The night was getting more and more crazier, and he was prepared to fight for Nylah, even if it meant going to jail tonight.

"No, Malik. NO! Please don't do this!" is what Bentley heard as he neared the front door.

His feet picked up speed against the concrete, and because the neighborhood was so still, his footsteps sounded heavier than normal in the night. With his shoulder, he lunged into the locked door several times. He could tell the bolts were loosening, but it never opened. He tried one last time, ignoring the pain that came with the forceful shoving. He was willing to dislocate his shoulder if it meant breaking down the door and protecting Nylah.

Bentley rushed around to the patio and pushed his way into the side entrance. What greeted him broke his heart and caused his blood pressure to skyrocket. What met his eyes angered him and made his breathing slow down and then pick up dangerously.

Malik was holding Nylah against the wall, and her face was moist with tears and whatever else. It looked like they had both been drinking—Nylah, unwillingly. Her skin was bruised, and her hair was mangled. A bath towel sat inches from her feet and had probably been snatched off her body.

All Bentley saw was red.

Without hesitation, he ran up to Malik who looked unexpected and fragile. He was long gone to the alcohol and fell limply as Bentley punched him over and over again. His head flopped around, and he tried to fight back pathetically, but Bentley's strength overpowered him. Nylah screamed in terror as she rushed to cover herself, and there was a trail of blood that ran down her thighs.

"Go in the room and call the cops," Bentley ordered Nylah.

She limped away and looked back every so often.

Bentley felt himself black out even more at the sight of her physical pain and with unforgiving hands, he choked Malik until the life nearly left his body. Then he sat on top of him until the police arrived. Only then did Bentley go outside, turn off his car, and then come back inside to comfort his sobbing ex-wife. Nylah had turned down the ambulance that had been sent, but seeking professional help was for the best. She didn't look so good.

"Let's get you to the hospital."

"No," she whimpered. "I'm okay."

"You're bleeding, Nylah! You have to get checked out, and then we can come back home. Now is NOT the time to be stubborn!" he screamed and yanked on her arm. "What did he do to you?"

She was quiet and still visibly shaken and crying.

"Nylah, answer me. What did he do?" Bentley smoothed her hair away from her face and then pulled her chin towards him. She refused to look him directly in the face, so he lowered his head to catch her eyes. "Did he…rape you? You can tell me anything."

Finally, she shook her head and spoke. Bentley almost had to strain to hear her gentle and painful words.

"No, h—he kicked me and said that if he couldn't have my babies or make love to me, then nobody else would ever have that opportunity. He said he was going to damage my body so badly that the next guy wouldn't want me."

Bentley watched as she wiped her tears gracefully and sniffed to clear her nostrils of mucus. Nylah finally looked him in the eye, whispering, "When you walked in, is when he was trying to force himself on me, but he never got to that point. I promise. He didn't do anything too crazy."

"That was crazy enough! I could KILL him!" Bentley screamed and punched the wall, causing her to gasp.

It did not matter that his knuckles were now sore or that the adrenaline was flowing through his veins. This was the only way that he could demonstrate just how mad he was without going on a manhunt. As if Malik had not already damaged the house, the indentation from Bentley's fists added to the destruction as he punched the wall over and over again.

"Bentley, STOP, before you hurt yourself! You're bleeding!" Nylah shouted and grabbed for his arms.

Reluctantly, he stopped punching the wall. He had stopped only because she asked him, but not because he wanted to. He breathed erratically, like a madman, and his eyes were narrow and darker than usual. Bloodstains now decorated the peach-colored wall. The two looked at each other for the longest time and then broke down crying together. Nylah held onto him as if her life depended on it and apologized.

"What are you sorry for? You have no reason to apologize to me," Bentley coaxed her.

"Because I let him in. Because I was stupid and trusted a monster! I let him into my life and my home. He's caused so much trouble between us, and he's the reason we're fighting for custody of Brooklyn. And now this," Nylah explained, motioning with her hands. "I should've known the red flags. All he wanted was sex, and that's all he talked about. Plus, he was always jealous of our relationship and made it known. I was so stupid!"

While she panicked, Bentley tried to offer some encouraging words, but she continued to cry and pour her heart out. It killed him to see his best friend, and the original beat of his heart, break down like this.

"You're not stupid, Nylah. Stop talkin' down on yourself that way."

"I—I don't know what I did in my past life but enough is enough!" Nylah looked up towards the ceiling.

She was now clothed in a pair of black jogging pants and a tank top, and she was as red as her shirt.

Fat tears rolled down her cheeks as she spoke, "God, what do You want from me? What did I ever do to *anybody* to deserve this? Why do You HATE me so much? Nothing has worked out for me. My marriage ended; my child was taken from me; I gave my heart to the wrong man. WHAT'S NEXT?"

Defeated, Nylah's body went limp against Bentley's and she let out an exasperated sigh. Her tearstained face relaxed against his chest, and then she wrapped her arms around his body.

"Can I please take you to the hospital?" he whispered as he stroked her head, feeling how warm she was.

Sleepily, and with exhaustion taking away the volume in her voice, she whispered back to him, "Yes."

## Chapter Fourteen

Thankfully, Bentley had followed his instincts.
Nylah was pretty much going into a shock from her
blood loss, and if they had waited any longer, things
could have been fatal. She was resting now with tubes
hooked up to her body, and fluids flowing through
her veins. She looked so peaceful, and Bentley was
glad that she could get some type of slumber. Since
Brooklyn was taken away, he was not sure how long it
had been since she actually slept.

The doctors would clear her to go home
tomorrow, and he vowed to stay at her side until then.
It wasn't like he had anyone to go home to anyway.
Tomorrow was also the day that they would get to see
their baby girl in a court-ordered visit with Bentley's
sister. Bentley could not wait to hold his sweetheart
again.

He still remembered the day that she came
home from the hospital. Brooklyn was as tiny as a
doll. For the longest time, he was scared to hold her
for fear that he would break something or injure her.
But the moment she looked into his eyes, all fears
subsided. Since the time that he knew Nylah was

pregnant, Bentley could admit that he had become a better man.

Only lately did he begin to feel indifferent.

It was like, no matter how hard he tried, he kept messing up. From allowing Jazlyn to walk over him, to cheating on her, to stirring up old feelings with Nylah, to forgetting their daughter at home, and the way he played with God was dangerous. Bentley just needed a breather. He needed help *ASAP*.

This would have been a perfect time to call his father for advice, but he was probably turning over in his grave with disappointment. Bentley could not confide in his mother either, since she was suffering from early stages of dementia and didn't need the added stress. Jazlyn certainly wouldn't be able to talk him through anything, and Nylah was probably sick of the back and forth.

He literally had no one.

As he sighed, and attempted to hold back tears, Bentley looked down at his hands and then pressed them together. Over the sounds of the machines in the hospital room and faint chatter down the hallway from nurses, he began to pray tranquilly.

"God, I know I've been messing up a lot lately," he chuckled painfully and looked towards the ceiling, "but I need You. I have fornicated. I have gotten drunk and cursed. I have hurt the women I love most. I have allowed my daughter to be taken away by the state. I even got into a fight."

Nylah moved around on the hospital bed, but never opened her eyes. Her chest moved up and down and seemed to match the tick of the hands on the clock.

"I need You to make sense of everything for me. I need You to show me the way again. Show me my purpose in life again, because obviously, I've lost it and I've RUN from it. I know You don't make any mistakes, but right now, I'm starting to question it all. What's the purpose for this season? What's the meaning of this heartache and this confusion I'm causing these women? What's the reason behind my daughter leaving? Why can't I seem to get it right?"

Bentley shook his head, and then balled his fists in frustration. He continued to keep his eyes lowered.

"I don't want to lose my faith, and I also don't want You to stop loving me. I'm desperate for You. Please give me a sign or show me what steps to take to get better. I'm just…so…so confused, Lord," he sighed with defeat.

As Bentley wiped the single tear from his eye, he decided to wrap up his pathetic plea. His prayer was as broken as he felt. God was probably looking down and laughing at him.

"I just pray that You heal Nylah. Please give her the strength to face the remainder of these hours without our daughter. Give her the strength to walk away completely from Malik, and never allow him back in. Give her peace from our divorce and take away any pain that I have caused her. Lord, I also ask that You heal me and my fiancée's relationship. If it's truly meant to be, I ask that You fix our marriage before it even starts. Make it holy and make it right. Continue to watch over, protect, and cover Brooklyn, and allow her to grow up to be as great as I've dreamed that she would be. Allow her to remain as innocent as possible and help us to create the best living situation that we can for her. In Your name I pray, amen."

As he ended the prayer, Bentley heard a faint word of confirmation. "Amen."

It was Nylah. She had heard the tail end of his conversation with God. She had her eyes closed still but there was a pleasant look on her face.

"You were always a great friend."

"Why do you say that?" Bentley questioned and reached out to hold her hand.

"You always pray for me even when we're at odds, or on each other's last nerve. Thank you for that," she said and finally opened her eyes. They were filled with tears. Judging by her grin, he assumed that they were tears of joy.

"I got you."

"Do you really?"

"I do," he affirmed as he still caressed her petite hand. "No other woman has *ever* come close to impacting my life the way you have. You hear me?"

"I hear you, and *you* better remember that."

"Of course, I'll remember. I remember everything about us. The day we met. The day we shared our first kiss. The day we got married and how we didn't go to sleep that night. We couldn't stop talking, laughing, or enjoying each other. I remember it all."

"Oh, you remember *everything*, huh? What was I wearing when we first met?" she joked.

Bentley thought for a second. Nylah was being sarcastic, but he had the memory of an elephant, especially when it came to her. He just had to *really* think on it.

"Things used to be so fun and exciting when we first started. Before these new relationships, and even before Brooklyn, it was just you and I. Late nights, sleeping in, traveling, and eating ice cream at our favorite college custard places. *Man!*" Nylah reminisced.

He looked over to see her struggling to find a comfortable position against the pillows. Bentley helped her sit up in bed and nodded.

"Those were the good ole days. Like seriously, the best time of my life."

"So, what happened? Did I really bore you like you said? Was I really that bad in bed or that uninteresting to you?"

She was hitting him with the 21 questions again and he was not sure that he could keep up, or even wanted to go there tonight. "Let's not start this conversation. I don't want you getting upset again with me or making yourself sicker."

"No." Nylah held up her hands, one of which had a needle sticking from the back of it. "I promise. I just want to know. Last time I reacted before really hearing you out. I know you said it was regarding our finances, but we both know that was a lie. Why did you really suggest a divorce? Why did you lose eyes for me?"

Bentley sighed and knew there was no way around the question. With a heavy heart, he decided it was time to finally stop running from the truth. Most importantly, Nylah knew him too well. At some point, he had to man up and be honest.

"Okay, this is the truth. I swear to God. It wasn't that you were boring in bed or that this marriage became a routine to me. To this day, you've given me my greatest laughs and memories, and not a day goes by where I don't think of all that we accomplished together. My fear of losing you pushed me away."

Nylah waited for him to continue, and her eyes stayed on his.

"It had everything to do with me constantly losing people in my life. You, of all people, have seen it throughout my life, and it's scary. My father passed, my youngest brother was murdered, and the other is locked up for decades. One of my sisters got married and moved overseas, and we haven't heard from her in a while. My mother developed dementia and Lord knows how long she'll be here on this earth when it really takes effect," Bentley explained.

He pushed back the emotions that threatened to overtake him. "I guess I was and still am scared to LOSE you."

Nylah was confused. "Lose me how? I'm not going anywhere unless God calls me home. We vowed 'till death do us part,' remember? Why did you think you would lose me?"

"Not lose you as far as death, but even your friendship. Your friendship has carried me since we were little. I was scared that we would get decades of marriage in, then separate, and then I would never be able to talk to you like I'm talking to you now. I was afraid of losing our history and our closeness. I've seen so many couples go that route, and I didn't want that same epidemic happening to us. Am I making sense?"

Nylah was quiet for a second and then chuckled. "You realize that is the dumbest thing you've EVER said? I mean, don't get me wrong, I get it, but honey, why didn't you come to me before the divorce? Why didn't you voice these concerns beforehand? You wouldn't have lost me then and you won't lose me now."

He began to explain himself again, but she held up her hand. Even with all the tubes in her, and with the olive-colored hospital gown wrapped around her body, she looked beautiful.

"Listen to me, Bentley. When we exchanged vows, I wasn't going into it thinking about the worst-case scenarios. If that's the case, no one could ever live and enjoy life because there's always tragedy or hardship. There will always be what ifs. I was excited that God had given me a soul mate to call my own. I PRAYED for you. I ASKED God for you, and I was willing to work at our marriage until we grew old together. You've been through a lot, and I get that, but we were beautiful as one. There was no reason for you to question any of that, or mess it up, for that matter," she added softly.

Bentley felt stupid. He wasn't sure why he was so pigheaded or selfish in his thinking, but he realized once again, Nylah always knew what to say and what to do. Her patience and gentle tone told him that he was forgiven, but he also knew that he had hurt her badly. Bentley had attempted to save himself from heartache and ended up causing more damage than intended.

"Wow. Love, what do I do now?"

She looked at him and shook her head. "You are about to marry a beautiful young lady who loves you. Mind you, y'all have some issues to work out, but I would suggest couple's counseling. That's all I can say. I'm here for you, but Bentley, realize that I did what I thought would make *you* happiest. I never wanted this divorce. I never wanted to say goodbye to what we had. Malik was only a distraction and, well, we see how that ended."

Bentley dropped his head in his hands in exasperation. He wanted to scream but figured that would be inappropriate in the hospital. He looked down at his bandaged hand, and then blew out hot air, "Are you still in love with me?"

"How can you even ask me that?" Nylah asked in incredulity.

"Why do you say that? We're talking. We're opening up to each other."

"We're talking, yes. But why ARE we talking about this? Like I said before, aside from your insecurities, you knew how much I loved you, Bentley. This isn't some mystery. I'll always love you."

"Loving me and being in love with me are two different things and you know that."

"It just seems like you're trying to embarrass me or force me to put my heart out on my sleeve."

"I'm not doing any of those things. That's coming out of your mouth," he told her calmly. "You don't have to answer…"

"Yes, Bentley! I'm IN love with you," she interrupted and screamed, "and I've been in love since the day you gave me that sweater in college when I started my period. I've been in love with you since you called me that same night and were more of a gentleman and rock to me than my FATHER has ever been. I've been in love with you for the last ten years and counting. Are you happy now? Is that what you wanted to hear?"

Bentley's heart soared. It was not the reaction that he was expecting from her. The tears rolling down his face were not the reaction he was anticipating either. It felt weird to hear her say those words, but it was also a relief. As selfish as it sounded, he could not help the joy that now pumped through his veins. She was in love with him, and he could not lie, it kind of felt good.

Nylah was visibly upset now as she struggled to stand.

Bentley stood up with his arms outstretched. "Where are you going? You need help?"

"I'm fine. I'm just ready to go home," her voice sounded shaky as she spoke. "Please don't feel like you have to stay. You've done enough."

"Girl, I'm not leaving you here. I don't care what you say. I want you to be well enough to go see Brooklyn tomorrow with me."

"Brooklyn," she repeated and stepped down from the bed. She headed to the bathroom leisurely and dragged the IV stand with her. "My sweet baby, and the *only* person who has never let me down besides God."

Bentley knew she was distraught and decided not to respond to her snide remarks. Instead, he said the only thing that came to mind. "Blue overalls and orange barrettes."

"What?" Nylah looked over her shoulder and paused.

"Blue overalls and orange barrettes," he repeated. "You asked me what you were wearing when we first met. Technically we met when we were too young to remember, but I can still see it as clear as day, when we started school together. We were in prekindergarten, remember?"

He watched as Nylah's pale but stunning face softened. She seemed to be speechless, and he watched as one of her hands opened, and out fell her cell phone with a crash. Instead of picking it up, she continued to stare at him, while he continued to recount their sweet memories.

"I can't remember what colored shirt you wore beneath it, but I know you had a million braids in your head," he chuckled with her, "some had beads on them; others had those orange, plastic barrettes that made sounds every time you turned your head."

Nylah continued to stand in the middle of the floor. She was unmoving and intently listening.

"I also remember standing in line behind you. We always had to line up by height and I was short for the longest time. You were just a few centimeters shorter than me before I hit that growth spurt in middle school," he added, and watched as her mind went back to their shared yesteryears.

Instantly, she seemed to forget that he had just angered her, and then burst into laughter. "Oh, my God! I sure did have that on because I remember I was angry with my mom for puttin' me in overalls! I have pictures of that day too! How do you remember that? We were soooo young."

"I already told you. I remember everything about you," Bentley asserted. Relief settled in his heart at the fact that she was now smiling.

Nylah hesitated and squinted her eyes. The single dimple in one of her cheeks became prominent, and then disappeared as she spoke again, "Okay, correct me if I'm wrong, but were you wearing green when we met?"

"I was."

"You gave me a Power Rangers card for Valentine's Day that following year too, remember? Oh, my God…it's all coming back to my remembrance now!"

"I did give you that." He shook his head in amusement. "That's crazy."

Nylah continued to stare at him. She was blushing as she relieved the sweet memories. All at once, his cell phone vibrated in his pocket.

It was Jazlyn, as expected, and she was calling at the worst possible time. She was probably checking to see where he was at this hour.

"Hey, beautiful. What's up?"

Out the corner of his eye, Nylah rolled her eyes, and then limped over to the bathroom. She slammed the door purposely.

"Hi, handsome," Jazlyn's voice was soft and remorseful. "Where are you? Can we talk?"

"I'm with Nylah, and before you say anything, remember what I told you so many times before."

Jazlyn sighed into the phone. He could tell that she was nodding with agreement. "I know, I know. She is your family, and until we're one, she comes first in your life. I get it. I don't even care that you're with her. I just…need to see you. Please come home so we can talk about this. I don't want to fight anymore."

"Neither do I, and we *will* talk it out…just not tonight. Please trust me and please understand," Bentley pleaded. "I'm all Nylah has right now, and she needs me. We'll figure this all out once my daughter is back home. You hear me?"

"I hear you. I love you," she whispered.

"I love you, too, baby. Thank you for sticking by me."

# Chapter Fifteen

As he had vowed, Bentley stayed the night with Nylah at the hospital. He slept, curled up in a chair near the window, and his snores were ridiculously loud. She had to laugh at the moisture collecting on his shoulder where his chin was tucked. He would probably be waking up any minute with a crook in his neck.

"Knock, knock," one of the nurses said in a singsong manner, as she knocked her knuckles against the door. She peeked her curly head in, and then gave Nylah a cheerful wave. "Good morning! You all ready to go home?"

Nylah motioned towards her overnight bag that was packed and zipped. "I am."

"I'm going to get your discharge papers and be right back. Did you or your husband need anything? It was such a pleasure meeting you two."

"Oh, no." Nylah smiled and decided not to correct her. Her ultimate goal was to leave and holding an even longer conversation would further keep her from being reunited with her daughter. "We're just fine, thank you."

The nurse ducked behind the curtain again, and left, and then Nylah turned to Bentley who was yawning.

"What time is it?"

"Time for you to wipe the slob from your mouth and get going. Brooklyn is probably waiting at the door already for us," Nylah said in excitement.

He grumbled about his neck hurting. "How are you feeling?"

"Much better." She smiled. "Whatever they gave me took away all of my pain. Can you pull the car around for me?"

"Of course," he said and then added, "anything for my wife!"

He was referring to what the nurse said, and Nylah could not help but to laugh. This man was a nut and had obviously been eavesdropping.

Bentley drove them home where he showered in record time, and then switched cars. Brooklyn's car seat now sat in the back of the two. They had even brought along her favorite blanket and stuffed animal. Bentley had also set up Brooklyn's tea party essentials so that when she got home, they could immediately catch up on all the time that they had been without each other. Although the visit was temporary, and

Brooklyn would have to return to his sister's care until the official court hearing, they wanted to make the best of the situation.

The car pulled up to the Bureau of Child Welfare, and silence fell among them. Nylah swallowed hard while Bentley exhaled deeply.

He said lowly, "Here we go."

He stepped from the car first, and then walked over to help Nylah out. Together, they walked hand in hand, and forced themselves to breathe. Time away from their baby girl had been nothing short of tortuous, but Nylah knew that God wouldn't let them down. Things would soon be back to normal.

"Hi, can I help you?" the receptionist asked and peered over her lime green glasses. She seemed warm and inviting, so Nylah leaned onto the desk, and motioned towards the back, while explaining the situation.

The woman collected their IDs and scanned them, and then gave them each a laminated visitor's pass. She showed them the way to the case manager's office with a smile.

"Good luck with everything, guys."

Bentley spoke up this time, "Thank you so much."

Together, they walked through the double doors as instructed. A Spanish woman seemed to recognize their faces, and then motioned them over.

"How are you two doing? I'm Esperanza, the case manager, you've been communicating with over the phone and by email."

"Nice to meet you." Nylah extended her hand.

"Thanks for all your help. We're ready to see our daughter. Has my sister made it yet?"

Esperanza cleared her throat as she tucked some hair behind her ears. "Mr. Rose, Ms. Christiansen, I know it's been quite a journey, but I'm so happy to inform you that Jessika Lewinski came forward and retracted her claims about the child neglect that was first reported to us. Brooklyn has been approved to return home."

"So, no trial? No court hearing or any of that?"

"None of that is necessary. She, along with a few witnesses in your dwelling, who wished to remain anonymous, all agreed that things were taken out of context that night. Your boyfriend was present *before* the time of her arrival, and according to a timestamp on the next-door neighbor's camera, you guys had only driven down the street before your boyfriend arrived from the opposite direction. There was only a three-minute timeframe that the child was technically left home alone. There was no other proof found that would suggest that this was neglect, abuse or abandonment, and Judge Meyers would rather not take this case to court or further drag out what we already know to be the truth. You guys are great parents."

"So that means…?"

"It means, Mr. Rose, Brooklyn has been cleared to return to your care, full-time."

Nylah began to cry softly behind her hands while Bentley pumped his fist towards the Heavens, "Thank you! Thank you! Where is she?"

"We left a message on your phone this morning, but your sister, Colette, took her back home. I just need you both to sign a few papers, and you're free to go pick her up. I must warn you, though."

"Warn us about what?" Bentley and Nylah asked in unison.

The woman presented them with clipboards so they could read over and sign the small stack of paperwork. "She keeps mentioning recycling. She seems very upset about something, and she is completely withdrawn, based on my last assessment of her."

"Completely withdrawn? What do you mean?"

"Your daughter hasn't spoken to any of our coordinators since she's been here, and understandably so, but when it was time for her to participate in some of the activities, she kept repeating that her recycling is over. I've never met a child so passionate about recycling," Esperanza chuckled lightly.

Nylah's eyes closed as she began to understand what the woman was saying. "Oh, no. Oh, no. I broke my promise."

"What? What's going on?" Bentley asked.

"I promised Brooklyn we would be there for her recital. She pronounces it *recycle*. Oh, my God. That was yesterday. She was looking forward to that," Nylah explained and covered her face with her hands again.

Bentley's heart seemed to sink right along with her.

"Dang it," Nylah cried out. "This is all my fault!"

"Ah, ah, ah. Remember we said we weren't going to be hard on ourselves anymore. We're starting fresh. We have to stop blaming ourselves. We can make it up to her."

Bentley had all the answers and Nylah could not help but to admire how calm he appeared. When they left from the Child Welfare offices, they headed straight for Colette's luxury townhome. Bentley called to give her a heads up that they were on the way, and Colette informed them that Brooklyn had gone to the park with Bentley's nieces and nephews.

When they arrived, Brooklyn still had not made it back with the other children, so they sat for nearly another hour before Colette's front doors opened.

Nylah's smile dropped when she saw that in the small group of family, none of the children were her daughter.

"Uncle B!" the younger kids cried, running to hug and greet Bentley. Colette had five children— three were adopted, one was a foster child, and her oldest, Cyan, was biological.

"Hey, guys, good to see you. What's up? What's up?" He smiled and rubbed the boys' heads and pulled playfully on the girls' ponytails. They all giggled and surrounded him. "I'm happy to see y'all too. Where's Brooklyn?"

Cyan stepped further into the room, fidgeting with the drawstring of her shorts. Colette crossed the room to stand in front of her daughter and ask the million-dollar question again.

"Cy, where's Brook?"

Tucked under Cyan's arm was a yellow blanket. Nylah could feel her stomach twist with the realization that it belonged to Brooklyn.

"I'm so sorry, Auntie and Uncle. I'm so sorry, Mom..."

"What HAPPENED?" Colette, Bentley and Nylah all screamed in unison.

"I—I lost her! I turned for one second while the twins were on the swing, and she was gone! I called the police, but my phone died shortly after, so I told everybody to pack up so we could go and get the grownups. I don't know where Brooklyn is. I'm so sorry!"

"She ran AWAY?" Nylah shouted.

Bentley let out a frustrated growl and ran his hands over his hair. "Cyan, Cyan...why didn't you call while you were there? How long ago was this?"

"We left as soon as she ran off. I wanted to get everybody home safe so I could tell you guys. I'm sorry. I didn't know what to do!" the 12-year-old cried.

Colette had gotten pregnant her freshman year in high school, and had grown up fast, but Cyan was a mature young lady. Bentley and Nylah knew this wasn't her fault nor had it been her intention; she had done her best to keep track of her siblings and cousin.

"Okay, okay, calm down," Bentley demanded. "Everybody, calm down and just breathe for a second. Cyan, what park did you go to? We're going to have to go look for her."

Nylah grabbed his forearm to try to follow him out of the door, but he shook his head. "Stay here with my nieces and nephews. You don't need to be hopping along on your foot like that."

"My daughter is out there! I don't care about a little pain. I need to help find her!"

Colette stepped up and spoke cautiously, "Listen, it was my daughter who lost yours. Let us make this right, Nylah. Stay back and monitor the phones in case someone calls with any news. I promise, we'll find her and bring her back home, sis!"

Nylah knew they were right. It was best for her to stay back, so reluctantly, she obliged and sat by the window with both the house phone and her cell phone in her lap.

She spoke to herself, "I don't believe my baby would just leave and run off like that. She had to have a plan in mind. Brooklyn, where are you, baby? Where did you go?"

She couldn't help but to think that in a matter of hours, what was sure to be a triumphant and restorative day, had quickly become another drama-filled and tragic night, and Nylah was not sure that she or her family could handle any more blows.

# Chapter Sixteen

*23 minutes later...*

It was like an answered prayer.

Seconds after Bentley text Nylah that they had made it to the police department to give a description of Brooklyn and try to file a report, she received a phone call back at the house.

"Hello, I am looking for Nylah Christiansen," the voice was professional and soft-spoken, yet oddly familiar.

"Yes. This is she," Nylah answered, sitting up a little straighter. She inhaled shakily and dabbed at her tear-stained cheeks with a tissue.

"Hi, yes, Ms. Christiansen. Good evening, I'm Shamya, the receptionist at the Restored and Renewed Family Counseling Services on State Street. Your daughter walked in our offices a few minutes ago, lost, and one of the therapists got her some warm blankets and a cot to lay on. She gave us your number. I have her here with me now, safe but shaken up."

"Oh, my God," Nylah exhaled. "Yes…*yes!* That's my baby! Brooklyn, right?"

"Yes." The woman was obviously smiling as she spoke, "It's Brooklyn. When can you come down to retrieve her? We will keep her safe and comfortable until you're here."

Nylah could literally feel as her broken heart became mended again. After a quick talk with her daughter over the phone to confirm that she was unharmed and okay, Nylah hung up and called Bentley. He stopped by the house to pick her up, and together, they went down to the State Street office.

Nylah recognized the building immediately, as she and Bentley had conducted their marriage counseling sessions there, many moons ago. Though there was a name change since her last visit, she even remembered the receptionists' and therapists' faces and warm demeanors.

Brooklyn was sitting in the waiting room, wrapped in a blanket, as they approached the door, and when she finally spotted her parents, she burst into tears and ran into their awaiting arms.

"Brooklyn! My baby!" Nylah wept.

Bentley held his girls snuggly against him, alternating between leaving kisses on Brooklyn's cheek to leaving kisses on Nylah's forehead. He wrapped his arms around them a little tighter as they both told Brooklyn how sorry they were and how much they loved her.

The surrounding employees allowed them a moment to be reunited with their daughter. The hugs, kisses, and gentle reprimanding went on for another few minutes, before Nylah glanced to one of the women standing around the front desk.

Apparently, she was the one who had spotted Brooklyn from her corner office.

"*Carlotta*? I mean, Dr. Bloomberg?" Nylah asked.

The woman, who no longer wore wire-rimmed glasses, and who was jazzier than Nylah remembered, looked up from speaking with her receptionist. The woman stared at Nylah, down to Brooklyn, and then back up for a second before her jaw dropped. Bentley looked over too and seemed to recall where they first met her.

"You gave us marriage counseling a couple years back!" Nylah exclaimed as she still held Brooklyn in her arms. "You look great. Oh, my goodness. Thank you again for taking care of my baby."

"It was my pleasure, and please, call me Carlotta," the woman said and motioned towards Brooklyn. "You've done an excellent job at teaching her your contact information."

"Thank you." Bentley smiled.

Nylah rubbed Brooklyn's back. She was in tears now that her parents were before her, and she appeared to be sleepy. An onsite medic examined her but did not find anything alarming, thankfully. Nylah could not have been happier.

"I'm happy to see you all together and still pressing forward," Carlotta added.

"Oh, we're divorced, but thank you for what you did for us."

Carlotta gave a knowing look.

It was time to go home and handle any further questioning and investigations at another time. Nylah's energy was drained, and her body ached, while Bentley's mind was tired. Brooklyn had fallen asleep on a full stomach of her favorite food, and they figured that the tea party could wait another day.

To Jazlyn's dismay, Bentley decided to stay overnight with Nylah and Brooklyn, and wrapped himself in the Doc McStuffins themed bedspread.

Sleep claimed him while Nylah closed the book she was reading and tiptoed to her bedroom.

There, she dropped to her knees and thanked God for bringing her daughter back to safety.

"God, it's been a long journey, but I thank You. I thank You because I still have my mind, my health, and my family even though this has been the test of the year. I thank You because You were with my baby, when she ran away, and You're still with her as she sleeps. Lord, I pray that You would cover this family tonight, tomorrow, and forevermore. Please help us to move forward from this with grace and peace. Lord, continue to bring us closer. I even thank You for Dr. Bloomberg and her involvement in getting Brooklyn back into my arms. There was a reason we reunited, and it was bigger than all of us. For that, I thank You."

Nylah concluded her prayer and looked up from her folded hands. She continued to kneel at her bedside and could feel the weight lifting off of her shoulders. God was so good, and although she had no idea where the next step of her life would take her, she was confident that God would be ordering her steps.

# Chapter Seventeen

Bentley slept well, knowing that his daughter was safe and sound, but there was just one more thing that he had to get off his chest. After spending the night and half the morning with Nylah and Brooklyn, Bentley bade a goodbye and made his departure. At some point, he had to make things right with Jazlyn and check in on a few of his businesses, but for now, he was a young man searching for his mother. He drove quietly across town. The lengthy journey over to the senior citizens' complex was done in complete silence without music or even his thoughts to entertain him.

He needed to speak to his mother. Whether she was up for company or not, he had to see her face and hear her voice. His only prayer was that she would remember his name. If nothing else, he needed to hear her whisper it. Bentley could feel his heartbeats quicken as he parked his truck and took two steps at a time up to the fourth floor. He was met with the familiar yellow door and chuckled as he thumped his knuckles against it. Although he hated this color, it was his mother's favorite. She had insisted that he paint her walls and ceilings that gaudy, God-awful hue.

"Come in," his mother called out weakly.

He would be getting married in less than five months, and he feared that her health would prevent her from attending the ceremony. But he knew she would be with him in spirit.

She looked so different. Her once beautiful, well-sculpted cheekbones no longer rose with her smile. The loose skin around her eyes was sunken in, and her flowing, sandy hair was thinning more each time that he visited her. Bentley hated what the medications were doing to her body, just as he hated what the dementia was doing to her once sharp mind.

"Momma," he whispered as he eased his shoes off and moved towards the woman, who had carried him for eight months, two weeks, and three days.

"Nurse, is that you?" his mother questioned. She glanced over a shoulder where she knitted.

Bentley settled in the loveseat across from her and then leaned to open the blinds. Light streamed into her apartment and touched her face. She looked like an angel the way she glowed in the warm sunlight.

"It's me, Momma. Bentley, your son," he spoke gently and slowly.

"*My* son?" she repeated. "Which one?"

"Bentley. Your favorite son," he joked and watched her as she placed her things on the table beside her.

She folded her hands in her lap and smiled at him. "You're my only son! The only one who visits me at least."

He was unsure if his sisters came out as often as he did, but he decided not to address her words. She wouldn't remember that one of her sons was dead and the other was locked up anyway. "You cool in here? You want me to turn off this fan, Momma?"

"Oh, no, I'm fine. My son said he was coming so I want him to be comfortable when he gets here," she explained and went back to knitting. "What was your name again, young man?"

Bentley's heart dropped at her words. Just that quickly, she had forgotten who he was.

"It's me, Momma. I'm your son."

His mother paused what she was doing and then chuckled. "Where is your wife? Where is Nylah?"

"Nylah's not my wife. I'm with Jazlyn now, and we'll be getting married soon," Bentley said and rubbed his hand over his face. Her child-like behavior was oftentimes frustrating, but he knew that she could not control her symptoms and forgetfulness. "You haven't met her yet, but..."

"I *have* met Nylah," she interrupted, and looked up from the quilt she was creating. "She was the best thing that ever happened to you. I've always loved and trusted her because she made you happier than I've ever seen you before. You hold onto her, you hear? God told me a long time ago that she was the woman for you."

Bentley kept quiet as he watched his mother. She spoke with authority, patted his hand, and then began to nod off. A smile tugged at the corners of his mouth as her head lolled to the side and she drifted off.

He was surprised at her memory. She could barely remember that he was her son, but she had no problem when it came to Nylah. For a moment longer, he stayed with her, and leaned into her as she slept. Tears came to his eyes as he thought about how much life had changed. He no longer had a mother. She was there physically, but mentally, she was another person, and it hurt badly. All he had now were sweet and beautiful memories.

After another hour of holding her sleeping, fragile body to his, and catching a few minutes of sleep himself, he decided to leave. He would now have to patch things up with his future wife.

"See you later, Momma," he whispered against his mother's cheek, seconds before he pressed his lips to it. "I love you. This is Bentley. I'll see you sometime next week."

His mother stirred awake, and she blinked a few times before she smoothed her hand against his. "Nurse, is that you?"

A single tear made its way down from his eye as he stood to his full height and then bade another goodbye.

As he walked towards the door, his mother's words sent a chill down his spine. "See you soon, baby. Thank you for always visiting and taking care of me. Bring Brooklyn and Nylah next time too, you hear?"

Bentley chuckled and reached for the doorknob. God had an amazing sense of humor. "Yes, ma'am. I'll bring them next time."

***

*Sixteen weeks later…*

Twentieth Street. *Dang it,* Nylah thought. She should have been on 32<sup>nd</sup> Street right now, but traffic would not let her be great. The day had finally arrived, and her fortitude was uncompromising. She had abandoned her car a few blocks back on the side of the road, so that she could get to her destination quicker. She knew she looked ridiculous as she ran with one bare foot while the other donned a half-broken stiletto. Its pale pink exterior was now scuffed, the bow on it was frayed, and the five-inch heel was inches shorter.

Her morning jogs at the gym seemed to prepare her for this moment while she took a back street and then accelerated even more. With her arms pumping at her sides, and with her full lips squeezed together, she proved to be a woman of determination and perseverance.

She had been running for over three blocks when she came to an unfamiliar intersection. Nylah's run slowed to a stop. She twirled tresses of her hair between her fingers in thought. Wisps of it had fallen from the bun at the center of her head. Its color, a chocolate brown and honey mixture, complimented her toffee skin tone perfectly.

"Come on, come on. Think, Nylah. *Think*!"

Her eyes were the shapes of fully-grown almonds, as they surveyed her surroundings leisurely. The ends of her long eyelashes kissed the tops of her cheekbones that were tinted with blush.

She was gorgeous to most people, and she knew it. Perhaps it was why she received so many stares from cars driving past and patrons walking by. It could also be because she wore a customized pale pink and cream-colored wedding dress, veil, and sparkling, silver-tone accessories. Nylah's button nose, speckled with tiny freckles, wrinkled in frustration. Clearly, she had no clue where she was going.

"'Scuse me." Her eyes looked down at the wedding invitation, and then back up to the young man who had stopped at a red light in front of her. He drove a freshly washed SUV; she could tell by the water that dripped from the truck's sleek exterior.

He rolled his window down more to hear her breathy inquiry. "Uh, yeah?"

"I'm looking for The McCall Worship Center. Do you know where that is?"

The stranger gnawed on his lip, thought about it, and then nodded. "Hop in. It's further up the street. Wait a minute. Are you late for your wedding?"

Nylah tucked her gown in around her, and then closed the door. She was sure that much of her train was now wedged in the door, but she had no more strength to fight with it. The material of the dress was now dingy and dirty along the bottom, and she knew she looked wild.

"Something like that," she said. "Thank you so much. I'm so sorry I don't have any money on me to repay you. What's your name?"

"Jhalil. Hey, don't worry about it. Congratulations on your big day," he said and looked over at her. He seemed to have a million other questions as to why she was alone, without a shoe or car, and out running on her wedding day.

Her thick but neatly waxed eyebrows shot up as she spoke, "Thank you. But please don't ask."

The guy who looked no older than 25 threw his hands up and laughed. "You read my mind. I won't."

Instead of being quiet as she promised herself before getting in the car, her eyes welled up with tears. Nylah was sure that by the end of this encounter, her makeup would be ruined, and she would resemble The Bride of Chucky.

"It's not my wedding. It's my best friend slash ex-husband's special day. I'm going to try to stop him from marrying his fiancée."

"*Whoa*," Jhalil whistled. "Seriously?"

"So serious." Nylah tucked her bottom lip between her teeth and shook her head. "I know it SOUNDS crazy and it IS crazy, but I *love* that man. I was always taught to fight for the people and things that mean the most to me."

Jhalil turned his music down as she poured out her heart.

"Since we were in kindergarten, I've been infatuated with Bentley Roderick Rose. We were married, had a child, and then got a divorce at *his* request, but I'm still in love. He was my first everything, and I know for sure his fiancée cannot love or take care of him the way I did."

Jhalil nodded. "Well, Bentley's a lucky guy if he has someone like you in his life. What do you think he'll say?"

Nylah sighed and looked out the window at the blurred houses and buildings. "Honestly, I've thought about that all night. Even if I look like a fool,

I'm going to say what I have to say, and be done with it. If it's meant to be, Bentley will come to his senses. If it's not meant to be, then our time together was beautiful. I'm woman enough to keep it moving if I'm not what he wants."

"That's incredible. I wish you the best, sweetheart."

The car rode in silence the remainder of the way to the massive church that she had never heard of. She skimmed the wedding invitation a final time, confirmed that it was the exact address, and then looked over at her new friend.

"Jhalil, you don't know how much you've helped me today. Thank you."

He shrugged and took her hand. "It was my pleasure...?"

"Nylah. Nylah Christiansen."

"It was my pleasure Nylah, and just remember the scripture. 'What God has joined together, let no man separate.' Go get your man," he whispered sincerely with a smile.

Nylah stared at him for a moment more, offered him a hug of gratitude, and then blew out hot air. It was now or never. She exited the car, smoothed out the gown that fit her body like a glove, and then walked towards the entrance.

Her hand closed around the door handle, and she entered the church. Nylah seemed to forget how to breathe while she looked at the ushers. They, too, looked confused as they examined what she wore, how erratically she breathed, and how she looked.

"Um, hello. Can we help you, ma'am?"

Nylah's hand went up, but she never said a word. The woman, who favored her late grandmother, looked shocked. She could hear the pastor officiating the wedding ceremony in the distance and walked a pace faster towards the sanctuary.

"Ma'am? Ma'am! This is a private wedding ceremony! Stop her!"

Nylah continued to walk and ignored the words of the concerned clergy. As she burst through the doors of the sanctuary, all eyes were on her. Nylah could hear gasps and whispers. A few ushers were running over to show her to a seat, but she only stared ahead at the couple positioned at the front of the mega church.

Her ex-husband and his fiancée were seconds away from being joined in marriage. She cringed at the thought of looking like a madwoman and disrupting a wedding ceremony, but her heart was overwhelmed with love as she focused on him.

Bentley was just as handsome as he was on their own big day. But quickly, her mind left his grown image and she suddenly saw him as a five-year-old again. She went back to a time where he was "just Bentley," the boy she knew and loved and had gotten to know before any Jazlyn came along.

They were five and had been told to stand next to each other for an icebreaker activity in class. Nylah, ever the leader and social butterfly, had grabbed his hand and introduced herself to their peers. Bentley, much shyer and socially awkward, began to cry. When the teacher walked over to ask why he was crying, Nylah had wiped his tears and gave him a kiss on the cheek. Later that day, during naptime, Nylah had offered him her hand again and they slept peacefully in their side-by-side cots.

"I've got your back," she had whispered to him then, and it had been the same thing since that day. She had *always* had his back, whether he realized it or not. She had *always* cared for his well-being and had his best interests at heart.

Today, he stood well over six feet and wore a velvet tuxedo. The low-cut Caesar on his head held waves as deep as the ocean, while his blemish-free skin favored silk. His eyes, the shade of coffee without creamer, widened and focused on her.

"Nylah? What are you doing here?" he asked. "What's wrong?"

Nylah looked to the confused and agitated bride. *Jazlyn*. Her cosmetically modified pouty lips, well-sculpted eyebrows, and skin that was a shade lighter than cinnamon, looked flawless. To top it all off, she wore long hair extensions that fell in layers of sandy brown and hints of burgundy around her petite shoulders. She would make any guy lucky, and the male beside her believed it was him.

But Nylah knew better.

Why Bentley had to settle for a woman that had an ego bigger than the moon, loved money just as much as she loved her next breath, and who was not a good fit for their daughter, was beyond comprehension. She could never understand his poor choices. Bentley deserved so much more. He deserved Nylah, and today, she would make sure that she proved her love.

"Mommy!" Brooklyn called out from the front row, and then was quickly shushed by Jazlyn's mother.

The officiator, who Nylah remembered as one of the community's well-respected pastors, looked back and forth between the three before he continued to speak, "If anyone feels these two should not be joined in holy matrimony, please speak now, or forever hold your peace."

Her presence had arrived on time, and those words were all that Nylah needed to hear. She cleared her throat and moved forward down the aisle. Beneath her feet, the custom runner held the names of Bentley and Jazlyn and the day's date. The thin paper bunched under her rushed footsteps, and her petite hand went up timidly as though she were answering a question in school.

"I don't feel they should be married."

Another round of gasps could be heard left and right, and hushed conversation broke out. Quite a few people knew who she was. After all, they had attended her dream wedding with Bentley years ago. Others looked confused. Her daughter ran down the aisle towards her, grabbing her hand. Nylah gave her a reassuring smile but answered to no one else. She only focused on the man standing less than ten feet from her.

"Bentley, you're making a mistake and you know it."

Jazlyn stepped forward and spoke up, "What do you think you're doing? You weren't even invited!"

"Jazlyn, this doesn't concern you. Bentley, can I speak with you in private?"

The bride stomped her foot. "You're messin' up my special day! Of course, this concerns me. What are you DOING?"

Nylah watched as her ex-husband began to panic. His eyes were wild with confusion, anger, and what she prayed was regret. "Please don't mess this day up for us. You know where we stand. I'll always love you, but...I'm *in* love with Jazlyn."

"You're in church, Bentley. Don't lie to me, to your family, or to yourself. What did you tell me on the phone yesterday? You said you were beginning to get cold feet."

"Nylah, please don't do this!"

"I love you. Our daughter misses you at home. Tell me you don't love me. Tell me you don't want that old thing back and I'll leave."

Bentley was silent as he dropped his fiancée's hand and ran his hands over his face in frustration.

A male family member from Jazlyn's side stood up and dared Nylah to step further. His arm closed around her forearm as he attempted to move her.

"Don't touch me!" she yelled. "And don't touch my daughter!"

"Don't touch her!" Bentley commanded at the same time.

"So, you're *really* condoning this? You're allowing her to ruin our wedding day? You're OKAY with this? Go to hell, Bentley!" Jazlyn burst into tears and ran off with an older woman in tow. It was most likely her mother, Nylah concluded.

"Bentley, can I *please* talk with you in private?" she asked one final time.

The church was still noiseless except for occasional mumbling from the family and friends, and someone's faint crying. One of Jazlyn's bridesmaids cried at the front, and Nylah imagined that a few of the women wanted to strangle her, but it was Bentley that she needed and could not seem to breathe without. No one had been more disappointed and upset about the divorce than Nylah, and she could not care less about interrupting this wedding that should have never been.

Finally, Bentley cleared his throat to address Nylah and the attendees, attempting to take the focus off the chaos and Jazlyn's hysterics in the room next to the sanctuary. His words were like a knife as they cut through the thick tension.

"No. Brooklyn, come back over here with Daddy. Nylah, please go back home," he said coldly. "I do love you, but not in the way you're thinking. We were best friends, and then college sweethearts, and nothing more. We grew apart and I fell in love with someone else. You will always be my first love—that'll never change. But what we had was just that. So, I would appreciate you letting me live my life. *Please*."

As if ice had been thrown at her, she received the shock of her life at his harsh words. His stare was cold and intense, and she could feel the growing hatred from where he stood. Whether his words were true or not, Nylah knew that she would not stick around to hear anything else.

Instead, with her head held high, she bent to grab the bottom of her wedding gown. She avoided the eyes of all the surrounding family members and friends and ignored the whispers of the ushers at the back of the church. With a single twirl, she walked back out of the church and never looked back. To her surprise, Jhalil's truck was still outside. He gave her a hopeful look, but then his expression dropped to match hers.

As she settled into the car, cooled with air conditioning, she let out the cry of her life. Pressing her head to the back of the seat, she screamed like she was auditioning for a horror film. Jhalil flinched beside her and then plugged his ears, still allowing her to get her emotions out.

When she got her scream and frustrations all out, she could feel the rawness and soreness of her throat. Her eyebrows wrinkled in pain, her nose burned, and then the river of warm tears came.

Jhalil cautiously reached over to rub her shoulder. "I take it things didn't go as you wanted them to?"

"He hates me," she sobbed into her hands. "I guess it…it wasn't meant to be."

Her new friend dropped her off back to her truck, they exchanged numbers, and she went home to cry herself to sleep. But fate had other plans. As

Nylah wiped under her sore eyelids with a half-balled piece of tissue, there was a knock at her door.

"Who is it?" she screamed out at the top of her lungs. Somehow, she still had the energy and voice. She had no tolerance for company right now, and certainly was not in the mood for a pity party from her friends. Several text messages and missed calls were on her phone, but she just wanted peace. She wanted silence to process what had taken place.

Her humiliation and self-confidence had taken a new low. She felt like the scum of the earth, and probably would not face the world for a long time. The rain outside poured as if all the deceased souls in Heaven were crying. The weather matched her mood perfectly. As the knocks continued, followed by the constant ring of her doorbell, she stood to her feet.

Her achy body maneuvered leisurely to the door. The house shoes on her size seven feet made a scrubbing sound as she forced herself to move. Without checking the window or peephole, she opened the door.

Bentley stood in the rain, still dressed in his tuxedo and was drenched from head to feet. His truck sat in the driveway and had a JUST MARRIED sign hanging from the hood.

Brooklyn sat in the passenger seat, out of the rain, and waved to her. But there was no bride in sight. There was no Jazlyn nagging him to hurry his visit along. He was alone at her door and looked like he had the world on his shoulders.

Nylah hated that she looked so horrific. Her hair was unruly and going in all different directions, and her face was pale and tear-stained.

All at once, Bentley dropped to his knees. He hugged Nylah around her waist and then buried his head near her womb. It was the same womb that had birthed their beautiful daughter, who sat watching their scene now. Bentley's shoulders shook as he cried. Nylah placed her hands on the back of his head, rubbing his moist hair and the nape of his neck.

"What's going on? What happened?" she spoke over the rain. Their daughter looked alarmed as she saw her father sobbing.

"Please forgive me for taking you through this. Please forgive me for almost compromising our history, Brooklyn's happiness, and our love. You were right. You were right all along. I can't live without you, and I was a fool to think that I could."

Nylah's heart soared at his raspy confessions. His voice was hoarse, but his message was clear.

He gripped her body tighter in his arms so much that she feared that she would fall over. "I *need* you, baby."

Bentley finally looked up at her and his face was drenched. It was not the rain, but his warm, salty tears. Nylah could not believe he was finally verbalizing the things that she always hoped he would say.

From day one, she knew God had written their love story, but it would take him pushing aside his insecurities and fears to see it. Speechless, Nylah closed her eyes, dropped to her knees, and cried with him.

"I love you," he spoke with relief that she did not turn him away.

"I love you too," she whispered back.

Their lips met in a kiss that was as sweet as cotton candy. Her cheeks became flushed immediately, and her heartbeats seemed to triple off the strength of their love, but it was really the swarming butterflies in her stomach. Bentley cupped the back of her head with his hands, and it had been so long since she felt this safe. She melted into his embrace and kissed him back with a gentleness that only her lips could give.

Her ears caught the sound of a door slamming and soon, Brooklyn joined them where they knelt. She wedged her face between theirs, and they chuckled as they leaned in to kiss her cheek from each side.

"Stop kissin' you guys! Or get a room!" Brooklyn exclaimed.

Nylah began to weep with joyful tears, but Bentley swiftly wiped them away.

"I don't want to ever make you cry again. With God and Brooklyn as my witness, I'm going to make you the happiest woman alive from this day forward," he vowed.

Nylah nodded to his promises and held Brooklyn against her. She sent a prayer up to God and thanked Him for Bentley's change of heart. There was a reason she had not stopped thinking of Bentley. There was a reason that her was still full of love for him, even after drowning herself in other men and habits.

Before they were twinkles in their parents' eyes, their love story had been fashioned by God. No matter what outside influences had to say, no time, separation, or relationship could keep them divided.

Nylah could already feel the glow in her face as he looked at her with his beautiful eyes.

"Marry me…" he questioned with sincerity. "…*again?*"

Nylah did not need to be asked more than once. With rain soaking them from head to toe, and with their daughter looking on with hopeful eyes, she nodded and accepted his proposal for the second and final time.

"Baby, I would marry you one hundred times more."

# Chapter Eighteen

Following her words, Bentley could not help but to smile and cry uncontrollably. He felt like the Heavens had personally opened up and shined a ray of sunlight on him. Despite the rain and gloominess of the day, he was elated to have his woman back—his *family* back.

He leaned in to kiss Nylah once more. Brooklyn, with excitement written all over her face, jumped up and down as her parents' mouths collided in a promising smooch. Bentley chuckled and pulled away.

"Let's get inside before we get sick in this rain," he said.

The three migrated inside.

Nylah helped Brooklyn change into a warm, dry pajama set, while Bentley went in his corner of the closet where a few articles of clothing were still there. He undressed leisurely in front of her as she shook her head in disbelief. Her cheeks were still moist from crying, and her eyelashes blinked slowly in thought.

"What…what was the change of heart?" Nylah sniffled and watched him struggle to take off his damp slacks. She got up to help him undress and skimmed her fingertips over his chest. "Hours ago, you literally looked at me and sounded like you hated my existence. I'm just still in shock right now."

"*Shhh,*" he shushed her and allowed her to unbutton his pants and work them down his legs. "I could never hate you. Even if you did the unthinkable, I would still find a way to love you and forgive you."

Bentley was quiet for a moment as he settled on the bed and then pulled Nylah down with him. She straddled his waist and nestled her forehead against his. Her arms curled around his neck, and they breathed in and out for a moment before he spoke again.

"God has been revealing His plan to me lately, and you were a major part of those visions I've been having. You knew it, my mom knew it, Brooklyn knew it, and even Jazlyn knew how much I was still in love with you. It was only a matter of time that I got it together and stopped running. I'm so sorry, baby. I…I can't apologize enough for what I did to you."

Nylah pressed her mouth to his for the twelfth time in the last hour. "Stop apologizing. This time away taught me so much and honestly, I'm thankful for the separation because it allowed us to come back stronger than ever and appreciate what we had."

"What we *have*," he corrected and held her backside with his hands.

"Bentley?"

"What's up?"

"What did Jaz say about all of this?"

The sound of him swallowing echoed throughout the room. The faint sounds of Brooklyn singing along to a made-for-TV children's movie could be heard down the hall. Nylah lifted an eyebrow in curiosity and Bentley rubbed his head as though her words had caused an instant headache.

"She didn't take it too well, as expected, and of course, her family didn't let me leave without giving me a piece of their minds."

"And that forming bruise on your jawline?"

"That was her doing as well," he said quietly and thought back to earlier in the day.

*A weird sensation came over Bentley as he ran down the hallways of the church. He was still in shock by Nylah's boldness to interrupt his wedding. It always felt good to hear that she still loved him. He searched for his wife-to-be while his heart thumped in his chest. He could hear her cries coming from one of the church's many rooms, so he followed the sound until he stood before the white door. "Jaz!"*

*"Go away!"*

*"Why are you pushing me away? It's not like I asked her to come do that," he explained and leaned into the doorframe. His voice was filled with desperation and perplexity. His knuckles knocked against the side of the door again. This time, his voice was more urgent and demanding. "Jaz, let me in!"*

*"She said you talked to her and told her you had cold feet. What is that? Why would you say something like that to her, instead of discussing it with me?" Jazlyn asked, and it seemed like more sobs formed in her throat by the shakiness of her voice. "How could you? I knew there was always something between you and her, and I should have never taken you back after you cheated with her."*

*"You said you forgave me for that!"*

*"Bentley, I'm very disappointed in you," Jazlyn's mother spoke up this time.*

"With all due respect, may I please speak with my fiancée ALONE? I don't know who's all in there, but this does not concern you."

The door flew open then, and Bentley fell into the room slightly. It smelled of pure estrogen, perfume, and the faint aroma of freshly flat-ironed hair. He assumed it was the room that they had all gotten dressed in because there were clothes, shoes, and other accessories strewn everywhere. Four women, including Jazlyn, stared back at him with their arms crossed and their lips twisted in disgust.

"So, I'm the bad guy now, huh? Jazlyn, let's go somewhere and talk. Please?" he all but begged and fidgeted under the stares of her family.

"No, Bentley. I need space right now."

"Naw, we need to talk this out. Let's get it all out in the open."

"Answer me this," she spoke lowly and carefully, "Are you in love with her?"

He expected to hear her ask this very question, but he did not think it would be in front of her mother, aunt, and bridesmaids. Bentley swallowed hard and the sound was the only thing that could be heard. Everyone remained quiet as they stared at him. He felt like he was a contestant on Family Feud and everyone was waiting on him to give his winning answer.

"Jaz, why can't we have this conversation in private?"

226

"Why can't you answer the question?" her mother piped up again and shook her head in disbelief. "Jaz, you can do so much better. He was always a pushover and God only knows how much that woman probably manipulates him."

"Right," one of the bridesmaids spoke up now and was sarcastic with her choice of words, "and to think that we all were jealous of what you had. He's not worth your tears, your time, or giving up your last name."

"Isn't he the same guy that you said was a lame in high school and college? Bentley, don't you know how many men who would LOVE to be with my friend? Yet she chose you, and you want to play games. You needed her more than she needed you!"

Jazlyn's aunt chuckled and looked down at her fingernails arrogantly. "I've always said you could do better. I mean, after all, he has a bratty daughter! You want your first marriage to be with someone who you can BUILD with, not take on other baggage."

"Baggage? Are y'all for real right now? Jaz, are you really going to let them talk to me like that?" Bentley spoke with anger and bitterness. The comment about his daughter was the last straw. "You're right. You weren't worth me marrying you if you could just give up on us that easily. I should've listened to my heart a long ago, instead of my head. I should have realized you were nothing more than good sex and a fun

227

*time while I matured and prepared for my REAL queen…Nylah."*

*Slap!*

*Bentley continued to talk although Jazlyn's hand to his face stung. He rubbed his jawline and walked back over to the door. He no longer cared about how much of a monster he looked to them, or that he was breaking his girlfriend's heart. He saw the light, and he had to make things right.*

*"You never tried to be a mother to Brooklyn or win her trust over. Not once did you try to visit with my mother and build a relationship with her, knowing her time on this earth is limited. All you did was spend my money and distract me from God's plans for my life. You hate to go church and you know that's the one thing I wanted to do every Sunday with you. My mother never cared for you even with her memory loss and warned me about you. If that isn't a sign, I don't know what it is! I should've seen the red flags before today. So, am I still in love with my ex-wife? YES!"*

*"Get out!" Jazlyn shouted. Her face was now reddened with anger and her voice had become hoarse from all her wailing. "Forget you, forget Nylah, and forget this entire relationship! You'll miss me when I'm gone!"*

*"No, you'll miss the way I spoiled and treated you! All you had to do was cook and clean, and I would handle the rest, but you couldn't even do that. Nylah has always held me*

228

*down; she's always been my backbone, even after the hell I put her through. When my daughter was taken away, you never showed concern. When my lupus flared up and I was hospital bound, it was always Nylah who stood by my side. You were never there through this relationship! All this time I was blinded by what your body did for me," he said his final words and opened up the door.*

*A few of her male family members stood around and began to push Bentley to the church exit.*

*"Get ya hands off of me!" he yelled and stood his ground. Then, he turned to the woman who he never really loved. "Jazlyn, I'm sorry things didn't work out, but you've proven to me time and time again that it wasn't meant to be. I'll pack up all your stuff and have it shipped to you."*

"Bentley?"

Bentley's head snapped up from his daydream, and he turned back to where Nylah looked at him like he was crazy.

"You're good?"

"I'm good. I just hate that I hurt her, but I would've hated it more to spend my life with her. I also would've hated myself because I KNOW some lucky man would've came along and taken you from me forever."

"And that would upset you?" Nylah teased and leaned into him.

"Upset me? No. It would have *killed* me. I don't want to pressure you into anything that you aren't ready for, but I know that I love you and want this marriage to work out badly. I know God will continue to guide us."

"He will," Nylah reaffirmed. "I know He will."

# *Chapter Nineteen*

As promised, Bentley and Nylah took it one day at a time and decided to downsize from their two homes to a cozy two-level condo, complete with a nice-sized backyard for Brooklyn. Life was good, and God was even greater. At their church home, they rededicated their lives and family to the Lord, and Brooklyn was baptized. An intimate wedding ceremony was scheduled to take place next month, and things could not have gotten any better.

They headed now to a family trip to Myrtle Beach. They would be staying at the city's stunning premiere resort. It was everyone's first time in South Carolina, and they planned to enjoy their week's worth of relaxation on the beach.

"It's so nice!" Brooklyn exclaimed as she stepped from the rental car. Her round face was lit up with childlike anticipation and the sunlight touched her eyes in a way that made them sparkle. Draped over her petite shoulders were the straps of her *Princess and the Frog* backpack that she clutched in excitement. "We've arrived? We're staying *HERE*?"

"Yes, baby," Bentley chuckled and rubbed a hand over her hair that was neatly braided with heart-shaped beads on the ends. "We've arrived, and we're staying here for the next seven days."

She looked from Nylah to Bentley, and then back again. "I'm so glad you're back together! Family trips are the best!" she shrieked and then ran up to the resort's revolving doors.

Nylah could not have agreed more.

After checking in, they unpacked and then headed down to the pool that stretched long and wide and was crystal clear. Nylah chose to stick her legs in, while Bentley and Brooklyn swam around in front of her.

"Mommy? Daddy?"

"Yes, baby?" Nylah splashed a handful of water on her body so that she could cool off in the beaming sunshine.

"Can I get a little brother or sister?" Brooklyn thought about it. "I would prefer a baby brother though."

Nylah began to choke on nothing while Bentley suppressed his laughter. "Um, maybe one day."

"Soon?" she asked and continued to swim around with her chunky legs kicking behind her.

"We'll ask God and see what He says," Nylah said. Her eyes widened as Bentley continued to laugh. "Would you stop?"

"Hey, that was my next question for you, too."

"So, you want another child too?"

"Of course. I mean, I know it's soon, especially since we just got back together but it's been on my mind. You remember our college days and premarital days? I would always talk about having four or five children with you. We can't have baby girl out here opening up gifts alone on Christmas." He motioned towards their daughter.

"Come back this way," Nylah called out to Brooklyn, who was nearing the deep end. Then, she turned back to Bentley's hopeful eyes. "Let's just focus on the *now*. Let's not look at our lives in five years. I just want to enjoy this vacation, enjoy my man again, and work on my tan."

"That melanin is already poppin', girl," he pointed out flirtatiously. "Do you need me to rub some sunscreen on you?"

"No, because I'm not sure if your hands can handle all of these curves. It's been a while since they've touched *gold*," Nylah teased him.

Bentley pulled himself up on the edge of the pool. His biceps looked particularly muscular as he propped himself between her legs. Water fell from his chest almost rhythmically, and then dripped onto her thighs. He leaned in slowly to kiss her lips and she could literally feel her insides melt.

"Just wait until I get my hands on you," he promised, speaking lowly, for only her ears to capture. His breath tickled the tiny hairs on the back of her neck as he kissed along her collarbone a few times. Then all at once he lowered himself back into the lukewarm pool and swam away.

"Next month," he said and winked.

"Next month," she repeated and could not wait for the day that they would consummate their wedding vows for the *second* time.

\*\*\*

Like all good things, the vacation came to an end, and it was time to go back to work and resume all everyday activities. Nylah, feeling refreshed and beautiful after a night of pillow talk with Bentley, saw him off to the office with breakfast and a long, sensual kiss.

"You comin' home right away?"

"Yeah, I'm not trying to workout tonight. We can watch a movie and chill. Need me to pick up any food on my way home?"

"Up to you," Nylah said and followed him down the driveway. "I had loaded nachos in mind."

"Loaded nachos it is," he said and leaned to pick up his briefcase. "See you soon, Love. Brooklyn, have a good day, baby, you hear?"

"See you later, handsome," Nylah called out with a wave.

"Bye, Daddy!" Brooklyn screamed with a mouth full of cereal. Tomorrow, she would be starting a new school in their new neighborhood. "Love you!"

"Love you more, Munchkin!" Bentley's words could be heard throughout the quiet morning. Soon, he settled in his car, started the quiet engine, and then zoomed off down the road.

Nylah smiled at the idea of how things used to be. She recalled how, before Brooklyn was born, she would see her husband off and then plan the evening right down to the candlelight dinner and full body massage. She catered to her man then and planned to cater to him now. All of her previous efforts were not in vain, and she was blessed to have their union back together.

She would continue to take things one day at a time but could not deny how excited she became whenever she envisioned the holidays, movie nights, and spontaneous date nights again like old times. It was almost too good to be true and she feared that she would wake up from this dream, although she did not want to.

Nylah spent the day cooking and cleaning and preparing the living room for their movie night. Brooklyn picked out a movie, took her bath early, and changed into her favorite blue pajamas without Nylah's help. Clearly, her big girl was growing up.

"Let's make some homemade popcorn," Nylah suggested and moved towards the kitchen.

"Mommy, why is Daddy taking so long to come home?"

Nylah's eyes scanned the room until they landed on the clock mounted on the wall. He had text her over two hours ago saying he was on his way home, and she swallowed hard at the thought that things may not have gone as planned. She hated to get Brooklyn's hopes up.

"Um, one of his clients may have made him late. Who knows? He's coming, so we have to make this bacon, caramel and cheddar cheese popcorn before he arrives, right?"

"Right!" Brooklyn said and seemed to forget all her concerns at the mention of her favorite snack.

Still, it did not stop Nylah's eyes from looking down at her phone, back up to the clock, and then over to the empty driveway where Bentley's car should have been. Then suddenly, like a movie scene, she got a phone call from an unknown number.

A scream tore from her unexpected lips and she jumped. In the process, her hands dropped her glass container of popcorn seeds. It shattered at the corner, and seeds spilled everywhere. Brooklyn continued to stand on the stepstool and put her hands up to her mouth in shock.

"Stay right there, baby." Nylah grabbed the vibrating phone, and decided to answer, "Ahem. Hello?"

"Hi, may I speak to Nylah Christiansen, please?"

Nylah frowned. It was a woman on the other end and there was silence in the background. It did not sound like the office, but she could not be too sure. "Speaking. How can I help you?"

"Hi. Yes, this is Cherry from Vincent Memorial Hospital downtown. We have your fiancé here. We found your contact information in his wallet. Are you able to get down…?"

Nylah did not need to hear anything else. She dropped the phone, sidestepped the mess that she had made, and then grabbed Brooklyn along the way.

"Baby, put your coat on while Mommy gets dressed."

"Where are we going? I have on my jammies! Why do I need to get my coat?"

"Don't backtalk me," Nylah scolded. "Do as I say!"

Her daughter never moved so quietly or swiftly. In record time, Nylah was on the road and racing down the highways of the still active city.

When she arrived to the hospital, she ran up to the receptionist desk and gave Bentley's information.

"Room 29, ma'am. *That* way," the young woman said, motioning with her finger. "He may still be in surgery."

"Surgery? For what?" Nylah began to panic and reached for Brooklyn's hand. "I know you don't know all the details. Thank you. C'mon, baby."

The two raced down the hallway until they got to the designated room. Only a curtain separated Nylah from seeing Bentley, and she was unsure of what to expect. She was unsure if he was down for surgery or if he was lying, unresponsive, with tubes everywhere. More than anything, she did not want Brooklyn to see him if things were very bad. She picked up her daughter, knocked twice on the doorframe, and then entered the room.

Bentley was not in the room, so the receptionist's assumptions were proven correct. He must have still been in surgery. A woman with a bandage around her head sat in the corner of the room, rocking back and forth. She was wearing professional attire and looked to be an employee from one of Bentley's offices.

His clothes and a few of his belongings were on the end of the bed.

"Hello," Nylah said lowly. She placed Brooklyn in the other chair that was positioned directly by the bed. "Stay there," she instructed.

The woman looked up, touched the bandage around her head, and then nodded to Nylah. "Hi."

"Um, I'm trying to see if I have the right room. I didn't see a name outside. Is this Bentley's room?"

"Yes. May I ask who you are? The doctors said he can't have any visitors right now."

Nylah exhaled to calm down. She did not care that the woman looked to be in pain or that the woman wore a bandage. Nylah was confused as to why she was being questioned like she was some woman off the street. "May I ask who *you* are? We're his family."

"Oh, I'm sorry," the woman chuckled and extended her hand. "I'm his coworker, La'Chelle. Sorry, I'm still a little loopy from the medications they gave me."

Nylah gnawed on her lip, debating if she even wanted to know what was going on and the woman's involvement with Bentley. "Do you remember what happened?"

"There was a car accident. He said something about his vision blurring, and before we knew it, the car had run into a tree. I think his collarbone and right knee was shattered. At least, that's what was explained to me."

"Before 'we' knew it?" Nylah repeated. "So, you were in the car as well? Where were you two coming from?"

The woman fidgeted. "We were coming from Happy Hour at…" she trailed off and then pretended to forget what she was saying. "Um, what was your name again?"

"Never mind what my name is—I didn't give it to you. Why weren't you two at *work*?" Nylah questioned loudly. Brooklyn's head looked up from the cartoon playing on the iPad in her small hands. Nylah forced herself to calm down and then spoke quieter, "Please tell me what's going on. Bentley said he was on his way home over two hours ago, and then we got the call to come down."

"Look, ma'am, I'm just his assistant. I'm engaged and I don't want your man. All I know is that we all stopped off for non-alcoholic drinks and appetizers and were heading back home. Mr. Rose volunteered to take me home and that's when everything spiraled out of control. I didn't mean to disrespect you in any way."

"No, you're fine," Nylah said with a sigh. "I'm just…on edge right now. I'm sorry for overreacting. I'm also sorry you were injured. Are you okay?"

"Just a little bump and bruise. God protected us from the worst and that's all that matters."

She had a point and Nylah could only nod and continue to calm down. Bentley's health was more important than anything right now, and she would get to the bottom of everything later. For now, she needed to find where the operating room was and find a doctor to give her updates. On cue, she turned and almost ran into the lanky, white man that entered the room with a stethoscope thrown around his neck.

"Good evening, ladies," the physician spoke solemnly as he removed the surgical mask from his face. "Are you all kin of Bentley Rose?"

"No," Nylah said and pointed to herself and then Brooklyn. "We are."

The handsome, aging doctor turned to La'Chelle and motioned towards the curtain that was half-open. "May I speak privately with the family? One of our nurses can assist you in the waiting room."

The woman reluctantly stood up, and Nylah took in her curves, tight clothing, and half-broken high heel. She was attractive, toned in all the right places, and she instantly disgusted Nylah. There was more to this story. There was no reason for Bentley to have had this woman in his car if he was truly on the way home like he had promised.

"Ma'am, would you like to sit down before I update you?"

Nylah broke free from her racing thoughts and focused on the man's chapped lips. "Sure." She sat down and then looked over to where her daughter had fallen asleep upright. *Perfect*, she thought. *Brooklyn doesn't need to hear this.*

"First and foremost, I'm Dr. Joel Weaver."

Nylah extended her hand. "Nylah Christiansen."

"Your fiancé's vehicle was discovered off the side of the road. It wrapped around a tree and all of the windows were smashed in. I have to tell you, Ms. Christiansen. I have *never* seen a victim so well put together after such an accident. He only came away with a shattered collarbone, shattered kneecap, and a few scrapes."

A heavy weight escaped Nylah's shoulders and she buried her face in her hands. Tears sprang to her eyes, but she tried her best not to let them escape. All she could do was shake her head in gratitude and relief. "Thank You, Jesus. That's amazing."

"A miracle is what we're all calling it," the physician said with a smile. "Now, of course, he'll require a lot of physical therapy and time off of work to rest, but I can assure you, your fiancé will be back and better than ever in no time at all."

"Thank you so much," Nylah exclaimed and stood up. Instead of shaking his outstretched hand, she gave him a hug. "Thank you for taking care of him."

"It's my job, and it was my pleasure." The man winked and then patted her shoulder gently. "The nurse will be wheeling him down any moment. You take care, Ms. Christiansen."

The moment the curtain closed behind the physician, Nylah fell to her knees and began to thank God for protecting and covering Bentley. There were so many things that could have gone wrong, and many people had died in more minor accidents. She was thankful and the tears could not stop flowing.

Brooklyn, hearing her cries, stirred awake and looked alarmed.

"Mommy, what's wrong?" she spoke half-asleep, half in concern.

"Nothing's wrong, baby," Nylah sniffed and wiped the corners of her eyes. "Mommy is just praising God."

"So those are happy tears?"

"Yes," Nylah said and laughed lightly. "These are *happy* tears."

# Chapter Twenty

Just as the doctor assured her, the nurse wheeled Bentley's bed into the clammy room. He was still heavily sedated, but Nylah could swear that he had a slight smile on his face. On his forehead was a deep gash that had been cleaned and stapled. A thin trail of blood seeped from under the gauze on his forearm, and a purple-blue bruise had formed on his chin and nose.

Although banged up, he still was handsome. She could not wait until he came to because she planned to tell him how much she loved him. She planned to give him kisses all over his muscular, mahogany-complected body, and against his lips. She was also excited that she could share this testimony with him. God had His hand over Bentley's life and there was not a thing that the devil could do about it.

For hours, Nylah stayed at his bedside with Brooklyn and the two kept him company. Nylah touched her hand to his chest and prayed for his speedy recovery. Almost instantly, his eyelashes fluttered open. A smile came to her lips as he finally awakened from his deep slumber.

"Hey, you."

His voice was hoarse when he spoke. "Hey, baby. What…what happened?"

"Don't try to move, just relax. You were in a car accident, but you only had a few injuries. It was nothing too serious, thank God."

"Am I…*paralyzed*?" he asked cautiously with tears in his eyes. "'Cause I can't feel my toes."

"No, you're just bandaged up pretty good, but you're okay otherwise. Give it some time, baby. You scared us," she added. "We were so worried."

"I'm sorry, Love. I can't even remember what happened but…I just remember reaching out and touching somebody before we crashed." His forehead wrinkled as he thought long and hard about what happened. He shook his head and seemed perplexed.

"Touching somebody?" she repeated. "That's all you remember?"

"It's like a blur. One minute we're talking and the next I'm being awakened from surgery."

Nylah decided not to address the whole La'Chelle situation. Some way or the other, the truth would be revealed. For now, she needed to get her man back in tiptop shape. There would be a long road ahead, but she was prepared for it. After all, so many moons ago, she had vowed before God and their family and friends to be with Bentley "in sickness and in health."

***

The road to recovery was a tumultuous one. It took patience, a lot of tumbles, and a *ton* of prayer. Bentley, unable to fully back away from his business, brought work into the hospital and physical therapy rooms. With Nylah's help, he conducted teleconferences, signed off on payroll checks, and headed major decisions. If not for his physical casts and restrictions, she would have thought that nothing changed about him. In addition to his drive, he was positive about everything.

"When will you be able to come out of your cast, Daddy?" Brooklyn asked one evening.

"Soon, baby," Bentley vowed with a smile. "We can go on our monthly father-daughter date when I'm better, you hear me?"

"You promise?" she asked. Looking just like her mother, she stuck out her lips and gave him the most pitiful, cutest, sweetest expression.

"I promise."

Brooklyn sat on the end of the bed as she drew a picture with a variety of colored pencils. Bentley dozed off here and there and Nylah watched the scene unfold with a soft smile on her face. Occasionally, she would walk off and run an errand or two, and then return to her spot to keep him company.

As he fell asleep from the effects of his medication, she scooted his laptop and phone away from him. She admired his relaxed face and then kissed along his cheek. He smelled good and that was one thing she admired about him. Even with being bed bound, he still took great care of himself; he'd trimmed his own facial hair and wore his favorite fragrance just for her. At that moment, his iPhone vibrated and lit up. Nylah was never one to be nosy, and Bentley had certainly never given her a reason to mistrust him, but she looked at who was texting him.

It was Jazlyn. *What does she want?* Nylah thought.

She was saying hello and asking Bentley how he was doing. Nylah rolled over onto her side and text her back.

*I'm good. Enjoying life. You?* Nylah text back.

A few, long moments passed before Jazlyn text back. *Glad to hear. Can we meet up and talk? It's really important.*

Nylah glanced over her shoulder when she heard Bentley move around. She hid the phone under her bosom and out of his view in case he opened his eyes. He continued to breathe deeply, so she went back to texting. *Important like what?*

Brooklyn began to talk in her loud, child-like volume and Nylah shook her head. "Be quiet, baby. Daddy's sleep."

"Sorry. I just was asking for that blue pencil by your hand."

"Oh, here," Nylah said distractedly and looked back down at the vibrating phone.

*I don't want to discuss it over the phone. Please don't tell your wife about this. Meet me at the restaurant where we had our engagement dinner. 6p tmrrw. That cool?*

Nylah's blood began to boil. She was sure that Jazlyn had lost her mind and she would be happy to help her find it. For a few more minutes, Nylah sent Jazlyn text messages, and then deleted the entire thread from Bentley's phone. She also blocked Jazlyn's number completely from the phone and was unsure why she still had Bentley's number in the first place.

In less than 24 hours, Nylah would be facing her fiancé's ex-fiancée. The entire situation was so ridiculous that it was comical, but Nylah was determined to get to the bottom of it. She vowed to keep her cool until then and prayed that God would hold her tongue for whatever was about to come.

The next day rolled around and with anxiousness, Nylah went to the restaurant early. She wanted to be ahead of the game and catch *everything*. She was seated at the bar, nursing a cranberry juice on the rocks, and trying to ward off happy hour patrons. A man sat beside her now, attempting to get her attention. She ignored him and kept her gaze outside of the building.

She was extra jazzy with a faux leather pleated skirt and the matching crop top. Gold accessories brought out the gold in her strappy, thigh-high stilettos. Her hair was slicked back, and the ends of her hair were curled in gentle spirals. She had no idea why she had gotten so dolled up. It could be her ego influencing her, and it could also be the bitter part of her. There were some areas of her life where she needed deliverance. This was one of them. To think that Bentley had been with them both irritated her, so she had to show up and show out for her fiancé's ex-woman. It was only right.

At that moment, she saw Jazlyn's Hyundai pull up outside. She stepped out in modest clothing—jeans and a grey T-shirt. There had to be at least ten to 15 more pounds on her than Nylah remembered. Jazlyn had never seen so much as a roll or jiggle, and yet, the woman before her seemed to have let herself go, even in the way that she dressed. There were large bags under Jazlyn's eyes, and her hair was not as full as it once was. Nylah felt that much more excited that she had come in such sexy attire. She would take pleasure in looking Bentley's ex in the eye while she told her to never text or contact her man again.

Nylah kept her head down until Jazlyn neared her. Only then did she glance up. Jazlyn spotted her immediately and stopped in her tracks. It was obvious that Jazlyn knew what was up by the way that she rolled her eyes and then pulled out the stool in anger. "What kind of game are you guys playing?"

"We're not playing any game. In fact, Bentley doesn't even know where I am right now."

"So what? He told you to come meet me? Figures. *Coward*."

"Excuse me? Don't call my man a coward. I could call you 'homewrecker,' if you want to start throwing out nicknames," Nylah challenged.

"What do you want? Why did Bentley tell me to meet him here and then send you?"

Nylah shook her head and then took a sip of her cold beverage. "You have to listen. Like I said, Bentley doesn't know where I am. He doesn't know that we're meeting. He doesn't even know that you text him. That was me all along yesterday."

Jazlyn huffed and finally took a seat. "You've got to be kidding me."

"Oh, no, I'm not kidding at all. Why did you want to meet with him? Whatever you have to tell him, you can tell me."

"I would rather he know first."

"Know *what?*" Nylah looked over at Jazlyn incredulously. "Get over it, Jaz. You were friends with him when he decided he wanted to divorce me originally. In the nicest way possible, hear my words. Respect out relationship and *stop* contacting him. You two are over and done with."

Jazlyn ordered water from the bartender before continuing to speak. She looked distraught, angry, and emotional. Her fingers shook and would occasionally sift through her mangled hair. It was so unlike her to go without her hair or makeup done, so Nylah was still in shock at her appearance. She looked almost…tacky.

Compassion fell from Nylah's lips as she examined the tears welling up in Jazlyn's eyes. "Are you…okay?"

As soon as the question touched the atmosphere, Jazlyn burst into tears and kept her head down for a while. Her shoulders and body shook as she cried hysterically, and her sobs grew louder and louder as time went on. Nylah was truly confused now as she watched Jazlyn weep. Finally, the nurturer in her came to the forefront. She looked around to see if anyone was looking at them, but only the bartender appeared concerned.

Nylah rubbed Jazlyn's back and whispered, "Whatever it is. I'm here for you. Get it all out."

Jazlyn continued to cry for a moment more. Then, with thickness in her throat, she spoke up, "I did everything to protect myself…to do things right…but…mistakes happen."

"They do, yes. But what are you saying?"

"I don't love him," Jazlyn confessed and sniffled. She raised her head and her face looked like she had been caught out in a rainstorm. There was moisture everywhere. Her breath was stale and warm as if she had not eaten in days, and she could not look Nylah in the eye if she tried. "I promise I don't. You can have him…I could never compete with what you two have and I won't try to," she continued.

Nylah kept quiet. She was still puzzled.

"I went to the doctor last week. I haven't been feeling like myself lately, and…" Jazlyn fumbled over her words nervously. "They ran tests, and…I, um…"

Nylah's heartbeat picked up speed and then broke in a million different pieces. She watched in horror as Jazlyn rubbed her slightly protruding stomach and then finally looked her in the eye. Before she could speak, Nylah dropped the glass of cranberry juice from her hands. It all made sense.

"No, no, no," she mumbled and backed away from the stool on shaky legs. She could feel her energy and mood hit a complete 180-degree turn. All she wanted to do was collapse in a heap of disappointment and tears, much like Jazlyn had done just a few minutes before. "Be quiet."

"I wanted to tell Bentley first. But since you're here, it's best you know, too. I'm pregnant, Nylah," Jazlyn said with a sigh of relief. It was like she had been holding it in for years.

Nylah's eyes involuntarily dropped back down to Jazlyn's growing belly. Indeed, there was a baby inside. She could tell because she, too, had been with child before. There was just a certain look and glow for a mother to be. The only exception was Jazlyn's current relationship status had gotten to her and she looked stressed out. Anger filled Nylah's heart.

"I said BE QUIET! Don't tell me that! You're—you're lying!" she screamed.

This time, several people's heads turned. Nylah could not care less about what type of scene that they created. In a matter of minutes, she now felt the slap of betrayal from so many years ago. It was like history was repeating itself and she had somehow become the other woman again.

"I figured you would say that." She shook her head and pulled out an envelope. Nylah knew what it was immediately and cringed as Jazlyn tugged on the ultrasound print off. Sure enough, a tiny baby was forming and had been captured for their eyes.

Nylah held her hand up to her mouth in shock. "I cannot believe this. I just...I don't get it."

"We always used protection, so imagine my surprise. I didn't mean for this to happen!" Jazlyn explained. "So please don't kill the messenger! I don't want to have this baby! My career is launching, and he or she's father doesn't want me. How do you think I feel?"

"You're right," Nylah said. She chuckled bitterly, shook her head, and then reached in her gold wristlet. She tossed a few dollar bills onto the counter for her drink, and then turned around. "You're not the one I'm pissed with or have a problem with! Thank you for being honest with me."

"Where are you going?"

Nylah never turned back around. "To congratulate our ex."

The second she got in her car, she pounded her fists against the dashboard and steering wheel. Her horn went off several times and surrounding cars jerked on brakes in surprise. Nylah could not believe that just as quickly as her world had turned around, it had now turned back upside down. Her heart ached and her mind raced a mile a minute. There was no way that she could face Bentley right now. She was much too irate and hurt. Instead, she took a deep breath, dialed his number, and allowed her car's Bluetooth feature to pick up his voice.

"Hello? Baby, where are you?"

He sounded like he had just awakened from a good nap. "I'm in my car. I need some space for a little bit, and by space, I mean, don't call or text me right now."

"Space? What are you talking about?" he sounded panicked as he asked.

"I'm going for a drive," she said simply, "Don't ask when I'll be back, or anything else. Don't worry or call the police. Just know that I'm okay."

"What's wrong, baby?"

"Didn't I say not to ask me anything? Oh, and one more thing."

"What's that?"

"*Congratulations.* I hope it looks just like you."

Click.

Nylah turned her smartphone off, and then tossed the device onto her passenger seat. She had no idea where she wanted to go, but she knew it would be a while before she returned to the house. Hopefully, Brooklyn was sound asleep and would not look for her. Lord knows, she hated to leave her daughter hanging like this. But she was not in a good headspace right now. She was liable to do anything.

She thought to call her mother but knew that the result would be even more angering. She thought to call Dr. Bloomberg, the therapist whom she had become good friends with, but was unsure if she still had the correct number. She even thought about going back to the bar and taking a sip of the variety of forbidden liquors. This would be her first drink in a while, since giving her life back to God, and she did not feel right. But even with her heartache, she did not do anything. All she could do was pray and cry. Life was so unfair sometimes, and this situation was no exception.

An entire hour passed before she stopped driving. She reached her destination and stayed outside in the car. She looked at the house with hatred and disgust, but she never went inside. She thought about all the times that she attempted to conceive with Bentley but to no avail. They had Brooklyn and prayed for another baby, but God always said otherwise when she was pregnant. Now, here she was, back with the love of her life, ready to rekindle the flame to their love, and another woman had given her fiancé a baby. None of it made sense.

Nylah monitored the lone light coming from their bedroom until it eventually turned off. Bentley was likely falling asleep and had given up the search for his woman. It was not like he could get up and do much of anything with his injuries. Nylah curled up in her car and fell asleep with tears staining her cheeks. She did not awaken until she heard the obnoxious birds on her block. It was just after five in the morning and the sky was still blanketed with darkness. The car was frosty from the chilly winds.

She decided to finally make her way inside. Brooklyn's bedroom was her first stop where she kissed her daughter and then tucked her in a little bit snugger.

"Love you, baby girl," she whispered.

Her throat was raspy and sore from spending the night in the midnight air. Her daughter's eyelashes fluttered as though she was watching a movie, and a soft smile tugged at her lips.

Then Nylah took off her clothes in the hallway and entered her bedroom. Bentley was pretty much still in the same spot that she had left him. He was sitting upright, and his head was lolled to the side uncomfortably. One of his pillows had fallen to the floor, and the remote had joined it. Completely naked, she mounted Bentley's legs and waited for him to stir awake.

"Baby? I was worried," he began to say. His hands moved to touch her waistline, but she knocked his hands out of the way. "What's the matter? What was all that about?"

With no hesitation, Nylah drew back her balled fists and began to hit him. She struck his face, chest, arms, and even down at his legs. Bentley, who was still in shock from being awakened, moaned in discomfort and confusion.

"Nylah! Stop it! What's going on?" he yelled and then grabbed her wrists. His strength was no match to hers even though he was still not fully himself.

"Are you happy now?" she asked and attempted to hit him one final time. Bentley held her body against his, and her voice was muffled when she asked again, "Are you? You ruined our family! It's all YOUR fault!"

Bentley was still baffled so he pulled back and wiped her tears. "Talk to me. Why are you crying? Did you have a nightmare? Where did you go last night? Is everything okay?"

There were so many questions and not enough answers. He looked so oblivious and innocent, and it made her sick to her stomach. He had no clue about her whereabouts the night before, and the fact that he was so clueless made her angrier. She expected him to be worried sick about her and yet he was relaxing in bed. She had no fight left in her. How could she compete with a baby?

Nylah sighed and looked him in the eye. "It's Jazlyn."

He looked surprised to hear that name. Still, he spoke calmly, "What about Jazlyn? Did you run into her, the reason you're so upset?"

"I ran into her all right, and she's with child."

He shook his head and did not make the connection right away. "She had a child with her? What are you saying?"

"Bentley...she's pregnant...with *your* child."

"What? We always used protection! That can't be right. Wait, she told you that?"

Nylah held up her hand in defeat. "Things happen, Bentley. You, of all people, know that."

"But…"

Nylah interrupted him again. "There's an ultrasound and a growing belly that says otherwise, so don't start denying it. Talk to her."

"I'm speechless."

"You and me both."

# Chapter Twenty-One

Bentley had pretty much gone into a shock following the news of Jazlyn's pregnancy. To make matters worse, his recovery seemed to slow down. The more stressed he became, the sicker he got. His lupus seemed to flare up and he was put back on an array of medications. Nylah, like the faithful woman she was, tended to his every need and was there for him emotionally and physically. Every night she prayed that he would find the strength to face the mess he had created.

It was not that he did not want his child, but it was the circumstances that hurt him most. He hated that his children would now have to grow up in different households with different mothers, one of which he no longer loved. It was the consequence of his sins so he could only blame himself and try to move forward.

To everyone's amazement, Jazlyn was just shy of seven months pregnant, and looked good physically. She claimed that she was still working out, the reason that she did not have much of a baby bump. Although Nylah did not believe anyone would stoop that low to claim a pregnancy, she had her doubts. Jazlyn was pregnant all right, but she distrusted that it was Bentley's baby. She kept quiet and vowed to do her research. With time, the truth would be out.

The cast around his leg was finally removed and he was able to return to the office to supervise and get things back in order. He would be getting off in another hour or so, where they planned to all have dinner, including Jazlyn.

Nylah felt uneasy about it but agreed to come. As she leisurely put on her formal clothes and played in her freshly washed hair, her phone vibrated against the countertop. It was a number she never expected, especially at a time where she needed it most. The caller was her mother.

"Hello?" Nylah tapped the speaker function on the phone.

"Hey, baby girl," her mother's voice filled the master bathroom. She sounded surprisingly happy. "How are you? This is Mom."

"Yeah, I know." Nylah combed through her tresses that smelled of fruity shampoo. "I'm all right. Yourself?"

"I'm good. I just needed to hear your voice. Do you have a minute to talk? It's been a while."

Nylah chuckled, "Oh yeah. A *lot* has changed since we've last talked."

"A lot like what? How's my Brooklyn?"

There was no skirting around the issue. Nylah knew she had to tell her mother the truth. She would probably look like a fool by the end of their conversation, but she could not care less. Who was her mother to judge?

"Brooklyn's healthy and happy, and she's about to be a big sister…I think."

"You think? Well, who's the father? Bentley?" her mother questioned. "How is that going to work with him getting married to the other woman?"

"He called off the wedding, Mom. He made things right, proposed to me again, and now, we just found out she's seven months pregnant."

Her mother was silent on the other end.

"So, yeah," Nylah continued. She already knew what the silence meant. Her mother was likely shaking her head. "Before you start judging and calling me every name in the book, know that I've turned my life around. I'm not the same person I used to be. I made bad decisions and I've moved on from them. I have God's approval, so I don't need yours or anyone else's. I don't need to hear your perfect stories on how you never made any mistakes, and I certainly don't need your opinions about what goes on in my life."

Her mother's voice cracked when she began to speak. "Baby, I didn't call to do any of that. I called to say I love you and I'm sorry."

Nylah froze in place. "Sorry for what?"

"I'm sorry for not being there for you!" she exclaimed through her tears. There was much remorse in her voice. "I'm sorry for always leaving and travelling when you were a child, and even now. The times that you needed me most, I've counted you out."

Nylah was shocked to hear the words, but her heart seemed to soar with every apology and confession. It felt good to hear her mother profess her love.

"I'm a horrible example of a mother, so despite anything I've ever told you, I would never criticize how you raise Brooklyn. You've always been a great mother to her, and a great wife to Bentley! I'm sorry that things aren't going as you hoped, but baby, nobody's relationship or life is perfect."

A single tear ran down each of Nylah's cheeks as she looked at herself in the mirror. While she hated that her makeup was now flawed, she needed to hear these words. If her mother could have held her, it would have been an answered prayer. "Thank you, Mom."

"Believe it or not, at 58, I'm still learning how to become a better person and your humility through all of the storms you've endured has inspired me. God has truly been working with me and showing me myself. I could do nothing but repent and call you. I really am sorry for all the times I've judged you or made you feel less than a woman. It's how my mother talked to me, and I should've broken the cycle."

"But you did, Mom. Don't you see? This is a step in the right direction. It all takes time. As you said, nobody's perfect."

"Thank you, baby girl. I promise, things will begin to look up for you. There is no denying Bentley's love for you, just like there's no doubt about your strength. As the saying goes, it takes village to raise a child. Although it won't be yours, it's Bentley's child, so it's a part of *you*," her mother added. "Love that baby and love that woman with the love of God. There's no way of stopping a child from entering the world, so you must make the best of it and just pray through it all. You don't have to live in one household, but you have to be a *loving* family."

Nylah nodded. She dabbed under her eyes with a makeup sponge and then exhaled. A weight seemed to fall from her shoulders. She felt ten times better already.

"What are you doing this evening? I've finally figured out how to use that darn FaceTime app."

"We're having dinner tonight; me, Bentley, and his ex. We're going to talk about everything. But other than that, feel free to call or FaceTime me."

"Yeah, let's talk so I can see your face, baby. I also want to fly up there for Thanksgiving if that's okay with you?"

Nylah smiled and nodded again as though her mother could see her. "I would love that. Brooklyn's going to be so excited to see you!"

"All right, baby. Take care. Let me know how everything goes tonight."

"I will, Mom. I love you."

There was silence on the other end. Finally, with another bout of emotions altering her voice, her mother spoke, "You don't know how much that means for me to hear that. I love you too."

The call ended and Nylah continued to look at the phone as though her mother was still there. Although father-daughter relationships were important, a mother-daughter bond was just as essential. It had to be God that allowed her mother to "see the light," at a time where she needed her most.

Many nights, Nylah would cry and pray for change, and it seemed that God had forsaken her when it came to this issue. Today's phone call debunked all those negative thoughts. She was elated to have her mother back in her life and vowed never to allow their relationship to go sour again. Life was much too precious.

Their reservation time rolled around, and Nylah figured she was as ready as she would ever be. Her nerves were surprisingly a lot calmer now that she had talked to her mother, so she figured she would be on her best behavior. Bentley could do nothing but compliment her, and she knew why. He was trying to butter her up for whatever was about to take place.

But she also could not blame him. Her slim-fitting, curve-hugging attire and five-inch heels were enough to make every man in the room take notice. It was almost as if they were going on their first date…with a little extra cargo.

They were seated and waited another 20 minutes for Jazlyn to show up. She finally waltzed in looking homely again. The only difference was her hair was done this time. The maître d' looked her up and down, turned his pointed nose up in the air, and then led her to where they sat. Bentley did not look shocked.

"Must be missin' out on my checks. She has *never* dressed like this," he mumbled before standing.

His eyes fell to her swollen waistline and sparkled involuntarily. Bentley loved children, so Nylah knew that this was bittersweet for him. He wanted another son or daughter, but certainly not from a woman he was no longer with. Jazlyn leaned in for a brief hug, whispered her 'hello' to him, and then stiffly hugged Nylah.

"Were you guys waiting long for me?"

Nylah kept quiet because she didn't trust herself not to say something out of line.

"You were always late to events, so nobody's trippin'," Bentley half-joked.

"Yeah, it's just been so hard for me now. So much going on," she said and picked up the menu. "You know?"

"So much like what? I've been pregnant before. I know what it feels like. Bentley's been through way worse than you, and he's *still* recovering. Stop being dramatic," Nylah snapped and rolled her eyes.

Jazlyn glanced over the menu and cut her eyes at Nylah. "Every pregnancy is different. Please don't flatter yourself."

"*Ladies*," Bentley cut in before the knives were thrown. "We did not come here for this, remember? We came to discuss the changes that are about to take place in ALL of our lives."

"You mean, the changes that's already taken place?" Jazlyn motioned to her belly.

"No, he meant exactly what he said. We're not obligated to do anything for that baby until we know who's the *real* father."

"Nylah!" Bentley hissed.

"You think you know it all, huh? You think you're all that because my man chose to be with you?"

"Let's not forget who he was with first. It certainly wasn't you, *homewrecker*."

"Nylah, be quiet," Bentley demanded. He looked around at the stares that they were getting and looked embarrassed. "Y'all are getting loud."

"Tell Bonquisha over there. She came in here looking and acting a fool. She started first."

"You're just mad because I'm carrying his baby!" she yelled with tears in her eyes. "Stop thinking you're better than me."

"Those words never left my mouth. I'm just trying to figure out why you show up seven months into a pregnancy and claim it's Bentley's child? We all know how you got down. It could be anybody's baby."

"Bentley, get your woman."

"Or *what?*" Nylah asked. She looked amused and unaffected, and if it were not for their surroundings, she would have said more. "I'm here to eat. What are you here for? Hm? Financial support? Sympathy? Need a hug? How's that modeling career working out for you?"

"ENOUGH!" Bentley finally shouted. It was obvious how upset he was, by the way he shook his head in disgust. "It's like we're in high school again.

Nylah, you promised at home you would keep your mouth closed, and Jazlyn, you know better. Stop talking tough with nothing to back it up with."

The waiter came over at that moment and took their orders for drinks and appetizers. When he walked away, Bentley continued to speak.

"Now, we came here to make things right. Jazlyn, I'm just as shocked as you about this, but I'm not going to leave you hanging with any of it," he spoke hesitantly. "I must admit though, I have my doubts."

"Doubts about what?" Jazlyn slammed her hand down on the table and made the silverware rattle. "Don't believe anything this…this woman has told you! I'm pregnant, Bentley."

"Yeah, but with whose baby? Let's not be foolish here. You were cheating on me, and as Nylah said, it could be anybody's child. I'm not trying to hurt your feelings or get out of any responsibilities, but would you be open to a DNA test?"

"No, no, no!" she cried out. "Absolutely not! You are the father, Bentley! Why are you doing this to me?"

"Can you blame me? It just seems a little suspect to me."

"No, Bentley! You're a little suspect to me. Of all people, I expected that you would have more decency and understanding."

Jazlyn stood up and held her hand under her stomach. Tears were flowing down her face now. She looked hot, humiliated, and hungry, but her pride would not allow her to sit and take their verbal beating any longer. "Look, until you're ready to be an adult, don't call me or bring Nylah along. Right now, this has nothing to do with her."

"It has everything to do with me! Are you crazy?"

"Waiter? Can you call me a cab?"

"That's not necessary, Jaz. We'll drive you home," Bentley volunteered and then looked back at Nylah. "You coming?"

"With *her*? Of course not. She had a car the last time we met up. Where is it now?"

"I was dropped off," she began to explain. "I live right up the street."

"Nylah, let's go." Bentley stood up and walked behind Jazlyn. "At some point, we *do* have to talk this out."

"Yeah, and at some point you do have to stop runnin' back to the same woman who split us up."

His entire demeanor changed. Jazlyn threw her hands up in defeat and wobbled out of the restaurant, while Bentley stared her down with controlled anger. His fists balled at his sides and his nostrils flared slightly. "So how are you getting home?"

"I'll call somebody, anybody." Nylah waved her hand in dismissal. "Bye, Bentley. If you can walk off with her and leave me here, then maybe we should be discussing a *lot* more than this baby."

He exhaled loudly. "I'll be back to get you," Bentley mumbled and walked off.

She eventually flagged down the waiter to cancel some of their orders, and then kept her head low. Her blood was boiling. Bentley had a habit of not protecting her when she needed it most. He was so gullible at times and this situation was no exception. Nylah could see right through the game Jazlyn was playing. It was only a matter of time before the truth came out.

"Excuse me?"

Nylah blew out hot air and looked up. She hated to be bothered at a time like this. Before her stood a gentleman with a gorgeous milk chocolate complexion. He smelled amazing and looked even more amazing in his all-black attire and expensive jewelry. Nylah was never one to gawk at *any* man, but he was worth the stare. She returned his polite smile and noticed that he had some of the whitest, straightest teeth she had ever seen. He was also very familiar.

"May I borrow your ketchup? The waiter is taking forever to bring me a bottle."

"Oh, sure," she said and fumbled to hand him the half-full glass bottle. "Here you are."

"Thank you." He began to turn around and then stopped. "Are you…okay? I saw your guests get up and leave you sitting here."

"I'm fine," she said dismissively.

"Are you sure?"

As he spoke, she could not suppress the frown that took over her beautiful features. A single tear escaped her eyelid, and she caught it with her hand before he could see but it was too late. The handsome stranger's smile dropped, and he walked off.

Nylah assumed that she had freaked him out as she put her head down on her folded arms. She could have waited outside or even in the restroom, but something told her to stay. Then, without warning, she felt a pair of hands trying to pry her arms apart.

She looked up, assuming it was Bentley who had returned, but it was still the mysterious man. He pulled her body against his, and asked, "Do you mind if I…? You look like you could use a hug."

She nodded against his chest. Never mind that he was a stranger—she just needed comfort. It was obvious that he worked out by his build, but especially because she could feel the muscles beneath his shirt. It felt wonderful to just be held while she cried out her frustrations and heartache. After all her snot and tears had made it to his shirt, she finally raised her head and exhaled.

"I am *so* sorry."

"I can honestly say I've had a girl spit on me, but never snot on me. It's cool," he joked and then motioned to his lone table and the food that was cooling more and more. "Do you mind if I sit with you? I came to get some paperwork done over dinner. Were you staying?"

"Yeah, I guess I have to because my fiancé won't be back to pick me up for awhile."

"Then it's a date. My wife is out of town on business, and I'm sure she won't mind me keeping you company." Nylah's eyes dropped down to his occupied left ring finger. "After all, I can't leave someone so beautiful unattended."

"Thanks, but why is that?" Nylah questioned and dabbed the napkin to her face.

"Just think about it. Diamonds are always enclosed in protective glass. They're never just sitting out for anyone to grab."

Nylah's smile grew as they stared at one another. "Thank you. That's sweet of you."

"It's the truth," he said and shrugged while he cut into his steak.

There was just something about this man that had her intrigued. He did not seem like a creep, or someone who was up to no good. He genuinely looked like he took care of home. She looked up at that moment when the waiter returned with her plate of chicken and ricotta flatbread.

"Can I get you guys anything else?" he asked while he looked confused. He was probably wondering why Nylah was now dining with him.

"Uh, no, thank you. I would like to pay the bill for the lady and myself though. Please keep the change," the handsome gentleman said nonchalantly as he held up a hundred-dollar bill.

"My food was less than twelve dollars," Nylah pointed out.

He shrugged and then winked one of his brilliant brown eyes. "I love being generous and making someone's night. It's no big deal."

She took a bite of her flatbread. "Thank you so much. You really didn't have to do it."

"My pleasure, queen. So, tell me about yourself? I don't know why you look so familiar," he mused and fingered his wine glass. To be so youthful, he said and did mature things. She was curious to know his age.

"Your face looks familiar to me, too," she whispered thoughtfully. "Did you go to school here?"

"No, I'm actually from Memphis. The wife and I moved up here six months ago."

She thought of his wife and how lucky the woman must have been. Her mind drifted back to Bentley and his whereabouts. He was probably trying to justify her behavior to Jazlyn right now. The ache in her heart returned as she thought of what life would be like, helping to take care of someone else's baby on the weekends. This was not how she envisioned that her relationship would turn out.

"What's on your mind? I keep losing you," he chuckled. "You don't have to tell me specifics, but it's obvious there's *something* wrong."

Nylah shook her head and rested her chin in her palm. She was leaning on one arm while the other arm was nestled in her lap. The tears welled up again in her saddened eyes. "You promise not to judge me?"

"Why would I? I'm not God. I'm just a friend right now."

She took a deep breath and exhaled. More tears seeped past her curly eyelashes. As she blinked, the moisture touched the tops of her cheeks.

"I married my best friend. We've known each other our entire lives and had a daughter together. However, things happened, and we ended up divorcing. He became engaged to a young lady, was *literally* about to marry her, and I interrupted their wedding. He came to his senses, proposed to me again, and now, we've just found out that she's pregnant."

The stranger's eyebrows shot up. He nodded and genuinely looked interested in what she was saying. "That was the woman here earlier?"

"Yes, and…I'm not saying this just because, but I truly believe she's lying about him being the father. So, you can imagine my frustrations. Not only that, but my fiancé seems to never protect me when I need it most. He left me while he took her home. What kind of mess is that?"

"Wow."

"*Exactly*. I can't win at this thing. It's like once I have one situation under control, then something else disrupts our relationship. I'm tired of it. I don't deserve any of it," she sighed. "I've been nothing but good to that man, and if he had appreciated me from the start, we would not be in this mess."

"That's tough for anyone to deal with; I'm not going to lie." He pushed his half-eaten plate of food away. "But it's life. We don't expect these things to happen. We have an expectation of perfection, and the truth is, life is far from perfect. It's just disappointing when we find that out firsthand. I also find it funny."

Nylah sipped her water. His baritone was soothing to her ears. "Why is this funny to you?"

"Believe it or not, I found myself in that *same* situation a few years back. Don't look so shocked. I wasn't always an angel," he explained with a hint of sarcasm. "I was unfaithful to my wife a few months into our marriage. One of my exes showed up at our door with a baby and told me I was the father. I, of course, reacted just like your fiancé. I believed her and fell in love with that baby. He even looked like me! But we did what any sane adults would do. We got tested and found out it was all a lie. She only wanted me to be the father because she knew I would take care of her and the baby. It hurt my marriage, but my wife was willing to fight through it, whether I was the father or not. You must take that same approach. Is your fiancé worth fighting for?"

Nylah thought about it. She was never surer about anything in her life. Still, it was difficult to comprehend that someone had potentially given him another child. "Yes. Bentley's worth it." A grin tugged at her lips. "I love him so much."

"I can tell you do—that's beautiful. Just take it one day at a time. Continue to pray for him and support him and allow the truth to sort of unfold on its own. Trust me, numbers don't lie."

"What do you mean? What numbers?"

"Any numbers. Birth dates, conception dates, DNA percentages…you know." He winked. "Do what's best for you. But don't let it take away your

283

spirit. You seem to have a good heart and that should never be tampered with."

"Just how old are you?" Nylah asked. His words had resonated in her spirit, so she just had to put an age with his baby face.

"I'll be 31 next week."

"Are you serious? Nah, I'm not believing that."

He nodded and laughed. Then he leaned to one side to pull out his wallet. It was real leather and was brimming with currency and what she assumed was a black card. He tugged at his ID. "You see my birthdate? I told you. Numbers don't lie," he repeated jokingly.

Nylah nearly spit out her water as she laughed. While she dabbed the corner of her mouth with the red linen napkin, she noticed how the stranger's face changed. He was looking over her shoulder while his smile faded.

She saw a shadow to the right of her. Her head turned to catch a better angle and was shocked to find Bentley standing and staring at her.

# Chapter Twenty-Two

Bentley's forehead was tight, and his gaze was unmoving. She knew things may have looked bad, but with a little explanation, she was sure she could smooth things over. One of his fists was balled at his side, and the other held a single rose that he had likely bought at the gift shop down the road.

"Nylah? I see you're making friends out here."

Nylah's heart thumped in her chest rapidly. "Huh? Oh, yes, this is…" she extended her hand towards the stranger and swallowed hard. "I don't even know your name, I'm sorry."

"No need to be sorry." He stood to his full height and reached out to shake Bentley's limp hand. "I'm Qwanell."

"I've never heard her mention your name before. Who exactly *are* you?"

"A married man who saw a woman in distress and decided to be a friend by eating with her. And you? Oh wait. You're the man who left her to tend to some other business. Ahhh. Got ya," Qwanell said smoothly and dropped his napkin in the plate.

"You have a problem with me, guy?" Bentley asked. "If you don't know the situation, it's best to be quiet."

Qwanell pretended to zip his lips sarcastically.

"I thought so. Qwanell, with all due respect, my fiancée and I have to leave. How much was your bill, Nylah?"

Bentley began to reach in his pocket, but Nylah stopped him. "It was…um, I paid for it already," she lied.

"Alright, then, let's go," Bentley commanded and turned to walk away.

Nylah turned back to where Qwanell was coolly shrugging on his suit jacket. "Thank you," she whispered.

"Take care, queen."

The car ride home was quiet and tense. Nylah wanted to ask him how everything went with Jazlyn, but she knew that he was upset with her. She did not want to tick him off more, and she certainly did not care to start an argument. No matter how friendly and innocent her conversation with Qwanell was, she knew that it looked bad from Bentley's eyes. He was already not in a good headspace from her spazzing out on Jazlyn, so she could only imagine how disappointed he was to find her sitting and laughing with another man. She would have probably reacted just as coldly if the shoe were on the other foot.

When they arrived home, Bentley quietly retreated to the den and slammed the door. She changed into comfortable clothing. As she washed her face free of the evening's makeup, Qwanell's words stuck with her. She was willing to fight for Bentley, just as long as he was willing to continue to fight for her. They were in this together. No matter the outcome, she decided that she would be there to support him through it all.

Bentley went to bed without so much as a goodnight or without their usual kiss and pillow talk. Nylah watched him lie down and turn his back on her. She would give him space and time to process everything. She planned to explain what had taken place at the restaurant another day and nestled her head in the pillow closest to his.

Sleep never claimed her, so she decided to try to talk things out.

"Baby?" she whispered into the dark atmosphere. The only light that touched the ceiling, in slivers, was the glow of the moon. "You sleep?"

"Nylah, go to bed."

"So, you're not asleep. Talk to me."

"Why do I need to talk to you? It seems like Quenell, Quintell, or whatever his name is, talked to you enough."

"It wasn't even like that, Bentley," Nylah said and turned her head towards the back of his. "He's happily married."

"Okay, *and?* When it comes to an attractive woman, a ring and a title stops *no* man. You're beautiful, I get that. But you could've easily gotten up and removed yourself from whatever game he was playing."

"There was no game, Bentley. The entire conversation was innocent. Heck, we talked about YOU!" she exclaimed. "It could've all been prevented if you had stayed in the first place. So, let's not play the blame game, because you're guilty too."

He whipped around and the sounds of the blankets rustling were startling. Through the dimness of the room, his cold eyes stared at her. "You realize I watched you two for a long time before walking up, right? I didn't take Jazlyn home either. After I followed her outside, I thought about it, and called her an Uber. I waited with her until the person came, and then I stopped by the floral shop to pick you up a rose."

"What are you implying, Bentley? You think I was cheating on you? That quickly, huh? So, you really believe I called someone to meet me in that short time to *cheat*? That's the dumbest thing you've ever said, Bentley. And if that's not the pot calling the kettle black, I don't know what is."

"I never cheated on you, Nylah, and you know that. Jaz and I were together when she conceived."

"Yeah, but you met her while we were still married, and if you had never stepped out on our marriage, none of this would have happened. The baby, the back and forth, the confusion—none of it!" she yelled. "Once again, this all stems back to you and *your* mistakes."

"Shut up, Nylah!"

"Don't tell me to shut up! I should be telling you that. After all you put me through and continue to put me through, you should be on your knees everyday thanking God for another chance with me."

"Like I said, shut up. I'm tired and this conversation is over," he mumbled groggily. "Your voice is beginning to really annoy me."

"Forget you!" Nylah reached around and smacked him as hard as she could with her open hand. It connected with his face and echoed off the room. She hit him a second time and then a third.

"Are you crazy?" he yelled and sat up. He leaned over to turn on the lamp while she continued to hit him. She balled her fist to get a final hit in, and it landed in his groin.

Bentley yelled out, smacked his head back against the headboard, and could not seem to control his reflexes as his elbow connected with her cheek. Nylah's head rocked to the side, and she was out for a few seconds.

"Baby!" Bentley looked over in panic. "Oh, my God! I'm so sorry, baby. That was an accident!"

Nylah blinked in shock and held her hand to her face. Her jaw felt as if it were yeast and was swelling by the second. She felt the sting of where her teeth had accidently bit down on the inside of her cheek. She also felt the twinge in her heart at the realization that for the first time ever, Bentley had hit her. Whether it was an accident or not, her mind could not wrap around that fact.

"Baby, are you…?"

"*Don't* touch me!" she commanded and dodged his hands. She kept her hand pressed to her jaw while her legs wrestled out of the covers. The moment her feet touched the ground, she raced to the bathroom and successfully closed and locked the door before he could get to her.

"Let me see, Nylah! It was a mistake. I didn't mean to!"

"You HIT me!"

"You hit me too! That doesn't justify what I did, but I'm just saying, why did you hit me? We've never been physical towards each other, and we aren't going to start now. Come out so I can see your face, Nylah. I'm sorry."

She could sense that he was leaned into the door, and all she could do was stare at the forming bruise along her face. Her skin felt thick and sore as her tongue slid across the inside of her cheek. The swelling was already visible, and no amount of makeup would be able to cover it up.

"Bentley, please go away right now. Remember you said I annoy you?"

"That was just me speaking out of frustration. You know I love you and can't get enough of you. Stop acting like this. Open this door, Nylah!" He kicked the bottom of the door, which made her scream out. "You know I would never hurt you intentionally. Please, let me see your face."

Nylah continued to stare at herself. The tips of her fingers gently skimmed over her skin, and then traced the mark his elbow had made. It looked like she had been hit with a baseball bat. What was this relationship becoming? They were fussing and fighting and arguing more than ever lately. She was about to become a possible stepmother, and now, Bentley had mistakenly slammed his elbow into her face. She was sick of crying and sick of trying to move forward only to go back several steps. God needed to step in soon, because she was not sure how much more she could endure.

Amid her tending to her face, she forgot that her mother was expecting a FaceTime call. It was probably a good thing that they had not talked, otherwise her mother would be furious at what she saw. Reluctantly, she turned the doorknob and peeked out into the room. She did not see Bentley anywhere, so she figured he had gone back to the den or had tucked himself away in some corner and thought about his actions.

She migrated to the kitchen and made an ice pack with a sandwich bag and six ice cubes. Her face stung as she pressed the coolness to it. When she turned to head back up, she could hear Bentley crying faintly from the den. As she tiptoed closer, she could hear him well. He was praying while crying and asking God to help him become a better man.

"I just keep messin' up, God! You know that I would never kill a fly, much less put my hands on my baby. Please forgive me. Fix this relationship, God, because I can't continue to hurt her and push her away. I don't want to lose her," he pleaded to the Heavens.

She thought about entering in and holding him, but she knew that this was his time with God. He had to figure out things for himself. As she wiped the tears that had puddled under her eye, she turned on her heels and went back up to the bedroom.

# Chapter Twenty-Three

It was exactly one week since Bentley struck Nylah on accident. While words had been exchanged and forgiveness had gone forth, her bruises remained and there was only so much makeup that could cover it up. Each time he looked at her, Bentley dealt with his own guilt. Still, she carried on her everyday life and avoided the questions from the people who knew her best.

Brooklyn was nibbling at the smoked turkey and cheese sandwich and chips that Nylah prepared for her. "Mommy?"

"Yes, baby." Nylah glanced over from washing a pot. She was tidying up the house before taking Brooklyn to her dance recital.

"I've been meaning to ask. What happened to your face?"

Nylah dropped the dishcloth that she was holding. Soapsuds plopped up and hit her chin. She was sure that she could get away with masking her scars from her baby, but Brooklyn was much too inquisitive.

Nylah attempted to play it off and chuckled, "You've been 'meaning to ask?' Girl, you are just too grown for your own good. Are you just about finished up with your lunch, baby?"

"Yep! All done." She hopped down from the wooden stool at the breakfast bar, and then handed her plate to Nylah. "It was really good."

"I'm glad you liked it. I added mustard, pickles, and a *whole* lot of kisses."

Brooklyn giggled as Nylah took her in her arms and then tossed her into the air. When she came back down, her giggles stopped and then she focused on Nylah's face again. Her small hand cupped her mother's cheek, and her big brown eyes took in the darkened skin. "You still never answered my question, Mommy."

Nylah sighed and knew she had to think of something quickly. She placed Brooklyn back on her feet and rinsed off the pot she had just washed. "I had an allergic reaction. No need to worry though. I'm not in any pain or anything."

"Oh…okay," Brooklyn said and continued to stare at the side of Nylah's face.

"Come on. Let's go get your dance bag."

Brooklyn ran off and Nylah sighed in relief. She hoped that it would be the end of her daughter's 21 questions. Bentley was with Jazlyn at a doctor's appointment. He would be joining them later at Brooklyn's dance studio so that they could witness their baby doing what she loved most.

Nylah had since apologized to Jazlyn about the night that she blew up and they were attempting to build a relationship…*kind of.* Nylah still wanted to keep her distance until the truth came out about Bentley not being the father. Because of the risks of prenatal DNA testing, they planned to wait until the baby was born. Until then, Bentley vowed to be there for Jazlyn through it all and he was already in love with the growing boy or girl.

"Are you ready, little lady?"

"Here I come!"

Nylah looked up as her daughter bounced through the hallway. She was one of the dancing bumblebees in her class and wore a costume with antennas and a Velcro stinger. She looked adorable with her long ponytails swinging, and her matching yellow and black barrettes.

"Can you take lots and lots and lots of pictures? Oh, and some video too?" Brooklyn asked as she scrambled into her car seat and buckled herself.

"Of course, I will. That's why I've been charging my phone," Nylah said and settled into the car.

"I'm so scaaaared!"

Nylah watched her daughter through the rearview mirror. "No reason to be scared. God doesn't give us the spirit of fear, but of power, love, and a sound mind. Do your best, baby, and don't think about the audience watching you. Just dance and sing your heart out, okay? Pretend it's just me and you."

Brooklyn nodded with a grin on her face. They made it to the Gregory Hines Dance School with less than 15 minutes to spare. Nylah sent Bentley a text on where she was sitting, and then sent Brooklyn off with a kiss. The auditorium was packed with other children and parents, and Nylah could not help but to chuckle at the different costumes running around her. Ladybugs, foxes, dogs, and even a porcupine.

The show's emcee took over the microphone and announced that the show would be starting in another five minutes, and that everyone should get to his or her seats. Nylah looked around but there was no Bentley in sight. She shook her head. "Please don't miss your daughter's show," she muttered to no one.

She felt the wooden seat beside her move, and then she soon felt something brush against her bare arms. It was a man settling in the seat that should have been Bentley's. Although he was on the phone, she tapped his shoulder and spoke up. "Oh, I'm sorry, this is my...*Qwanell?*"

The man looked over and his eyes grew wide. A smile tugged at the corner of his mouth before he wrapped up his call. "Nylah. Wow. I never expected to run into you again."

"I could say the same thing. What are you doing here?"

"Supporting my daughter's recital debut. My wife had to work, so I'm holding it down for her. Yourself?"

"Oh, wow. Same here. My daughter's playing a bumblebee. This is her second year in the program."

"My daughter's one of the ladybugs," he laughed and motioned to the stage. "I guess we have a lot more in common than we thought. How old is your daughter?"

"Brooklyn's five, almost six." Nylah noticed that the auditorium had filled up. If Bentley did decide to show up, he was going to miss out now. There was no way that she was going to tell Qwanell to get up.

"Oh, okay, so she's in the same class with Nyomee then. Cool." Qwanell looked around for a moment, down at the folded white program, and then back up towards the stage. "Is Bradley here?"

"*Bentley*," she corrected with a chuckle. "No, he was supposed to come but once again, his other obligations got in the way."

"I, uh…I didn't get you in any trouble, did I?" Qwanell asked.

From what she could see, he was dressed nothing like when she initially met him. He was much more casual and fatherly looking in a tall T-shirt, cardigan, and slightly baggy jeans. On his feet was a brand-new pair of expensive tennis shoes that were named after some overly paid basketball player. Perched on his knee was the cap he had just pulled from his head of curly hair.

"Excuse my head. I need a good cut."

"Oh, no. You have a nice texture of hair," she pointed out and without thinking, ran her fingers

299

through his dark curls. She caught herself and yanked her hand back, "and no, you didn't cause me any trouble."

"You sure?" he asked with his eyes focused on the stage. "Because I really don't recall you have any blemishes the last time I saw you. What's up with that mark on the side of your face?"

Nylah froze in shock. Another woman sitting beside them seemed to hear his question and turned to look at her before facing forward again. Nylah's cheeks warmed in a blush as she put her hand over her face and leaned against it. "Must be the lighting," she whispered dismissively.

The show began at that moment and Nylah was relieved. Qwanell looked concerned for the longest time, but then his expression softened when a little girl dressed in red and black polka dots entered the stage. It had to be his daughter, Nyomee. She favored him in every way, and had the cutest singing voice—besides Brooklyn, of course.

The two girls held hands, danced, and even giggled together when it was not their time to talk. How ironic was it that she and Qwanell's daughters got along so well? Nylah took as many pictures and recorded as much video as she could before her phone's charge reached the lower twenties. She turned it off completely before it went dead and Qwanell agreed to send her more of the footage from his phone.

Another hour passed before the recital ended. Nylah still could not see Bentley amid the other parents and children in the audience. She found herself growing angrier at the thought. He should have been there. Nylah understood how sometimes work, duties, and other obligations came up unexpectedly, but their daughter came first with everything…period.

"Well, Ms. Nylah, it was good seeing you again."

Qwanell volunteered to walk her out to the car while the girls lagged behind and giggled about God only knows what.

"You too," she said sincerely. "I'm still confused as to where we know each other from. That's going to bug me until I figure it out."

"Maybe a parent meeting here?"

"I never attend them," she said with a laugh. "Facebook?"

"I hate social media," he added. "I don't know. It'll come to us one way or the other."

At that moment, a bus rode past them and on the side of the bus was the name of a local gym that Nylah frequented. Her eyes grew big as she turned to look at Qwanell, who was already nodding his head.

"All Day Fitness," they said in unison.

"Oh, wow. Yeah, you're the guy who was in my kickboxing class last year. Oh, my goodness! No wonder you look so familiar," Nylah recalled. She was all smiles as she thought back to the exercises that the trainers had them doing.

"I haven't been there in about a month," he mused and placed his cap over his head. "But I'm getting back to it. Been so busy lately with my business."

"What do you do?"

"You're going to laugh."

"I promise I won't."

Qwanell looked around to be sure nobody heard their conversation. He blushed a little bit and then said no louder than a whisper, "I own a boutique."

"Okay? Why is that embarrassing?"

He chuckled and shrugged. He gave her a boyish look. "You know, sometimes it can be a little emasculating. I sell women's clothing."

"I'm still waiting on the embarrassing part. That's awesome. You definitely have an eye for fashion, so it's not surprising," she motioned towards his clothing as she spoke. "Where's your boutique located?"

"Downtown. We sell all kinds of accessories and jewelry, and we're working on getting a few high heels in there."

"We?"

"My wife and I," he said.

The wind whipped around them, and Nylah shivered. He shrugged off his cardigan and wrapped her shoulders in it. She nodded, impressed. "Thank you. I'll have to check out your store the next time I'm in the area."

"Please do. You have a nice style already, but I'm sure I can help you find a few pieces that'll complement your…uh…frame." His eyes instinctively fell to her curves that were handcrafted by God Himself. Neither her ample breasts nor buttocks could be hidden in any outfit that she wore. He bit on his bottom lip for a second and shook his head. "I apologize. Let me get you out of this cool air."

Nylah looked halfway down the block thoughtfully. "The girls are having the time of their lives over there. I already know they're going to hate to separate."

"Maybe they don't have to."

"What do you mean?"

"Pizza on me? That is, of course, if it's okay with your man. I already know wifey won't mind."

"I'm beginning to think you don't have a wife. I think you just want me to tag along with you all the time," Nylah joked and handed him his cardigan as she backed away. She called for Brooklyn, who pouted for a few seconds, and then eventually grabbed her hand. "We'll pass. We have leftovers at home. Thanks, though. Next time, however, I won't say 'no'."

"I'll be looking forward to it. Goodnight, Miss Brooklyn," he said with a wave.

Brooklyn waved back sadly and then waved to her friend a final time. "G'night, Mister."

Later that night, in bed, Nylah knew she should have been angry with Bentley. She knew that she should have fussed at him for missing their baby's recital. She knew she should have been disgusted with the fact that he was beginning to spend most of his time at work and with Jazlyn at her random appointments and parent preparation classes, but all she could do was smile and think of Qwanell's charm, good looks, and easy conversation.

# Chapter Twenty-Four

"Aye, baby?"

Bentley scrubbed his skin with his fingertips roughly. The scent of body wash was fresh and clean, and permeated his nostrils. Any sleepiness that had plagued him soon disappeared as his skin grew redder and redder with every warm droplet that touched him. The bathroom was filled with steam from the hot water and had completely fogged up the mirrors. He called out to Nylah again but did not hear her.

He stepped out of the shower one foot at a time and tied a towel around his waist. Unable to see out of the foggy mirrors, he blindly brushed his teeth, brushed his hair, and then trimmed up his goatee.

Bentley looked towards the cracked door, and asked one more time, "Boo? You still in there?"

Still, no answer and no Nylah.

As he left the bathroom, a trail of steam followed him. He quickly dressed and then searched the house for his fiancée. She had been in the bedroom talking with him right before he showered so he was confused by her disappearing acts. Lately, she had been acting so strange with him and he could only blame it on the baby and Jazlyn situation.

He could not blame her for lashing out, but he prayed that something turned around. He could not and would not continue to live like this, especially if it was hurting her. He loved Nylah too much. In fact, he had gone out of his way to treat her to a romantic, candlelit dinner on the beach tonight. He planned to present her with an engagement ring and discuss their wedding that had been pushed back because of the baby.

"So much for taking her on a dinner date," he mumbled.

He decided to send a text to ask about her whereabouts. She returned his message not even a minute later stating that she was picking up the perfect outfit for their night out on the town. She promised to be home within the hour.

Bentley smiled in relief as he went to his walk-in closet and prepared for his lady.

*** 

Nylah turned off her phone as she entered the women's boutique and immediately spotted out what she wanted. It was not the chic clothing or the sparkling, high-end accessories. It was the towering gentleman who was coolly leaned over onto the counter as he spoke into a cordless, black phone. It was obviously a customer on the other end, the way he read off their business hours. She watched him from afar until he hung up the phone. Only then did his eyes take her in and brighten up.

"Oh, wow, I wasn't expecting you! How are you, gorgeous?"

"I'm good. I was in the area and decided to stop by," she lied. She had purposely driven over 20 minutes to be in his presence, if only for a few minutes. She just knew this was a recipe for disaster.

Qwanell grinned. "You must've known I was here alone."

"Not exactly. I wanted to pick up a dress— something sexy but tasteful. I have a little date with my fiancé and wanted to remind him of what he has, if you know what I mean."

"I know *exactly* what you mean." He came around the counter and extended his hand. She took it and felt a shiver run through her womanly parts. "Welcome to my boutique, by the way."

Nylah looked around in thought. "It's intimate and beautiful. I like it."

"I did the décor and everything," he added and led her to the back of the store where both formal and casual garments hung. "Let me guess. You're a…size ten?"

She was impressed. "Twelve but thank you." Her eyes caught a red jumpsuit that was sleeveless and had a dangerously low neckline. It was not a dress, but it certainly featured everything she wanted as far as style, class, and affordability. "What about something like this? Can you see me in it?"

Qwanell looked her up and down and then perused the article of clothing that she was referring to. He began to picture her in it, and then shook his head free of any crazy thoughts. "I think you'd look great in it. Would you like to try it on? It's on sale, too."

She agreed and disappeared in one of the fitting rooms. The entire time she tugged on the jumpsuit, she kept scolding her reflection in the mirror. Why was she playing with fire? Why was she entertaining Qwanell?

Soon, she emerged with bare feet and the jumpsuit on. It was still half-zipped and revealed the cream-colored bra that she wore. Her body looked appetizing in the stretchy material, and her hair was slightly tousled from the wind outside. He was quiet for a long time as he examined the skintight garment that was stretched over her endless curves.

"So that's a 'no' from you?" she asked. Her insecurities set in as she turned to the side and frowned. "I look fat, don't I? I wonder if my cellulite is peeking through?"

"No, no," Qwanell rushed to assure her. "I was speechless in a *good* way. He's going to love the way you look in this."

"You think so?"

"I promise you," he whispered and stood behind her in the mirror. He took her hand and twirled her around as he kept his eyes locked on hers. "I mean, the way it hugs your hips, and accentuates your backside is incredible. It was like it was made just for you. It even brings out that hazel color in your eyes that I never noticed until today," he added.

Nylah swallowed hard. If it were any other man, she probably would have felt uneasy by his words. Instead, she became hot and bothered and thought about Qwanell removing her jumpsuit right then and there. She thought about nasty things, inappropriate things. As much as she wanted to fight temptation, she could not deny the look in his eyes. It was like he was undressing her right then and there, and the thought drove her crazy.

"I just…feel so stuffed in this."

"Stuffed?" He turned her so that she was facing the mirror. His hands fell against the curve of her hips, and he pulled her back until she was pressed against him.

"Lately, I've been eating so much more, and I feel so huge." She looked down but he reached around and brought her head up.

"Hey, stop that. You're gorgeous, Nylah," he assured her with his lips close to her ear. He lightly brushed away her hair that had fallen against her neckline. "I wish you could see what I see."

She closed her eyes as his lips went from her ear to her collarbone. He kissed her skin softly, and then his mouth closed around her earlobe. Her breath caught in her throat, and she stepped forward to try to escape his addicting touch.

Qwanell wasn't having it. He yanked her back against his body with his large hands. This time, she slammed into the front of him. She gasped into the quiet atmosphere, and he moaned at the thought of having her to himself finally. Her backside was pressed directly against him now, and she could feel every inch of him.

Although it felt good, it was so wrong.

"Qwa—Qwanell, I can't do this," she said and snapped out of her trance. She stopped one of his hands as it eased up past her stomach and was ready to cup one of her breasts.

"Can't do what? Don't fight the feeling, Nylah," he commanded her and tugged at the material of the jumpsuit.

"I shouldn't have even come. I'm so sorry," she said with tears in her eyes. She had committed adultery. Nylah had cheated on Bentley and dipped into the pool of sin. She felt horrible and the guilt stayed with her as she scurried back into the fitting room and changed into her original clothes. She waved awkwardly to him and bade a final goodbye.

"Where are you going?" he called after her. "Let's talk about this!"

"I'm going back home to my family. I'm so sorry. You have a wife…I'm engaged. It just won't work."

Nylah never ran so fast in her life. Qwanell looked regretful as he watched her leave, and she could only ask God for forgiveness. This was not in the plan. He was so sweet and so nice, and yet, things had gone way too far, and she had allowed it. Nylah's guilt stayed with her as she sped home, parked in the driveway recklessly, and then ran inside to hug Bentley. She jumped in his arms and did not let go.

"Hey, baby. I missed you. What's wrong?"

"Nothing. I was just thinking about you and wanted to hug you," she mumbled in the crook of his neck. Her words were muffled but sincere. He held her waist and kissed against the side of her face until she pulled her head up. Then he kissed her lips softly.

"Mmm. You taste good." He seemed to look deeper into her eyes. "What's wrong? Where's your outfit? Did you find anything?"

"I missed you too much and had to get home to you. Let's just order something and chill for the night, okay?"

"Yeah, that's cool with me, baby," he said. "Are you sure you're alright?"

"I'm fine."

"Yes, you are." Bentley stooped down and picked her up around the waist. His head nestled in her chest, and he inhaled her jasmine-smelling perfume. "You would be even better with Tiffany."

"Tiffany?" she repeated with confusion. Her body slid down his until her feet were planted on the ground. Then she watched as he knelt and pulled out the distinctive Tiffany & Co. ring box. "Bentley, you didn't!"

"Of course, I did. You deserve the world but for now, I would be honored if you wore this ring. It's a token of our love and our commitment to one another. I've said it a thousand times and I'll say it again. You complete me and I will never stray from you ever again. I, for sure, don't want a man to come along and treat you better than me. So, from this day forward, I'm asking you to accept my ring, my proposal, and my promise. I know we've had more downs than ups, it seems, but I vow that you'll never want for anything. You'll never cry over me again unless it's tears of joy, and you'll always feel loved and appreciated. You hear me?"

It was as if he knew just where she had been. It was like Bentley sensed that he was losing her over another man. She felt much better now that he was rededicating himself to their love. With everything that was going on with Jazlyn, it felt good to hear him say this. Chills ran up and down Nylah's spine as she nodded and agreed to his words.

"I hear you, and I'm not going anywhere! I've loved you my entire life, and you know that. Our love is forever, baby."

Nylah never planned to tell Bentley about her affair because she knew some things were better left unsaid. Nothing seemed to hurt a man as much as the thought of another man taking his place in a woman's life. This would be her secret and she would have to forgive herself. Still, it did not stop the uneasiness that she felt. She prayed to God that it never came back out.

# Chapter Twenty-Five

*Two months later…*

It was in the wee hours of the morning when Nylah heard the buzz of the cell phone. There was just something about the ring that jolted Bentley from his sleep and that confirmed to Nylah it was time. When he answered, she heard the anxiousness in his voice and waited for him to hang up.

"The baby's coming!" Bentley exclaimed. "The baby's coming. That was Jaz."

Nylah looked alarmed but did not right away move from the warm confinements of the king-sized bed. "Should I go? What do you want me to do?"

Bentley scrambled around the room like he did not know what his first move was. "Where are my keys?"

"Start by putting on some clothes," she giggled and handed him a pair of joggers.

He chuckled nervously and did as she suggested. The socks and T-shirt went on next. Both were inside out. Nylah shook her head and ordered that he calmed down. Then he took a deep breath while they kissed briefly.

"I'm about to be a father again. This is crazy," he said.

Nylah's heart dropped. Call her selfish but she felt some type of way. For so long, it had been their sweet little Brooklyn, so for him to call another person his child stung a little. All she could do was push aside her emotions and just pray for a safe delivery for both Jaz and the baby. She would not dare visit them while he and his child met. That was a bond that she could not compete with even if she tried.

As Bentley threw on a coat and headed out the door, he yelled out, "I love you!"

She did not right away respond as she watched him race to the driveway, jump in his car, and halfway start it up, before he peeled off down the road. Only the red of his taillights could be seen after awhile.

Nylah made sure her phone was nearby. She would support him and Jazlyn from a distance, and she believed that was truly okay. Less than 15 minutes later, Bentley sent her a text saying that the baby had arrived after only a few pushes from Jazlyn and a couple pulls from the doctor. He wanted her to join them at the hospital and with little hesitation, she headed out and only stopped to pick up a bouquet from the gift shop.

Nylah rounded the corner to Jazlyn's room and saw a curtain pulled back. She saw no faces, but heard the voices of Bentley and Jazlyn, and of course, she heard the distinctive cries of the newborn girl or boy. Nylah braced herself with a deep breath and stepped forward to make her presence known. Suddenly, she heard Bentley's whispers.

"Man, this is the son I've always wanted."

Nylah's heart dropped. As foolish as she sounded, she was disappointed that he had a son. She wanted to be the first woman to give him both a son and daughter, and Jazlyn had come along and taken that opportunity from her. No matter how much she hated the idea, she knew every child was a blessing, and every move under the Heavens was purposeful and intentional.

Jazlyn chuckled. Nylah could hear that they were fussing over the baby. As she stepped forward, Jazlyn's voice sounded again, "You know, we would make a beautiful family."

Bentley grew quiet for a second. "We would but that's not going to happen."

Nylah smirked. *Good answer*, she thought.

"Why can't it?" Jazlyn asked. "I love you. I don't want our son to grow up in two separate households."

"Jaz, why are we even getting into this conversation? You know what's up. Nylah has my heart and nothing you say or do can change that. Junior will be well taken care of, and he'll receive love from all angles, so that's all that matters."

"You're impossible," she said.

"Naw, you're impossible. Why is it so hard for you to move forward? You told Nylah you no longer loved me, and yet, now you want to make me feel guilty for no longer being with you. That's not right, and you know it."

"So, you can honestly say my sex wasn't good?"

"It was incredible, but that's not the point."

"And my kisses?" Jazlyn continued. "How were my kisses? Was I one of your best?"

"You've definitely got skills, but…"

Bentley was cut off, and Nylah heard nothing but silence. Her eyebrows furrowed as she finally slipped past the curtain and made her presence known. No one heard the faint thuds of her shoes or saw the shocked look on her face. Bentley and Jazlyn were tongue-deep in a lip-lock that made Nylah's stomach churn. It was as if they could not get enough of each other. Bentley still held their son, and Jazlyn was still sweaty and clothed in her scrubs.

Nylah watched the scene in disgust and then dropped the bouquet down on the ground. She cleared her throat and cocked one hip to the side until they broke apart. "Are y'all done, or should I step out so y'all can finish?"

"Nylah! It's not what it looks like," Jazlyn was the first to say.

"Oh, it's not?" Nylah removed her earrings and stepped out of one of her shoes. "Because according to your conversation just now, you've lost your mind. I'll help you find it just as soon as I wipe the floor with your desperate behind!"

"Hey, hey!" Bentley called out. He stood up and tried not to raise his voice too much. The little bundle of joy in his arms began to stir awake. "Really? You're ready to fight the mother of my child? She just gave birth!"

"The mother of your child? Hello? Are you forgetting I was the ORIGINAL baby's momma and wife? So, I see you've lost your mind too?" Nylah bent down to put her shoe back on. "You know what? Neither one of you are worth it. Enjoy your beautiful son and enjoy each other."

Nylah looked the baby in the face and smiled with bitterness. "He really is handsome…just precious. But last time I checked, two full, black parents couldn't birth a biracial baby, but hey, what do I know?"

She walked out, picked Brooklyn up from the neighbor's and cried herself into a migraine.

Sunday rolled around and Nylah knew that she needed a little more Jesus. After all, she was liable to do something everlasting while she dealt with the hurt of Bentley's sins, once again. She had given Bentley the silent treatment much of the week, and she decided that today—because it was the Lord's day—she would finally put away her boxing gloves and open her arms to him. She knew he was in a shock and just as unexpected as she was. It did not make things right, but she knew that forgiveness went both ways.

"You ready, Love?" he asked cautiously.

They could hear Brooklyn's soft snores coming from the living room. She was fully clothed in a pink pantsuit and a matching patent leather purse. She had fallen asleep while she waited for her parents to finish dressing.

Nylah shrugged on her floral blazer and nodded. "Yes. I just have to put on my shoes, and I'm done."

"Let me get that for you," he said hurriedly.

He dropped to his knees and took one of her legs in his arms. With his eyes locked on hers, he caressed her foot and then eased it into the high heel. She bit her lip shyly but continued to stare at him. Then he took her other foot, massaged it with just as much attention and gentleness, and then leaned down to kiss the tips of her toes. They were polished in a nude color, and her skin smelled of the body wash that she used earlier. His lips kissed the length of her legs and towards the inside of her thighs, all the while he massaged her calves and inner thighs.

"Bentley…"

"Shhh."

"We have to go."

"I would never put the church before you. How can I claim to be a man of God, and put all my other responsibilities, duties, and titles before you?"

"I know, but…we're late," she added softly.

Truth was, her body was calling out to him, and it made her uncomfortable that she was having such thoughts on a Sunday morning. Whether angry or not, the man was handsome on so many levels and knew just the right things to say and do to bring that old spark back. She was reminded of the late nights where they would make love on the balcony of their apartment building or have spontaneous lunch break sex. So much of the world thought that being a Christian was boring, but she had just as much fun as the next person with her man.

There was her thinking again, going to the left. She shook her head free of any impure thoughts and reminded herself that they weren't yet married. Nylah gently guided his face away from her legs and cleared her throat.

"Baby, get Brooklyn while I finish up."

"Do you forgive me?" he asked and ignored her previous question.

"I do," she said simply. "Now *go*." He did as told and soon, they were on their way.

Church was everything that she needed. The message was 'Why Are You Afraid? God is Yet in Control!' She knew the Holy Spirit was speaking to her specifically, especially after everything that was going on. There was no reason for her to fear the unknown or to be upset about life's changes because God was still the head of her life. As the pastor wrapped up the message, he called for those in need of prayer to the altar.

Nylah was first in line with her hands lifted high and her eyes lowered. She wept soundlessly and tucked her chin in her chest. She did not care who saw her crying, and she certainly did not care about who speculated what. She felt helpless at this point. Her emotions were all over the place lately, and it was getting the best of her. Every little bit of excitement that she had about their rekindled love seemed to diminish. She wanted her joy back. Her emotions got the best of her, and she collapsed onto her knees until she felt a hand land on her shoulder.

"Young lady, God says 'arise, My child.'"

Nylah looked up. Her hair had fallen in her face and had stuck to her face because of the moisture. She peered at the woman standing over her and took heed to the voice of God. She struggled to stand up. Once she was eye level with the minister, the woman formed a cross on her forehead with blessed oil. Then she grabbed Nylah's hands.

"Now, darling, God drew me to you. He drew me to you because I am you…I *was* you. God said He is trying to get your attention. After all these years, you have been DISTRACTED by love. You have been distracted by intangible things like men and relationships, and you've focused on everything but Him. He has placed you in a position where you MUST worship and praise Him as much as you've been worshipping and praising the man—or men—in your life."

Nylah was shocked. She knew that the minister was right. She had never met this woman a day in her life, and yet she was reading her like a best-selling novel. Nylah had become so focused on Bentley and his problems and had gotten mixed up with Qwanell because of her own flesh and worldly desires. None of it was right, and most importantly, none of it pleased God.

"Things have been going haywire in your life, am I right?" the woman asked and waited for Nylah to nod. "God says He intentionally allowed chaos to enter your life, but this is only temporary. I repeat, this is ONLY temporary! You must repent immediately and go back to that place where God was the head of your life. You know that little feeling in your gut, and that little voice in your head? That's the voice of God! You must trust Him and hold steadfast to your faith. Only then will the storms calm and your situations will begin to make sense and work themselves out. You hear me?"

Oh, Nylah heard loud and clear. She felt warm all over and began to pray for forgiveness as the woman rested her palm against her forehead. The woman spoke in tongues and then Nylah succumbed to the power of the Holy Spirit. She began to fall backward but was gently guided to the floor by a pair of strong arms. Her eyes were closed, and her mind was on God, but she could smell Bentley's cologne.

He was crying from what she could hear, but just as the minister told her, she could not be concerned with what he was doing, thinking, and feeling anymore. It was time for a change. She knew that she had to get herself together and continue to follow God's will. As the woman said, only then would things begin to look up for the better.

Following service, she felt refreshed and renewed. It was like she got her second wind. She received the shock of her life when, during dinner, Bentley cleared his throat and announced that he had planned their wedding. It would take place in December, in Hawaii, and had been already orchestrated from the reception and flights, down to the cruise departure ports and arrival time. All Nylah needed was a wedding gown.

"How did you pull this off?" she asked dryly.

A wedding was honestly the furthest thing from her mind. She was now focused on getting herself together. She knew that it could have waited, especially with the birth of his son and everything else that was going on. Still, she vowed to hear him out.

"I've been putting you on the backburner, and I wanted to do something special for you."

"I appreciate it. I really do," she said. "But we can't do things on your own time anymore. I have to do what's best for me, and most importantly, I have to do what God says is best for me."

He put his fork down and stopped eating the mesquite chicken that she had prepared. "I get that. So, you don't think it's in His will for us to get remarried?"

"Of course, I do. That's not the point. There's a time and season for everything, and I just don't know if *now* is the right time."

Bentley grew quiet. He glanced over to Brooklyn who was looking back and forth between her parents. "Baby girl, take your food in the living room for a second, okay?"

"Yes, Daddy," she said with a mouthful of red beans and rice. She carefully took her plate, climbed down from the chair, and then trotted off to the next room.

"Have you prayed about this? What inclined you to plan everything without asking?"

"I thought I was being romantic. I didn't think it would be a problem. My goodness, Nylah. Do you hear yourself when you talk? You never used to tear me down."

"So, talking is tearing you down now? Oh, okay. Can we refer to your past mistakes and the high road I've always taken when dealing with them? Honestly, Bentley, if you had not divorced me in the first place, we would not be having this conversation right now. Am I right? Am I RIGHT?"

"Here we go again." He slammed his arms down on the table and scooted away. The chair made a screeching sound against the hardwood. "Stay out of the past, Nylah. Let's focus on our future."

"That's fine. We can focus on our future, but let's make sure God is in it too. That's all I'm saying. We've been doing so much out of flesh, and it's done nothing but put this relationship in shambles. That's all I'm saying."

"I'll tell you what. Let's fast on it, pray on it. If this season is right, everything will flow and God will confirm that it's time. But if the season is wrong, we'll wait on God and hold off on our wedding. Deal?"

"All right," she said with a shrug. "Deal."

# Chapter Twenty-Six

Summer departed, the leaves on the trees turned various hues of burnt orange and gold, and Thanksgiving crept upon them. It was Nylah's favorite season. It was time for the sweet potato pies, black-eyed peas, macaroni and cheese, and endless dinner rolls. Her parents found time to fly in and finally visit for a couple of days. Instead of staying at an overly priced hotel, Bentley agreed to allow them to stay in their house. Nylah cleaned each room from top to bottom, and ran all her errands ahead of time, because she knew that there would be a lot going on.

Brooklyn was excited to finally be reunited with her grandparents and had prepared a few hand-drawn cards and bead bracelets. Bentley decided to invite his own mother over and was going to cook *every* single dish this year. It was not often that his in-laws were in town, and he wanted to make it special for them. Plus, he wanted to continue to spoil and prove to Nylah that he had her best interests at heart. His only request was that she made her famous peach cobbler.

They were setting up the table now while the sounds of Jonathan McReynolds blasted from the entertainment system. Brooklyn was folding the napkins and putting silverware in its rightful place, while Nylah poured non-alcoholic sparkling grape juice in everyone's champagne glasses. She had a lot to be thankful for as she looked around the room with a smile.

Bentley's mother, Adalynn, was still aging gracefully although her dementia was growing worse by the day. Nylah's parents, Doreatha and Austin, on the other hand, were fresh off a cruise and had brought different sized gifts for everyone.

"You can't open up until Christmas though," Doreatha ordered.

"Christmas? You trying to torture me, Mom?" Bentley asked. He was always a big kid when it came to surprises.

"You'll be all right," she chuckled and rubbed his cheek. "You look good, son. Sis, you do too," she said to Adalynn who was dozing off.

Nylah smiled in pure gratitude. No matter the circumstances leading up to this pivotal moment, she was just happy to have everyone under one roof. Life was too short not to enjoy each other's presence.

Bentley carved the final piece of turkey, and then wiped his hands on the apron that Brooklyn had created in school for him. "Dad, will you do the honors of praying over the food?"

"Absolutely. All heads bowed and all minds clear," he said with great timbre in his voice. "Father God, we thank You for allowing us to see another Thanksgiving. We thank You for family, laughter, and love. Most importantly, we thank You for Your Son who died so that we may live. We ask that You take out anything that is not like You, and to make it nourishing for our bodies so that, as a family, we may see many, many more Thanksgivings, birthdays, graduations and even weddings. What You've brought together, we know that no one can separate."

Nylah's heart soared. She felt her mother and Brooklyn's hand, but she opened one eye to peer over at Bentley who was already looking at her. She felt warm all over and he nodded with a knowing look. It was God's confirmation for the very thing that they had been fasting for. She smiled and closed her eyes as her father finished the prayer.

"In Jesus' name we pray, amen. Now may we eat? 'Cause I'm ready to throw down and these greens are lookin' heavenly!" he joked.

"Amen!" Brooklyn said and everyone erupted in laughter.

Over dinner, they discussed everything from Brooklyn's upcoming dances and straight As, to Doreatha's plan to write a self-help book and give all the proceeds to Brooklyn's college fund. It felt so good to catch up and talk endlessly without tension or negativity surrounding their conversation. Bentley even mentioned their upcoming wedding, to which Adalynn had a few words for.

"Do it before I pass. Lord knows, I want to see my babies wed again."

"Yes, ma'am," Bentley vowed. "I will, Momma. But stop talking like that. Everything's going to be okay. You're not going anywhere."

She picked over her cornbread and shook her head sadly. "God is a healer. We all know that to be true. But my time is almost up, baby. Momma is tired."

"Why are you tired, Grandma?" Brooklyn asked innocently. "Would you like to take a nap in my bed?"

"Oh, no, baby." Adalynn chuckled and rubbed her granddaughter's cheek. "God has a bed in Heaven waiting for me."

This was one topic that Nylah was dreading because she knew it would upset Bentley. No matter how much preparing he did, he did not want to lose his mother. His eyes welled up with tears and he excused himself.

"God is only keeping me for so long," she added. "I don't mean to put a damper on things, but promise me something, baby. Promise me that you two will STAY together long after I'm gone."

Nylah cleared her throat and nodded. "I promise, Mom." Her voice cracked with emotion.

"You promise what?" Adalynn questioned. She went back to eating quietly and was completely oblivious to the conversation that had just taken place. Just that quickly, she had forgotten what they were talking about, and Nylah's heart dropped.

Dementia truly was a cruel disease.

She got up to check on Bentley. After a couple minutes of searching, she found him outside, pacing near the driveway. She approached him with caution and hugged him from behind. "Baby?"

He breathed in and out heavily. She could feel his heart pumping as she pressed her cheek to his back and wrapped her arms tightly around him. "It's not fair," he said softly. "Why does *my* mother have to suffer?"

"I know, baby. We can't question God, but we do have to trust Him. He has a master plan even during your pain and confusion," Nylah whispered. She kept her arms wrapped around him as they rocked back and forth.

"What do I do? How can I be so strong when everything seems to be falling apart?" he questioned with sadness. He looked and sounded like a little boy.

"You don't have to be strong. That's what I'm here for." She wiped the tear from his eye. "We're going to enjoy life, just as your mom requested. We're going to celebrate her while she's still with us. Let's not think about the what ifs, okay?"

He nodded but remained silent. As they continued to hug, a car drove up in the distance. It was unfamiliar, so Nylah assumed Bentley invited an additional family member over. As she squinted, she saw the silhouette of a woman and figured it was one of his distant sisters. But as the car moved up further, she saw that it was the least person she expected to be in the driveway of her home. The realization nearly made her sick to her stomach.

"Why is she here? No, correction: how does she even know where we live?" Nylah asked as an attitude crept up. She could feel her blood begin to boil and she suddenly felt hot all over. "You know what? Don't even answer that. Let me just go inside. Let me know when she's GONE."

The car stopped abruptly, and Jazlyn rolled the window down. "Wait! Nylah, stay right here. I have to talk to you both."

Nylah exhaled and said a quick prayer so that she would not go completely off and ruin her holiday. Bentley grabbed her hand and they watched as Jazlyn retreated from the driver's seat to the back passenger seat. She unstrapped and unlocked the car seat that held a peacefully sleeping Bentley Junior.

Jazlyn faced them again and she looked like she had lost a lot of weight. True, her body had bounced back immediately as there was no baby weight in sight, but she almost looked...*too* thin.

There were deep bags under her eyes, and her lips appeared raw from biting on them. A soft cry came from the bundle of blankets. Nylah swallowed hard at the thought of finally being face to face with the baby.

"What are you doing here, Jaz? I told you to bring him next week, since we'll be having family over for the holiday."

"I know, I know," she said. Her voice sounded different today. There was something wrong, but Nylah could not pinpoint it. "I need you guys to keep him. I just...I can't do this."

"What are you talking about?" Nylah asked this time.

Bentley chimed in. "You can't do *what?*" He reached out and grabbed his son. The blanket had fallen from his face, so he kissed his forehead twice gently, and then covered him back up. "Hey, man."

Jazlyn smirked at the perfect picture they made. "You look like a family right now. As a matter of fact, you always have. It's beautiful, really. This just confirms my choice. He's right where he needs to be."

"Right where he needs to be? What are you saying?" Bentley asked as he gritted his teeth together. He placed his son in Nylah's unexpected arms and approached Jazlyn. "Please tell me you're not trying to abandon your son."

She confirmed his words with her nod. "Not abandon—just handing him off to people who can take good care of him. Please take him for me. I'm not fit to be a mother. You two would be the perfect parents for him."

"Jazlyn…" He grabbed for her arm, but she began to back away.

"No, Bentley! I was never mother material. You, of all people, know that my career means everything to me and…"

"Get over yourself! You're well over 30 years old and have been saying this stuff since I've met you! You don't even have an agency or contract, Jaz! Let that modeling stuff go and come back to the real world where you have real bills and real responsibilities."

Nylah could not believe what this woman was saying. She switched Junior from one shoulder to the next and cradled his head as she raised her voice. "What kind of mother puts her career over her child? Girl, you have life ALL mixed up!"

"Don't judge me!" Jazlyn screamed. "Don't you DARE judge me! You don't know what I've been through or what I'm going through."

"We all go through circumstances. You're no different than anybody else!" Bentley shouted. "You know how many people go through messed up situations and bounce back? As a mother, you still must be strong for your child. You can't just give in like this when problems come."

Jazlyn ignored him. "I'll send you guys his medical records and the clothes that I have for him. He's allergic to bananas."

Behind them, the door opened and Doreatha peeked her head out in concern. "Um, guys? We can hear you all from the living room. Is everything okay?"

Bentley answered her question but kept his eyes on Jazlyn. He was unmoving and unapologetically staring her down as if she was the scum of the earth. He could not believe she was doing this to him or their child. "We're fine, Mom. Go back inside."

Nylah walked over and handed the baby over. "Can you please get him out of the cool air?"

"Sure," Doreatha agreed and smiled as she held her step-grandson. She disappeared back into the house a few moments later and they could hear her coos briefly before the door closed. "Look at the little prince. Hiiiii, baby boy."

Nylah turned back around and charged towards Jazlyn but before she could get to her,

Bentley grabbed her by the arm. "Calm down!" he ordered.

Just because her arm was bound did not mean her lips were bound. "So, you're saying you don't want any part of Junior's life? Is that what I'm hearing?"

With tears now coating her cheeks, Jazlyn dropped her head and openly cried, "Yes. Please forgive me."

Bentley looked up towards the sky. Clouds filled the blue canvas. It was chilly but beautiful out and was the opposite of his mood. He could not believe his Thanksgiving had turned around for the worse. He had no doubt that he and Nylah would be a great fit for Junior, but it was the idea that Jazlyn would be missing out on their son's life that bothered him.

"You know what, Jazlyn?" Nylah spoke up this time. "It's best you leave. I don't know why you're doing this but if you're giving up your rights as a parent then you can go to hell and miss out on Junior's birthdays, graduations, and all his firsts. If you leave, don't EVER come back again, you hear me?"

Jazlyn said nothing. She placed a hand over her face and turned to walk away without another word. She placed the car seat on the pavement, glanced at them once more as she got in her car, and then sped off down the driveway. The tires screeched loudly as she drove as fast as she could away from their judgmental and pained expressions.

Nylah had a few more choice words for her but chose to keep quiet. She glanced over at Bentley who looked hurt and confused. All things considered; this was too much for him. She grabbed his hand and tugged on it until he followed her back in the house.

"What's going on, kids?" Austin asked. He was now cradling the baby in his arms. "Is Jazlyn coming in?"

"No, Dad, she's uh…she's gone."

"Well, is she coming back? I wanted to congratulate and hug her on this handsome little fella. Is that okay with you, Nylah?"

"That would've been fine if she hadn't tucked her tail between her legs and ran off like a little girl."

"What do you mean?"

"She left him with us...for good."

"Wait a minute. She *left* him with you? What for?"

"Because she wasn't woman enough to handle her responsibilities," Nylah answered. "Well, I guess that's the end of dinner. You guys can start on dessert. I have to run to Wal-Mart and grab some formula and diapers for him."

"Wait a minute." Austin shook his head in confusion. He was still trying to grasp what she was telling him. "She gave up her rights as a mother is what you're saying?"

"*Yes*, Dad!" Nylah snapped with tears in her eyes. Her lips quivered as she spoke, "What kind of mother would give up her child? I would DIE at the thought of losing Brooklyn, much less willingly giving her up."

Bentley rubbed the back of his neck where there was tension building up. He sighed and shook his head. "I'm sorry that this ruined dinner, you guys."

"Dinner wasn't ruined. We're family. God knew that you two would need the love and support of family, so I'm glad we could be here at this time. Trust me, son, it's no big deal. What can we do to help?"

Nylah grabbed her faux leather jacket and keys. "Can someone go with me to the store? Are they open today?"

"Yeah, they close a little early, but they're still open now. I'll go with you," Doreatha volunteered. "Can you two handle staying here with the baby, or do we need to take him too?"

"Naw, we got it. Plus, Mom is here too," Bentley added although his mother had fallen asleep on the large reclining chair with Brooklyn in her lap.

Yet again, life was throwing them a curveball and it hit them hardest this time around. Nylah was not Junior's mother, but she was a mother nonetheless, and she would love this child as her own. She would show him unconditional love not only because the baby deserved a good upbringing and home, but also because she was in love with Bentley, and she vowed to be there for him through it all.

"Hey, what's on your mind?" Doreatha's question broke through Nylah's thoughts.

She shrugged and then cried as they drove down the road. "It's not the baby's fault at all. He didn't ask to be here. But it just hurts, you know? I was supposed to be the only woman in his life, and we were supposed to have children TOGETHER.

What started off as a fairy tale ended up like a nightmare. What do I do, Momma?"

Doreatha grabbed her hand. She had her full attention on the road ahead but made sure to comfort her daughter in the process. "I guess now is the time to share some secrets with you. After all, you're mature enough now. Do you remember when your father and I separated for a few months?"

Nylah looked over thoughtfully and wiped her tears. "When I was a child? Yes. I remember that well."

"That was the hardest three months of my life! He was unfaithful on a number of occasions, and as a result, a baby was born."

"I have a sister or brother?" Nylah interrupted.

"*Had.* The baby was stillborn. I wanted to teach him a lesson, so I separated from him. I thought I was doing the best thing for me, but it ended up hurting our relationship more because I shut him out, left the church, and did my own thing for a while."

Nylah was in shock. "Wow. I never knew this."

Doreatha nodded. "This is something your father wanted to take to the grave with us, but I know that I went through that very experience to help you now. But you know what's the craziest thing about that?"

"What's that, Ma?"

"I would have stayed regardless with your dad—I loved him *that* much," Doreatha said with a smile. She seemed to reminisce on their precious yesteryears. "God joined us together long before we were thought of, and I knew that early on. Of course, I didn't think infidelity would creep in the way it did, but forgiveness is a powerful thing. I know you didn't expect to become a mother to *another* woman's child either, but God is faithful, and He will lighten your load through this. Plus, you have me and your father, and the support of family and friends. Lean on us."

"Thank you, Momma. That means so much to me."

"Of course. I'm trying to right these wrongs and that includes supporting you in whatever endeavors you have. We're even thinking about moving closer so we can take Brooklyn sometimes, and just be closer."

"I would love that."

"Me too, baby. Me too."

They smiled at one another, embraced at the stoplight, and then continued their drive to the nearest Wal-Mart.

# Chapter Twenty-Seven

Life with Bentley Junior was much more enjoyable than Nylah could have ever imagined. Although they were only two weeks in, she loved him and could not get enough of his smile. He did not favor Jazlyn thankfully. Instead, it was as if she was looking at her fiancé every time their eyes met. It was clear that Bentley was the father by the identical shape of his lips, nose, and eyes. She took it as a blessing that she did not have to carry a son for nine months, but God had given her another child.

Brooklyn took to her little brother well and was an excellent big sister. She volunteered to help Nylah change his diaper and feed him as much as she could. Nylah was thankful to God that with every changing season, He continued to have His hand over their lives. Things were different but had changed for the better.

As planned, Bentley still stuck true to his promises and encouraged her to take a day off from mommy duties and to just relax and pamper herself. He wanted her to be good and ready for their weekend in Maui.

They packed now with the baby propped in his car seat and looking on. "I just feel like I'm missing something."

"Missing something like what?"

"I don't know. Are babies okay to travel on planes? Do we need anything special for him?"

"Naw. BJ is good. But I did pick up something for *you*. Doctors said everybody should have it when visiting Maui."

"Have what?" she questioned.

"Close your eyes," he ordered.

She did as told and grinned as she heard him move around. Junior began to cry, and she almost opened her eyes, but Bentley told her to remain still. "I got 'im, I got 'im. Keep those beautiful eyes closed."

Nylah smiled and held out her hands naturally. Soon, she felt plastic touch her palms. Whatever he was handing her grew heavy, so she extended her arms, but continued to keep her eyelids shut. Finally, he rounded her, kissed the sensitive skin just below her ear, and then whispered, "Open up."

Nylah's eyes landed on the package in her arms. From what she could see it was a wedding gown that was brand new, striking, and flowy. Its train hung low to the floor, and she noticed that it was mermaid-style and strapless. "Wh—what is this?"

"I know you were stressing out about everything, soooo, I gave your mother some money and she picked out what she believed would be your perfect wedding gown. It was also as close to your original dress as she could get. I haven't seen it personally—just what's visible through the plastic—but I hope you like it, baby."

"This is one of the sweetest things you've ever done for me," she said. "Oh, my goodness. Thank you! I can't wait to see it. What size is it?"

He shrugged. "Mom said she took your measurements a while back?"

"You're always pulling something special off," she mused and leaned in to kiss him. "Seriously, that means everything to me and takes a load off of my shoulders."

"It was my pleasure." He winked and rolled a shirt down so that he could tuck it in his suitcase tightly. His large hands folded the cotton material with ease and then he took her hand. "This trip is so much more than the ceremony and kicking back with family and friends. It's rediscovering ourselves and focusing on you and I like I've failed to do time and time again. I just want you to know how special you are to me."

She nodded to his sincere words and felt herself melt a little bit more. "I do, baby."

"Now what do you say we do something really romantic?"

"Like what?"

Bentley leaned in close and wrapped his arms snugly around her waist. He pressed their bodies together and whispered in her ear, "Mmm. Something we haven't done in a while."

She swallowed hard and her mind raced at what they used to do. "We're celibate. What are you referring to exactly?"

"Something freaky…" Bentley growled.

"Bentley, no."

"…like go to the store and use a bunch of coupons."

"Wait. Whaaaa?" Nylah paused for a second, realized the joke had almost gone over her head, and then she burst out laughing. "You are so goofy! *Move!*"

He chuckled. "No, for real though. I need some more socks."

"I feel like we've been going to Wal-Mart every other day lately," Nylah said and grabbed her purse. "I'll drive. You got Junior?"

Bentley picked up the car seat and smiled down at his spitting image. "Got him. Brooklyn, grab your coat! We're going on a field trip."

When they arrived at the store, there was hardly anyone in the aisles. Brooklyn was placed in the larger part of the cart, and the baby was situated at the front in his car seat. They strolled through the store as a family of four, and bought a few necessary items, and a handful of unnecessary items. At some point, Brooklyn's legs became completely covered with items. The cart slowly but surely began to fill up and became hard to push. Nylah could only laugh.

"That's a shame."

"What's a shame?" Bentley asked while he distractedly looked down at his phone.

"We can never come in here for just ONE item," Nylah said, seconds before she rounded the corner and her cart slammed into another cart. "Oops. I am so sorry!"

"Oh, it's my fault. I wasn't paying atten…" the woman's voice trailed off, which made Nylah's head look up. The women both stopped and stared at each other in silence before Nylah dropped the pair of undershirts that she held. She looked to the woman's cart that was spilling over in fragrances, clothes, and lacy panties.

"Really? You give up your child so you can go on a shopping spree?"

Jazlyn stared back at Nylah and then sighed. "I'd hardly call picking up items at Wal-Mart an ideal shopping spree. Please don't start."

"No, I'm going to start. Look at my cart and look at yours. I'm buying stuff so that YOUR son can live comfortably, and you're purchasing items for *yourself*? But you couldn't send your child with anything while we take on YOUR responsibilities? How selfish and arrogant is that? What kind of game are you playing, Jazlyn?"

"I'm not playing any game. I told you why I made my decision. Please don't keep crucifying me each time you see, and especially not in public." Her voice was much softer in humiliation as she looked around to see if anyone was listening.

"Oh, did I embarrass you? Would you like me to lower my voice?"

"It's clear you think you're better than me. Okay! You've won! You've got it all; you're the better mother. You're the better woman for Bentley. Would you like a handclap?" She began to clap her hands in sarcasm. "*God*, Nylah! I expected more from you, being a woman of God and all."

Bentley was nowhere to be found and she was happy that she could give this woman a piece of her mind without interruptions. She was saying everything she wanted to say in the last two weeks, and there was no telling when she stopped.

"I'm not judging you. I'm stating facts, am I not? There's nothing in the Bible that says I can't state facts."

"Whatever, Nylah." Jazlyn turned to walk away.

"Yup. Run away like you always do," Nylah chuckled and waved her hand in dismissal. "Have a good life. Enjoy yourself. You're free now from your responsibilities. Do you, boo."

"Yeah, well, according to doctors, I have only a month or so left of this 'good and free life,' as you put it," Jazlyn said solemnly as she continued to walk in the other direction.

"What did you say?"

Jazlyn whipped around so quickly that her thin frame nearly toppled over as she was thrown off balance. There were tears in her eyes as she declared, "You HEARD me, Nylah! Don't act like you didn't. I'm *dying!*" she exclaimed and began to cry. "Inoperable brain cancer! Are you happy now? Do you see why I would have rather dropped Junior off than explain this tragedy to you? Huh? Do you get it now why I left him in you and Bentley's care? Oh, don't look at me like that. Just a second ago you had so much to say; what happened?"

Nylah could feel her heart literally rip in her chest. She felt low for all the jabs that she had verbally given Jazlyn and felt like crying right then and there. She looked at Jazlyn's receding hairline, sporadic balding, and unhealthy weight loss. It all became so clear. This woman was telling the truth and suffering in silence and all Nylah had done was kicked her while she was down instead of attempting to understand and empathize.

"Oh, my goodness. I am so sorry, but why didn't you say that? Bentley and I could've handled it."

"It kills me. Literally every day, I'm one step closer to death and it hurts more than anyone will ever know or understand. I can't carry out my God-given duties as a mother or woman because of something out of my control."

Nylah was still in shock as she tried to process everything. "How long have you known?"

"Three months ago, the diagnosis was given to me, along with a countdown of what was to become of my life."

"Why didn't you tell anyone?"

"I guess I just wanted to be normal and feel normal." She shrugged. "I was in denial at first. I couldn't live out my last days like that—dying in a hospital room. I'm supposed to be hooked up to a monitor and everyday I should be taking six pills at the minimum. I decided not to do any of that and just enjoy the remainder of what I have left."

Nylah had to admit. She felt a little bit better about Jazlyn's reasoning for leaving Junior in their hands. But she was also confused by her logic. This woman truly needed to be guided in her thinking; there was first a pregnancy and then a terminal illness that she chose to withhold from the people it affected most. While it was difficult to deal with, Nylah was not sure that she would have hid these things from her loved ones.

"The truth is, though, honey, I could get in a car crash TODAY and leave *two* babies without a mother. Don't you want to spend the time you have left with your son? I know it hurts because you'll get too attached but embrace these moments. Hug and kiss him as much as possible. Take some pictures with him so that we can show him years from now who his mother was. Show him love while you still have breath in your body. Don't you want that?"

Jazlyn began to speak but then trailed off as she looked behind Nylah.

"What's going on over here?" Bentley walked up. He looked back and forth between the two women. "What happened now? Jaz, what are you doing here?"

"Bentley, I um…"

Nylah cut Jazlyn off before she could say too much. She grabbed Bentley and then Jazlyn's hands. "We all need to sit down and talk. Now is not the time or place. We've got some things to discuss and figure out."

\*\*\*

The talk lasted over an hour and was filled with a lot of emotions, prayers, and repentance. Bentley sat at the head position of their living room table, hours later, with both women on either side of him. Jazlyn held her sleeping son against her chest, and Brooklyn was fast asleep on Nylah's lap.

"Come with us to Maui. I'll get you a ticket."

"No, I don't want to impose on your special day. That's not necessary. God willing, I'll be able to see you all when you return."

"That's nonsense," Bentley said, and Nylah agreed. "You can stay in the resort with our parents. It's just for a few days. You need to get away."

"Is that okay with you?" she turned to Nylah and asked.

"Of course."

"Then it's settled," Bentley said. "Grab my phone, baby." He dialed a long number, put it on speaker, and the women watched as he used his notoriety to add a plane and cruise ticket to their existing vacation package.

As he ended the call, Jazlyn rubbed a hand over Junior's head and then nestled her chin against the top of his head. Her hand rubbed up and down his back and soon, tears were rushing down to puddle onto his onesie.

"You guys don't have to do this for me. Really. I've made my peace with God and I'm ready to go whenever He calls me."

"Look, Jaz. I know you and I have not always been the best of friends, and we met under crazy circumstances. But I just want you to know, woman to woman, I forgive you. I don't think I've ever really just told you that."

"Thank you, Nylah. I am also sorry for the hurt I've caused you both. You two are beautiful together and I pray God continues to have His hand over your relationship. Bentley Junior is in great hands."

The two women stood up and embraced as best they could with their children still lying against them. Bentley looked on with tears in his eyes and shook his head.

"I've told you both a million times how apologetic I am. As a man, I'm sorry for the tears I've caused. I truly learned my lesson, but I'm sorry that it took so many heartbreaks and heartaches to get it right."

Nylah watched as he turned to her and spoke sincerely, "I love you, Nylah, as the woman of my dreams, mother of my daughter, confidant, and best friend."

They kissed.

He turned to Jazlyn, then, and said with genuineness, "And you, Jaz. I love you for the season that you held me down, and for blessing me with my little man."

The room grew silent as the peace of God swept over the room. Healing seemed to flow from one adult to the next. It felt good to forgive and move forward.

# Chapter Twenty-Eight

"Good morning, passengers, this is your pilot for the last time. Please buckle your seatbelts as we prepare for our final descend into the beautiful state of Hawaii. Right now, the temperature is 83 degrees with low humidity and a few clouds in sight. On behalf of the entire airline, I want to thank you for choosing us, and we hope you fly with us again. Enjoy your visit."

Nylah stirred awake as people around her moved around and buckled their seatbelts. Bentley was still asleep, so she checked to see if he was buckled in, and then looked across the row at Brooklyn. She opted to sit by herself, next to another cute little black girl, named Jordyn, and her mother. They talked much of the flight and seemed to establish a friendship.

"Are you excited?" Jordyn asked. She was missing several teeth and had the sweetest snaggle-tooth smile.

"Yes! 'Cause I heard you get laid when you arrive!" Brooklyn exclaimed loudly.

Nylah, was who was still looking over, begin to choke on nothing. Bentley woke up at the sound of his daughter's quirky announcement, and several other passengers erupted into laughter at the innocence of her words.

Jordyn's mother put her hand over her heart and chuckled. "Oh, that is too funny!"

"She means, everyone gets a lei when they arrive," Nylah explained in embarrassment. She was half-amused at the intelligence of her daughter. "I'm so sorry."

After another few minutes, the wheels of the airplane touched the runway with a gentle bump. Nylah could feel her excitement soar at the thought of relaxing on a real beach, with real seashells, real sand, and real sunshine. A vacation was long overdue, and she was ecstatic that, not only would she be able to kick back, but she was remarrying the love of her life.

The only difference is their nuptials would be unbreakable this time around.

Nylah looked towards the back of the plane where their parents, Jazlyn, and Junior were. She waved and then gave the universal sign for a phone call. She planned to give them a call once she entered the airport so that they could meet up and board the shuttle that would take them to their resort together.

"Gimme a kiss witcho' fine self," Bentley said and smacked her buttocks.

She leaned in and did as told with a schoolgirl giggle. "My daddy's going to get you!"

"You ready to be Mrs. Rose again?" he asked.

"Is that even a question?"

They gathered their belongings, and bade a goodbye to Jordyn and her mother, but not before taking a picture of the girls. Soon, everyone was reunited just as the shuttle arrived to take them to their resort. A short, scenic ride over resulted in lots of pictures, selfies, and video recording. Maui was incredible, and tomorrow for the ceremony, they would be taking a smaller boat to the shores of Honolulu to explore more.

Nylah could not believe her dream wedding was taking place. Her first wedding ceremony was beautiful, but this time around, God had truly blessed them financially to do it even bigger. She could not be any more thankful to have her family there, celebrating with her.

She looked over to Jazlyn, who looked in awe at the passing palm trees and villages and was cradling

Junior against her breasts. Nylah smiled and was glad that Bentley had invited her along. Even if it was temporary, she deserved a final vacation to take her to the Father in peace. Jazlyn looked over at that moment and caught her eyes. Nylah winked and then leaned more into Bentley.

"You okay?"

"I'm perfect, baby."

After a restful night, the group awakened early and set out for the sailboat that would take them to the private wedding ceremony. A pastor waited for their arrival with a Bible in his hand and smile on his middle-aged face.

"Welcome to Hawaii!" he called out.

Nylah, who was all dolled up, held her hair against the strong winds while Bentley helped her with the bottom of her flowing gown. Everything fit and looked flawless. Even her curls had turned out as she wanted them to.

"You two look stunning," the man complimented and situated them across from one another. "Are we all ready?"

Both Bentley and Nylah nodded and held hands. The wind seemed to stop blowing as violently, and the chilliness that hung in the air grew warmer suddenly. It was like a sign that God was showing them that this marriage, although disrupted and nearly torn apart, it was made to withstand all tests and trials.

"We are gathered together on this day to witness and celebrate the marriage of Bentley and Nylah. We come together not to mark the start of a relationship, but to acknowledge and strengthen a bond that already exists," the pastor said and opened his Bible. "This ceremony is a public affirmation of that bond and as their dearest family and friends, it is our honor and privilege to stand witness to this event. This day is made possible not only because of your love for each other, but through the grace and support of your family and friends. It is our hope that your fulfillment and joy in each other will increase with each passing year."

Although they had not previously met the man, he had called them twice and asked about their past. Bentley gave a watered-down version of their history and had pieced together their love story beautifully with his words. Nylah smiled as she looked at their parents' and children's faces, and then turned back to Bentley.

The pastor continued over the sounds of birds chirping, and the horn of an approaching ship. "Marriage is a commitment in life, where two people can find and bring out the very best in each other. What you have, Bentley, she needs. What you have, Nylah, he needs. Marriage offers opportunities for sharing and growth that no other human relationship can equal. It is a physical and emotional joining that has the promise of a lifetime."

A tear sprang to Nylah's eye as she thought about their love story. Never in a million years did she phantom she would be wedding him again. Still, it did not change the fact that she had fallen more in love with him.

"Please, bow your heads in prayer."

The group did as told and listened to the pastor's resonating voice. "Lord, we thank You for Bentley, Nylah, and the surrounding family that is gathered here today. We ask that You help Bentley and Nylah to *always* remember the strong love that they share. We ask that during the good times, they would uphold each other, and in the bad times, never leave one another. May their love always inspire them to be kind in their words, considerate of the other's feelings, and concerned for the other's needs and desires. Increase their faith and trust in You, Lord. Bless their marriage with peace and happiness and make their love fruitful for Your glory and their joy, both here and in eternity. Amen."

"Amen," everyone echoed.

"Now for the good part. I see that you each already have your rings on. That's fine. Please repeat after me, Nylah."

She cleared her throat and looked at the love of her life. "I, Nylah, take you Bentley, to be my lawfully wedded husband. I give to you in the presence of God and these witnesses, my promise to stay by your side in sickness and in health, in joy and in sorrow, as well as through the good times and the bad. I promise to love you without reservation; I'll comfort you in times of suffering; I'll submit to you, laugh with you and cry with you. I vow to grow with you in mind and spirit, always be open and honest with you, and cherish you for as long as we both shall live."

Doreatha cupped a hand over her mouth as the day's emotions overtook her.

"Now, Bentley, please repeat after me."

Bentley stood up straighter, squeezed her hands a little bit tighter, and then spoke with authority and confidence, "I, Bentley, take you Nylah, to be my lawfully wedded wife. I give to you in the presence of God and these witnesses, my promise to stay by your side in sickness and in health, in joy and in sorrow, as well as through the good times and the bad. I promise to love you without reservation, comfort you in times of sorrow, encourage you to chase after your dreams, and respect and protect you. I vow to grow with you in mind and spirit, always be open and honest with you, and cherish you for as long as we both shall live."

The pastor began to speak, but Bentley lifted his hand. "I'm sorry, Rev. I also vow to my children, Brooklyn and Bentley Junior, that I will be the best father you could ever ask for. You will never want for anything with Daddy. I promise to provide for you, love you, and raise you up in the way that you should go according to the Word of God."

"Amen," Austin confirmed as he held Junior.

The pastor continued, "Bentley and Nylah, as you hold hands, may you see the gift that they are to you. These are the hands that are holding yours on your wedding day as you promise to love each other today, tomorrow, and forever. These are the hands that will countlessly wipe tears from your eyes—tears of joy and sorrow. These are the hands that will passionately love you and cherish you through the years. These are the hands that will help hold your family together as one as you overcome adversity. These are the hands that will give you strength when you need it. These are the hands that will work alongside yours as together you build your future."

'I love you,' Bentley mouthed.

'I love you too,' Nylah mouthed back.

"May the rings that you two wear be from this day forward, your most treasured adornment, and may the love they symbolize, be your most precious possession. As you wear these rings, may they be constant reminders of these promises you are making today. You have pledged yourselves to a lifetime of caring for one another this afternoon. May this be a commitment made in love, kept in faith, lived in hope, and eternally renewed. As you stand before us, it is our hope that you will go through life loving, trusting, and caring for one another, completely and forever."

The pastor touched each of their foreheads and then cupped his hand over theirs as he prayed a final prayer. Nylah's shoulder now shook as she tried her best not to cry. Adalynn handed her a tissue that she dabbed gently under her eyes so that she would not smear her makeup. Nylah realized she was now seconds away from reclaiming her title to Bentley's throne. She would be his eternal queen. A broken piece to her heart was finally mending itself.

"Having pledged their fidelity to one another, to love, honor and cherish one another in the presence of this gathering and by the authority vested in me by the constitution and the laws of this state, it is my honor to now pronounce you husband and wife. You may kiss your bride, Bentley!"

He did not have to be told twice. Before the words fully left the pastor's mouth, Bentley was leaning in and kissing Nylah's lips. His hands closed around her hips, and he held her in place as he dipped their bodies dramatically. She dug her toes into the sand and hugged him so that she would not lose her balance.

"Baby!" she exclaimed with a giggle.

Their parents cheered and took pictures, as Jazlyn clapped and smiled, and Brooklyn jumped up and down in elation. Nylah looked back to her handsome husband and knew that this time around was forever. Nothing or no one would get between them, and she was sure of it. She had no regrets for their past mistakes or failures because she knew it was all needed to get to this very moment.

God was so good, and so faithful. She looked up towards the Heavens and lifted her arms. Bentley dipped low and picked her up. She was sure that his all-white, neatly ironed and assembled tuxedo would be wrinkled by the time he put her down, but he did not seem to care.

"I's married now!" she joked.

# Chapter Twenty-Nine

It was exactly 365 days later. Bentley and Nylah's life had changed forever in just a short time. Junior was growing bigger and stronger each day, and Brooklyn was thriving in her six-year-old glory. Their lives had taken a pretty big loss. It was a realization that they were dreading, but a change that was inevitable because God had revealed His master plan through many prayers and signs. Bentley was deep in his paperwork at the office, Junior was at home with Nylah, and Brooklyn was playing tag on her school's playground during recess when Adalynn passed away peacefully in her sleep. Not even a month later, Jazlyn went on to be with the Lord as well.

Nylah remembered it all so well. Her petite hands had fallen from around the cordless landline phone from the news on the other end, and the device crashed to the floor with a loud bang. Junior, who was startled, began to cry at the top of his lungs, and Nylah lowered her head in sadness.

"I'm sorry, baby boy," she said. She dialed Bentley in panic as she threw on her snow boots and a jacket. "Mommy didn't mean to."

She did not in the least bit feel weird referring to herself as Junior's mother. Following the wedding, God had completely done a new thing in her life. Things had looked up in a major way. Bentley had secured many new accounts with his firm, so financially, they were in an overflow. Life was good, but Nylah knew that the enemy always had a way of ruining things when God's people were feeling and doing their best.

This time was no exception. Two deaths in two months were tough in every sense of the word. Apparently, Jazlyn had collapsed while she was getting into her car. Because of the duration that she was unconscious, she suffered major brain damage, liver damage, and heart failure. Jazlyn had been taken off life support at the request of her mother and siblings. Jazlyn was gone...*dead*. Adalynn was gone...*dead*.

It was bittersweet and hard to grasp. On one hand, Nylah was happy that both women were no longer in pain, had to be medicated, or were supervised by doctors. On the other hand, Junior was

372

now without his biological mother, Bentley was without his mother, and a family would now have to mourn at two lives gone much too soon.

Currently, Nylah and Bentley sat in the cemetery that was his mother's final resting place. They had a thick blanket out on the snowy ground and were sitting directly in front of Adalynn's tombstone. The kids were asleep in the car not even five feet from them. Although it was cold out, they reminisced on the memories of both women and could not help but to laugh, cry, and smile.

"I'm glad she got her wish," Nylah added.

"Me too," Bentley added. "That was her dying wish and I believe God allowed her to stick around so she could see it. Momma knew a long time ago that we would be together."

"Promise me you won't ever leave me."

"I promise."

She nestled her head against his chest for a moment. "I think your mom would fuss at us right now though."

"Why's that?"

"Because we're out in this cold weather like we have NO sense," Nylah said with a chuckle. "Baby, I can't feel my nose. It's *so* cold."

"All right, we can go back home." He got up first and then helped her up. "I love you."

"I love you too," she said and gathered the blanket in her arms. She folded it neatly before they turned and walked hand in hand towards the car.

They made their way back to their family—their happy and healthy children. Their relationship had been through many twists, turns, roadblocks, and reconstructions, but God had restored all. She was happy, honored, and blessed to be the mother of two children, and the wife of a man who loved her more than she would ever know.

Never mind any outside relationships or influences, she had Bentley's heart, and he had hers. She planned to protect it with everything within her, and with God at the head of their lives, she knew forever was theirs.

## *The End*

# ABOUT THE AUTHOR

Olivia Shaw-Reel has written nearly 30 books before her 30th birthday. Her award-winning novels, *Soul Cry, What God Has Joined Together, and Matters of the Hart: A Tale of the Dysfunctional Hart Sisters*, have become her biggest-selling books to date.

She also hosts *The Reel Love Podcast* with her husband, Paris. Olivia lives in Milwaukee, WI.

Visit the official storefront for updates and to purchase autographed paperbacks at ***osrbooks.com***.

Follow her on Instagram, TikTok, and Facebook at ***@oliviashawreel***.

## OTHER TITLES FROM THE AUTHOR

Soul Cry, Vol. 3
What God Has Joined Together, *2-Book Series*
Baptized in Her Seduction: A Church Love Affair,
*2-Book Series*
Lord, Save Me From Myself, Vol. 2
Meet Me at the Altar
Full Court Mess
The Only Gift
Andrue & Sy'mone: An Urban Love Affair, *3-Book
Series*
Can't Leave Him Alone After the Love We Made,
*Book 1*
Kiss Me @ Midnight
Stuck Wit'chu
Sins of a Mafia Princess
Matters of the Hart: A Tale of the Dysfunctional
Hart Sisters, *3-Book Series*
In Love With Everything You Could Be
Stalked by My Pastor, *Book 1*
A Christmas Miracle
Who's Loving You This Christmas?
Saved, Sanctified, & Filled With Anxiety
Compilation

www.ingramcontent.com/pod-product-compliance
Lightning Source LLC
Chambersburg PA
CBHW060928030726
47503CB00003B/513